CAT
PEOPLE

Illustration credit: Priya Kuriyan

CAT PEOPLE

Edited by Devapriya Roy

SIMON &
SCHUSTER

London • New York • Sydney • Toronto • New Delhi

First published in India by Simon & Schuster India, 2021

The copyright © for the individual pieces rests with the respective authors.

1 3 5 7 9 10 8 6 4 2

Simon & Schuster India
818, Indraprakash Building,
21, Barakhamba Road,
New Delhi 110001

www.simonandschuster.co.in

Paperback ISBN: 978-93-92099-12-0
eBook ISBN: 978-93-92099-13-7

Typeset in India by Mridu Agarwal, Simon & Schuster, New Delhi

Printed and bound in India by Replika Press Pvt. Ltd.

Contents

this book is for gitanjali and nayantara chatterjee, cat ladies of E-936

Introduction

How does a cat-less person come to edit an anthology of cat-essays?

A True Story in Three Parts

PART ONE

New Delhi, 2018. An evening in February. We are in the metro, my friend Janice and I, doing our usual thing: cooing into her phone at the latest photos of her cat.

Around us, people eat and chat, bob to music, nap. We have a long commute from the university where Janice teaches, and where I have recently begun to adjunct, and we fill the journey, first the shuttle from college and then the train from Jahangirpuri to Hauz Khas, with talk of cats and food and books—mostly cats. The adventures of Vincent are our mainstay: one weekday he might get stranded on a high perch and need to be rescued by a whole team of neighbourhood bravehearts, only to repeat the feat the very next afternoon; one season he might fall in obsessive love; one mid-term break, he might give the cat-sitter a slip and vanish, causing Janice and her partner to frantically cut their trip short and return from Shillong to look for him.

This February evening though, as the compartment judders and the announcements drone on, I have a cat-story of my own for Janice. I have had the honour, this afternoon, of acquiring a novelty: a human-cat.

This is (the very short version of) how it happened.

One of the students in my creative writing class, P, is a great reader. She reads a book a day, while managing to still stay on top of all her other courses and assignments. The rest of us in class admire that greatly—though we are all a little scared of her. I bring P books every week, which she comes into my office to collect. Last week, delighted at the offerings I had humbly placed upon the table, she asked me if I could adopt her, so she would have complete and unfettered access to all my bookshelves forever. I had replied that, alas, I was too poor to adopt her; also, too useless.

This afternoon, upon her friend's suggestion, she presents an alternative: what if she is my *cat*?

Cats look after themselves, she says, and are writer-friendly. Useless-person-friendly too, she adds helpfully.

It is an offer I can hardly refuse.

And now, in the unnatural warmth of the compartment, I am telling Janice this story, and she is listening with her writer's curiosity. 'I want to meet your cat,' she says finally. With that remark, it is settled.

We alight from the train into the press of crowds in the station. Outside, it is dark and cold, and the halogen light pools in a little circle of warmth where we stand.

'You know what would be nice?' I tell Janice. 'If there were an anthology of cat essays and everyone would write about their actual cats and I would write about P.'

(If you think it is odd that I thought of instrumentalising this lark so quickly, that I wanted to begin writing about it *already*, then you don't know enough about writers. We are contemptible creatures.)

'Of course,' I say, 'You remember P's bête noire, T? She will implode if I do that.'

Janice laughs. She has heard about this cat-fight before.

'But darling, there *should* be a book like that,' she says reflectively. 'If there were, I would write a sestina about Vincent.'

PART TWO

New Delhi, February 2019, a café in SDA. I am sitting with H and S, book editors, and we are talking about this and that, books we have just read and books we are about to read, and writers we love and, well, writers we hate. I no longer teach, and my human cat is now my Research Associate, an official position we created so she can boss over me at will. (T claims she has grown up and is completely above any petty competition whatsoever. I privately think the lady doth protest too much.)

A couple of days ago, my RA had accompanied me to a children's litfest, where I was talking about *Indira*, a book I had created with the artist Priya Kuriyan. Kuriyan is the one who manages our kid-crowds—all she needs is a blackboard and a piece of chalk and as she turns a scratch into a squirrel, or a curl into a cat, the young ones begin to eat out of her palm. Without her, my RA and I are somewhat tense about handling the bright and bouncy middle-schoolers. As a tactic, I opened the session by introducing the human cat. The kids were instantly captivated. 'Miss Cat, Miss Cat,' they called her from all directions, 'I need a sketch-pen, I need some paper, can I touch your hair, are you a real cat under a spell, Please Miss Cat, come heeeere.'

'It's Ms Cat,' a very sophisticated young lady in the first row spoke up, correcting her hapless classmates with withering charm.

Ms Cat had purred with pleasure.

Somehow, my mouth full of cheese garlic bread, I tell H and S that there should be an anthology of cat essays. They should publish one.

'Oh, yes,' S replies immediately, 'Cats are all the rage.'

'Why don't you curate it?' H asks me.

What can I say—my mouth is full of cheese. Maybe I nod, maybe I hem and haw. But somehow, apparently, by the end of tea, I am doing this.

Ms Cat is not amused. 'You are still in the middle of your serial novel, you have all these other commitments, *contracts*, did you really just get into something sticky again without thinking things through?'

Like all cat-owners—sorry, like all who are owned by cats—I gulp and look penitent.

PART THREE

As I start reaching out to writers to send me cat essays or cat fiction or cat lists, almost by magic, other cat stories begin to come my way too, in ones and twos, and sixes and sevens.

Our housekeeper Rupa didi acquires a cat. 'It is in my horoscope,' she tells me, 'Four-legged creatures are naturally drawn to me. Especially cats.'

Come mating season, I get daily reports about Bhuntu's obsession with a most unsuitable black Tom, the Mawali of Munirka. Soon, there are kittens. Bhuntu ignores the runt and outraged at this dereliction of maternal duties Rupa didi drips milk into her mouth with a plastic dropper. Laila, the neglected kitten, is the princess of the family now.

In a train back from Kathgodam, the lady sitting next to me tells me—unbidden—about Sureeli, the cat who lives in her brother's house in Almora, along with many dogs, so named because she sings along to the radio.

My niece Priyanka is the original cat-girl in the family. When she was five, I had gifted her a Barbie with a pet cat called Seraphina, and I like to think that was what triggered her cat obsession. (Though I am reasonably sure that it was because of her cat obsession that I'd got her this particular doll in the first place—but let's go with my trigger theory for now.) Since then, she has sought out cats wherever she is, and I have sent her cat memorabilia from wherever I have travelled to.

Once, when her father was posted in Bombay, a beautiful white cat with beautiful blue eyes had walked into their house—she must have charmed the heavy security at the gate since it was an army base and no one without AADHAR or PAN was allowed in—and made herself at home. As Priyanka's father, the Brigadier, later told the story:

'When I came home and saw her, I announced that *either the cat stays or I stay*. Mother and daughter walked inside with the cat. I got the message, showed myself in, and did not say anything anymore.'

These days, my brother-in-law is posted in Delhi, and Krystal-the-blue-eyed-being throws the iciest looks at the regular billis who haunt the cantonment area, and walk past the clerestory windows their old house is full of, hungrily looking in, at the loving light that shines on the blue-eyed goddess.

She yawns, she burrows into a wardrobe shelf, she sleeps. She never acknowledges them.

And then my best friend Gee gets a cat. During the pandemic, they multiply. Her house is now full of cats.

T's mother Nina, by now my friend, has been feeding strays in Carter Road in Bombay for many years. During the pandemic, she would awaken at dawn and go feed the cats, who were hungrier than usual, since all other establishments that patronised them were closed. Soon, word spread on the network, and cats began to turn up from far away. In T's view, they came primarily from fisher settlements like the Khar Danda or the Versova koliwada, which were completely shut. Towards the end, Nina was feeding around thirty-five or forty cats every day.

The cat grapevine is an actual thing though, and not a T-invention.

My friend Sharm's friend Sriparna also confirms this. Sriparna must have been born under a configuration of stars similar to Rupa didi's, because cats find her *wherever* she is, whether Tokyo or Tollygunge. Once she began to rescue strays and nurse them back to health, the news spread on the cat grapevine of Vasant Kunj, and injured cats began to routinely make their way to her doorstep. She never turned anyone away.

The human-cat leaves for the US, to study for a degree in fiction. A week from that day, I am in the kitchen, looking for something, when a cat perches on the window and mews. Food is found for her. The next day, my husband goes for a walk. She appears and rolls about on his feet, first the right, then the left, and finally she follows him on his rounds. She becomes a regular visitor, always and only perching on the window ledge outside the kitchen, never anywhere else. We name her 'Noorie'.

It is the season of departures. T is about to leave for London. A lot of things are ordered on Amazon, and the day before her flight, she gives one large cardboard box to her cat, Goofy. Since that day, Goofy has stayed loyal to the box. Sleeping in it every night, loafing in it during the day. T keeps sending me pictures from London—the box is now ragged, but Goofy is like Casabianca, waiting solidly for her to return.

The book of essays takes a long time to come together. Through multiple Covid waves and other illnesses, through misfortunes and chance goodwill, through ups and downs, my writers send me their nuanced thoughtful pieces. I am grateful they marshal their words for this project, at a time when I have run out of mine. I am glad they are able to say almost everything there is to be said on this most inexhaustible of subjects, and I hope you will discover their rare wisdom—and humour—in the pages that follow.

As for me, in the end, I don't end up writing an essay on the human cat, and my friend Janice does not write a sestina. But then neither Vincent nor Ms Cat worry about such things. That we loved them enough to plan so expansively is probably enough; with stoic generosity, they forgive our lapses.

Devapriya Roy, Lonavala
21 November 2021

Cats of Summer

by Saba Imtiaz

It was that time of the morning, a time when you're not sure if sunrise is five minutes away or five hours, because you're not quite sure when, exactly, the sun rises. It's when the only acceptable reason to be awake if a) you're walking into the house after a crappy, crappy night spent, inexplicably, at the beach, b) you got hooked onto a *Sex and the City* marathon that, also inexplicably, began at 1 am, c) you went online to look one thing up and are now so far into Instagram Explore that you have no idea why you're watching a video of Queen Elizabeth's corgi.

I was doing none of this. Instead, I was upright and attempting to talk to a cat. More specifically, I was offering bite-sized pieces of raw chicken to Smoky, my 12-year-old tabby-Persian mix, who was sitting there, nose upturned, staring as if she'd never seen it—or me—before, even though she ate chicken every day, and we'd lived together for over a decade.

My summer with Smoky had just begun. By the end of the summer, Smoky would learn to talk, and I'd earn the dubious distinction of owning a bullet-ridden AC.

Smoky wasn't my first cat, but she quickly eclipsed the pets who'd come before her: the kitten who died young because she was born with underdeveloped lungs, and the rabbit who cosied up next to you and tried to steal your crisps. (Food and pets, you will learn, is a recurring theme in our house.) Losing a pet is devastating, and each time, we vowed to never go through this again. But one of my closest friends wanted me to get another cat, so she took charge, looked up a notice on a bulletin-board on campus offering a cat for sale, and took me to see the cat.

That cat was then a fluffy, six-month-old called Smoky. Her only vice, the seller grumbled, was that she was obsessed with the air-conditioner. Over the next decade, my father would add many more things to Smoky's list of obsessions: ironed white sheets, kheer (from two specific shops, not your run-of-the-mill dairies), fries (but only from KFC), warm custard, finely chopped sausages, and the flaky tops of chicken patties. This is not an exhaustive list.

I may have brought her into the house, but she instantly became my father's cat. He could be in the throes of a migraine, completely unable to function or even speak, but would remember to feed Smoky. He finally had a child who, in true Punjabi fashion, he could constantly check in on and feed, and then grumble about how said child was spoiled. Smoky, in turn, sprawled out onto his entire bed, leaving him with a narrow space to sleep.

But Smoky also turned out to be the perfect child, who didn't mind spending time in the kitchen, observing him so intently I was sure she, too, could make biryani from scratch. She would watch warily if I ever asked my father for money. If I woke up in the middle of the night, I could hear the fridge opening and closing, Smoky meowing, and my father cajoling her to eat something, anything.

She was never the kind of cat that curls up in your lap and purrs. For the first few years of her life, we barely had any photos with her, since most photos resembled a ransom shot with Smoky struggling to get free from our clutches. She was aloof, stalking in and out of rooms at will, determinedly ignoring visitors, sometimes hiding in some dark corner under the bed while we organised search parties.

But my father insisted that she did love us. She showed her affection in random, disconnected ways: she waited by the door if she heard our footsteps, but then walked off as soon as we entered. Her ears perked when a rickshaw rolled up in front of the building. She could get extremely annoyed if we argued, meowing loudly to get us to stop shouting. If my father was unwell, she would keep vigil by his door, only venturing in every few hours to check in on him.

But that summer, my father was planning to travel to the US for a few months. Smoky and my father had been apart before, during my father's various rounds of hospitalisation, or his short trips out of town, but this would be their longest separation. That left me bound to the cat—and to Karachi for the summer.

Karachi can be a strange place any time of the year but the summer is particularly strange. The humidity makes it impossible to walk, work, or think. Karachi's residents perpetuate myths like 'July in Karachi is nice' whereas July as just as terrible as June and just as terrible as May. My extended circles of upper-middle-class acquaintances decamp to the easiest places they can get visas for—Thailand, Turkey, the confines of the Dubai Mall. The city doesn't quite empty out, but there is no one to eavesdrop on at the coffee shop, no one to run into in the crowded aisles of the supermarket, and more importantly, no one to avoid.

In any case, I was set to have a strange summer. Earlier that year, I'd started to withdraw from most people I'd been friends with recently. I'd grown tired of the nature of one-sided friendships, and of my inability to address that imbalance. Instead, something inside me snapped. I let most phone calls go to voice mail, my text messages went unanswered. I was well and truly ghosting everyone I could.

Except for Smoky.

Our summer did not get off to a great start. After my father left, Smoky went on a day-long hunger strike to express her dismay that her saviour did not appear to be walking through the door. The next day, she resigned herself to her fate and deigned to eat. It was only then I discovered that feeding Smoky wasn't as simple as putting down a plate of food. Over the years, Smoky and my father had developed some sort of a routine in our small apartment, an obstacle course that when combined with an exacting schedule was like being in an extremely not-fun version of Crystal Maze where you did not win any crystals and did not get to geek out in the Medieval Zone but went from room to room, desperate to try and win.

After a day of wondering why Smoky wouldn't eat despite the right hour (5:30 am), the right food (chicken), the right room (the drawing room), I asked my father why Smoky didn't eat food on the sofa. He explained the headrest situation as if it was a matter of common sense. (It wasn't.) Smoky would only eat the *first half* of breakfast—the second half was due an hour later—on the headrest of a specific sofa, not on the sofa cushions, or the table, or in the window.

Over the next few days, Smoky expressed displeasure with her deteriorating living standards at every turn. One evening, she sat on the kitchen floor, watching me chop sausages. My father always managed to dice them perfectly. Mine were misshapen chunks mixed in with shreds. As I slowly chopped, Smoky meowed incessantly like an American cooking show host shouting at a scared contestant, her yowls translating to 'chop faster, bitch!' I gave her the half I'd gotten through already, and her look of distaste before she deigned to eat them seared through my soul before I turned back to the chopping board.

Nothing was quite right: if I gave her warm milk, she walked away in distaste at the steam rising from the bowl; I cooked custard, but it wasn't as smooth as the one my father made. If I bought kheer from her favourite shop, she would lap it up gratefully, as if she'd been starving for days. Smoky had never been a very vocal cat, except when she was on heat and could meow the neighbourhood down, but everything I did elicited a meow that sounded distinctly like 'nooooooo' or 'pleaseeeeeeee.'

I was on a hunger strike of my own. Like every summer, I'd decided this would be the summer I'd remake my physical self: I decided to go on the ketogenic diet and doubled down by combining it with intermittent fasting, which meant I was either constantly hungry, or buying expensive avocados, or staving off my hunger with a blended concoction of butter, ghee, and coffee. One evening, as Smoky watched me suspiciously in the kitchen—she couldn't quite fathom that I could take over my father's (or her?) territory—the blender lid blew off. I valiantly threw myself at it so Smoky wouldn't get scalded. Her fur remained dry. I ended up with a ghee-and-caffeine conditioning treatment.

Over the next couple of weeks, Smoky and I formed a kind of routine. It mostly involved me being perpetually sleep-deprived and Smoky forcing herself to eat sausages that were not perfectly diced. I would haul myself out of bed at 5 am, and set a plate in front of Smoky. Sometimes Smoky would climb up on the bed and let out a meow so blood-curdling it sounded like the house was on fire.

There was no room for complacency. I had to get up, and I had to make the bed—because Smoky refused to lie on an unmade bed with wrinkled sheets and a twisted duvet. Her face—I don't quite know how—contorted into a grim expression at seeing a sheet that hadn't been straightened out, or clothes that hadn't been folded away. Some evenings—when the sausages were particularly dissatisfactory—she would sit alone in my father's darkened room as if mourning her fall from grace and culinary perfection. She would sit by my laptop as I struggled to write workable ledes, or let me sleep on the same sofa at night, her paws digging into my hair while I curled up in a ball.

The summer would have been calm. Uneventful, even, had it not been for the plagues.

First came the cockroaches—big, massive, terrible creatures—that I had to destroy using a bizarrely named insecticide called Czar which had to be smeared into corners. The roaches were otherworldly, not even put off by the large feline in the house. One even skirted past Smoky, but she could not be bothered to even attempt to swat at it, since over the past decade she'd wizened up to the fact that humans were perfectly capable of using their sandals to kill insects and there was no need for her to dirty her paws. She couldn't be bothered with killing lizards either, and so one evening, on discovering a lizard darting across the closet doors, I ran to my neighbours', handed them a jharoo, and asked them to take care of the reptile while Smoky and I took shelter in another room.

Smoky wandered into the room one afternoon and discovered that I had pulled out my entire closet—clothes meant for weddings, 20,000 hangers, t-shirts I hadn't worn since 2004. I'd just read Marie Kondo's *The Life-Changing Magic of Tidying Up* and got commissioned to write a piece based on my experience trying to achieve an ideal of minimalism. As the plague of unwanted possessions took over the room, Smoky gingerly tried to find a stable surface to walk. Eventually, she took refuge in one of the empty closet spaces—which she'd barely gotten to explore over the years—while I sat despondently amid piles of clothes, wondering why I was holding onto ripped trousers and a sequinned orange-and-yellow tunic. Over the next few days, I packed boxes and filled bags with clothes and books, marvelling at how I had managed to amass so much that seemingly meant so little.

I would have thought this process of ghosting, of re-examining my closets and my diet and my life would be therapeutic, that somehow I would remake myself into a new person. It wasn't so much that I wanted to find something new. After I stripped bare the layers of clothing and the social circles, I discovered I did not like anything: the people around me, the stories I wrote, the ideas I had, the fact that I didn't feel like any of the people I'd been friends with in recent years would ever turn around and ask if I needed help. Instead, I found more comfort in my old friends, in spending evenings in a cafe, in my pared-down possessions, in the comfort that I did not have to be anywhere, see anyone, do anything. But even though I seemed to have Marie Kondoed my life—shedding too much, too quickly—it never felt isolating. I had Smoky.

The plagues kept descending, one after the other. There was the brain-eating amoeba that infiltrated Karachi's already-toxic water supply. I stocked up on chlorine tablets and stopped washing my face for fear I would die a horrendous death by inadvertently putting water up my nose. I had to bar Smoky from drinking out of a bucket in the bathroom, and instead pushed her to a constantly replenished supply of mineral water.

Then one day, the air-conditioner mysteriously stopped working, even though—as every AC repairman pronounces at the beginning of the summer—the 'gas' had been filled and the grilles cleaned.

The AC repairman arrived, took one look out the window, and declared: 'It's been hit by a bullet.'

At this point, I'd lived in Karachi for 20 years, during which I'd had a gun pointed at me several times, and had heard stories of a man's head being lopped off and used as a football. I've also heard every manner of reason for an AC not working: the perpetual 'the gas has finished' to the 'there is ice in the AC'. A bullet was a new one, and I refused to believe that this could be true.

But the next day, the AC unit was pulled in and much to the smirking repairman's satisfaction—and one for his CV—we could all see the hole where a bullet had ripped through, causing seven thousand rupees of damage for some trigger-happy idiot's night out on the town.

Then on my thirtieth birthday, came the heatwave. Over the next few days, hundreds of people would die in Karachi. The power broke down. The city felt like someone had turned on the heating and forgot to turn it off. Smoky and I were two marooned souls, staring mournfully at the AC that refused to work. I paced around the house updating editors around the world about the heatwave while wishing I could rip off my skin. I never want to have children, but the extreme heat made me terrified of the young living being in my care. I was determined to do anything to protect her. I doused Smoky with a wet towel every few hours, while I wrote about morgues that had overrun capacity. I would wake up from my perch on the bed, confused about whether I'd taken a nap or had passed out from the heat, while Smoky sprawled out on the tiled floor. Smoky and I made it through, shielded by our privilege, a UPS that worked, and my incessant fear that I had to safeguard the only other living being in the house. (The roaches could die for all I cared.)

Smoky would never know what it meant. We can make all kinds of choices—who to love, who to be with, who to never see again. You can unfriend a person, ghost them, never want to hang out with them again. But a cat is more intuitive than your close friends, the ones who couldn't tell that something had fundamentally broken.

And then my father returned. Their reunion was punctuated by Smoky's plaintive meows—first, her anger at the fact that he had left her, then, trying to impress upon him the indignity of eating non-perfectly-diced sausages, then, her annoyance at the extremely jarring tune of a cat toy he had picked for her, followed by her enjoying the supply of treats he had brought to appease her. But instead of abandoning me altogether, she circled back to me for a hug, something she only permitted if she wanted you to save her from her weekly shower.

That summer, I was convinced that Smoky and I would be together for a long time, that she was somehow immortal. She would see me through everything, we would grow old together, and I would eventually take her around the world, wherever I ended up. In 2017, Smoky fell sick—a long-running infection took hold of her liver, and her body could not cope. I was abroad at the time. I arrived in Karachi the next morning to a quiet house, with the unshakeable feeling that she was just about to pop her head in the door, to check that we were all present and accounted for, and then go off to nap on a sofa. Years later, I still sometimes come home—in a different city, in a different country—and imagine that Smoky is sitting by the door, ready to walk off in a huff because I didn't get the right brand of kheer. Perhaps somewhere in cat heaven, an angel is deputed with changing the sheets and chopping up sausages, and pleading with Smoky to eat something, anything.

Vincent

by Janice Pariat

Last month, Vincent entered my life.

Vincent of the bitten ear, so named for obvious reasons. He doesn't bear any resemblance to his namesake, the Dutch Post-Impressionist painter, but I would venture to say he's quite the artist at heart. Once, when a friend left a wet oil painting on my floor, Vincent padded all over it leaving tiny paw-marks across the portrait.

Vincent is a rescue cat.

He was found abandoned at a dumpster, small, malnourished, unwell, and eventually fostered by well-meaning friends, who already had three cats of their own.

I saw his face first on Instagram. 'Take me home' the caption said, and my heart flip-flopped like a fish. Cannot. Must not. I live alone. I travel. Who will feed him? Take care of him? It's a struggle. A juggle. Don't be stupid.

Obviously then there was nothing else to be done but go across and pick him up.

And just like that he slipped into my heart, and my barsati.

We get along splendidly. Mostly because we leave each other alone.

The first few days, I thought, would be difficult. Perhaps he'd be mewing for lost friends and companions, at the strangeness of his new surroundings. But he quickly picked his favourite spots—under the sofa, under the bed, in a flower pot (especially if it had just been watered), under the moon chair in the corner—and fell asleep.

I picked out a few toys from the pet store, found an old shoe lace he could chase, and voila! That took care of all entertainment requirements. After a week, he was allowed to venture out into the terrace where more adventures awaited—with moths and bees and unreachable birds picking at ripened jamuns.

It is so easy to look after a cat, I tell everyone.

I write. He sleeps.

And I'm afraid by now I'm living up to all the clichés there are about cats and writers.

'That's why you brought kitty home,' a friend teased. 'You've always wanted to be a writer with a cat!'

And though I protested—I love animals, when I was little I wanted to be a vet, I grew up around animals in Assam, and have mostly always had pets at home—I must confess there might be something there. Writers are well paired with certain things—coffee, windows with a view, lovely fountain pens—and cats seem to fit snugly into the crook of this list. Obviously they aren't inanimate, immovable *things*, but living, breathing beings determined to turn you into their slave. (Vincent knows he will get fresh yoghurt every time he follows me into the kitchen and meows mournfully. A friend's cat will only drink water that's been chilled to his preferred temperature.) Blame it on writers before us, Hemingway, Doris Lessing, Mark Twain, Poe, Plath, Eliot, William Burroughs, who assailed the world with portraits alongside their felines, and cat-books and poems.

There are theories, of course, to explain this affinity.

Cats are lap-size, and hence more ergonomically suited to the writing exercise. As opposed to dogs. Or kangaroos (Elvis), anteaters (Dali), orangutans (Napoleon). (Although there are exceptions—Byron kept a bear, Baudelaire a tarantula.) Generally though, writers prefer small, quiet creatures, well-suited to someone who will be spending long hours sitting at a desk, staring out a window. The other explanation proffered is that there are several cat–writer characteristic overlaps conducive to cohabitation: they're observant, curious beings, leading lives largely in their own minds. In other words, both are happy to leave the other well alone. They create their own routines, are largely nocturnal, and are perfectly content to amuse themselves on their own.

Some are convinced that cats are a muse. They inspire, with their weirdness and comic traits and aloofness. Perhaps the fact that cats, no matter how domesticated, are never entirely tamed. For the cat is social outlier. The animal appeals to our romantic notion of a singular lonely genius endowed with not wholly benevolent powers. Or, as Poe said, 'I wish I could write as mysterious as a cat.'

But I'm convinced there's something more.

In an article in *The New Yorker*, 'Virginia Woolf's Idea of Privacy', Joshua Rothman writes of how Woolf seems to have strongly believed in 'preserving life's mystery'. And doing this by leaving certain things undescribed, unspecified, and unknown. It has to do, Rothman continues, with a kind of inner privacy, by means of which you shield yourself not just from others' prying eyes, but from your own. Call it an artist's sense of privacy. A certain resolute innerness. A 'kernel of selfhood' that we can't share with others. Cats, I think, share this with writers. Why else would Joyce Carol Oates say, 'The writer, like any artist, is inhabited by an unknowable and unpredictable core of being which, by custom, we designate the "imagination" or "the unconscious" (as if naming were equivalent to knowing, let alone controlling), and so in the accessibility of Felis catus we sense the secret, demonic, wholly inaccessible presence of Felis sylvestris. For like calls out to like, across even the abyss of species.'

First published as "Writers, Practical(ly) Cats" in The Hindu BusinessLine *on 14 July 2017.*

A Home for Eecha
by Anushka Ravishankar

I always felt I was a dog person. There really was no reason for this conviction. I never had a pet, growing up—canine or feline or even piscine. So I had no reason or opportunity to prefer one over the other.

My first close encounter with a cat was when my daughter, A, was around two years old. I heard her yowling in the backyard. I rushed out in a panic and found her standing with a cat almost as big as she was, in her arms. She had evidently picked it up and didn't know how to put it down. I released the cat (and A) and laughed till I cried. The cat seemed unfazed.

A was animal-mad and wanted a pet dog. My husband, R, was all in favour of the idea, having grown up in a zoo. (Honestly. I'm not making that up.) But I stood firm in my refusal. I had no time, energy or inclination to manage a pet. Besides, I'd noticed that dogs barked. And they needed to be walked. I could do without the exercise.

I did give in to A's entreaties for a pet and get some fish, at one point, but that ended in tragedy, as fish stories often do (for the fish, at least).

In between, we had another cat encounter. A kitten used to come to the door of our apartment in Chennai and A and R used to feed him regularly. A few days later, he turned out to be a she, and gave birth to many more kittens. The mother cat was then named Juno. She went away with her kittens after a couple of weeks.

Many years later, when we lived in Gurgaon, a cat brought three kittens to our terrace. A immediately set out a little tub, about one foot in diameter. So while the mother came and went, the three kittens cuddled with each other in the tub. Whenever we stepped onto the terrace, they would scuttle away and hide behind the washing machine.

Then one evening, when A had gone away to spend the night with friends, I heard a mournful mewling on the terrace. Two of the kittens had disappeared—the mother cat had taken them away. But the third, a scrawny unappealing-looking black thing, had been left behind.

I had no idea what to do. I called A at once, as the cat expert of the family. A said that since there was a chance that the mother cat might come back for the kitten, we should leave it on the balcony. But there were some big tomcats around; I was afraid one of them might find the kitten and attack it. So, since I couldn't bring it in, I sat vigil just inside the door, all night. The kitten didn't stop mewling for a minute. After days of cuddling and cavorting with its siblings, it was suddenly alone and motherless. It was heartbreaking.

Amazingly, though, every time we stepped onto the terrace, instead of running away as it used to, the kitten would come towards us. As if it knew we were now its only hope. *We* knew nothing of the kind, though. I still hoped the mother might come back.

In the morning, I knew she wouldn't. The kitten's eyes were shut with something oozy. The mother had taken away the other two to save them from the infection. I panicked. I had no idea what to do with a healthy pet, let alone one that was ill. R had to leave early for work. I called A again, and she dropped all her plans for the day and came charging back. We took the kitten to the nearby vet. The kitten may have been ill and practically blind, but it was full of beans and tried to bite his way out of the tub, which we'd covered with a flimsy lid made of newspaper.

Long story short, he (we found out at the vet's that he was a he) was injected, fed, and we came home with a kitten. We discussed it and decided that
we would have to find him a home, but until then, we would take care of him.
Meanwhile, he needed a name. He was black and tiny and we felt he looked
more like a fly (eecha) than a cat (poocha). So Eecha he was.

Eecha sat around and mewled sadly for two days straight. At night, he
slept if we kept him on our laps, but the moment we set him down, he woke
up and started mewling again. Most of the time he slept in my cupped palms.
A and R looked at one another and raised their eyebrows, remembering my
rants against pets.

This is different, I said defensively. The poor thing has been abandoned.
Of course we have to look after him. Until we find a home for him.

Finding a home for Eecha was the next project, then. A put word and pictures out on Facebook and some enquiries came in. What followed was like
something out of The Great Indian Wedding. Finding a match for a pet is
much the same as finding a match for an offspring, we found.

The first candidates called. They were a young couple, not long married.
We asked them to come over to see Eecha.

By this time, it must be said, Eecha had fully recovered, decided he was
the boss of the house, and was completely unafraid of human beings, since
the specimens he'd encountered were wont to give in to his every whim and
endure his every misconduct. He had grown sharp teeth and he bit us all the
time. We found it cute.

There was one evening, that I remember clearly. I had gone out to dinner
with friends and R was alone with the kitten. In the middle of dinner, I got a
call from R asking me to buy cigarettes. Why don't you go down to the shop

and buy them, I asked? He replied that the kitten was sleeping on his lap and he didn't want to disturb him. One of the friends I was with told me, you will never give away this cat. I laughed at him. People are coming to see the cat this week. By next week he'll be gone, I said.

The young couple turned up the next day. They looked nice. The young man (YM) and young woman (YW) sat down on the sofa and we called Eecha, who came trotting in to see who had come.

Anyone who knows anything about cats knows that you don't pick up a cat until the cat says you may. YM clearly doesn't know this. He grabs Eecha. Eecha is not happy. Young man drops Eecha like a hot brick, nursing his hand, which has some rather cute (from my besotted POV) teeth marks.

We asked YM if he wanted some antiseptic ointment. No, no I'm used to all this, YM said, and laughed in a macho sort of way. While our attention was thus diverted, Eecha had climbed onto YW's shoulder, presumably to get a good look at her face. YW was clearly terrified of cats. YM, slightly jealous, I felt, of the attention his wife was getting, told her ominously that she should watch out in case he scratched her eyes. YW froze, eyes closed, breath held.

A took pity on her and took Eecha away.

YM was still pooh-poohing the idea of ointments. I am an animal lover, he declared. As an example he told us of the time he was bitten by a monkey. We were fascinated and asked him how it happened. We carefully refrained from asking the question which immediately occurred to both of us: how does being bitten by an animal prove you are an animal lover?

Turns out, a monkey was playing on his neighbour's car and YM, as an unafraid animal lover, went right up to the monkey, to try and stop it. And the silly monkey, not recognizing an animal lover when it saw one, bit him.

A and I avoided each other's eye and almost choked from trying not to laugh.

YW was still looking at Eecha in a horrified manner. YM, oblivious to his wife's horror, was holding forth on how he loved animals and how he wanted his wife to get used to animals, which is why he wanted a cat.

Not this one, A and I told each other with a look. Not after the way he handled Eecha. And the monkey.

That evening, Eecha was fussed over and was told he'd had a narrow escape. Unimpressed, he bit my ankle.

We should have stopped him, I know. But he was too tiny for his biting to be anything but amusing.

He was so small, he had to crawl up the sofa hanging on precariously with his claws. The sofa was also his scratchpad, and it was beginning to look ragged, so on the advice of experienced cat owners and the vet, we decided to get his nails trimmed. He came back from the vet's and tried to climb up onto the sofa where we were sitting. But without his sharp nails, he slipped and slid and fell off. His look of wounded bewilderment was so sad to see, we decided never to trim his nails again.

In any case, it's just till we find him a home.

We got another call in a week or so. It was another youngish couple. They had lost their kitten and wanted another one to replace it. When we asked them how they'd lost it, the man told us that one day they'd left the door open and the kitten had run out as they were leaving for work. They didn't have the time to look for it and by the time they got back, it had been killed by a passing car.

We told them not to bother to come.

We weren't handing Eecha over to a couple as careless as that. Eecha showed his gratitude by chewing A's hands. She still has the scars.

When he was not biting us, or sometimes even when he was, Eecha was a source of endless delight. Since he had no mother to train him to be a cat, he created his own training schedule. One day was running. He ran like a loon, round and round the room. One day was stalking. He'd find something to stalk (usually someone's feet) and crouch unmoving for a while. Then his bum would begin to wiggle and he'd pounce. One day would be given over to jumping. He'd leap as high as he could. I could watch for hours, fascinated by the catness of him. He was such a lively kitten, we were sure anyone would be happy to have him.

The third candidate was a young man. He came over and we all really liked him. Eecha seemed to not be too inclined to bite him, which was a very good sign. He was an adventurous young man, who had a couple of cats already and, if I remember right, even a dog. They all lived in his parents' home. His job involved travelling, so he travelled a lot to the hills, he said, in an SUV, with his friends and his pets.

We imagined Eecha going on swashbuckling adventures with many other cats. I pictured him sitting at the window, the wind in his fur, the mountains reflected in his yellow eyes. We felt this might be a life he would enjoy.

But how were we to know if the young man was reliable? That all these animals that lived together were taken good care of?

A told him that we would like to see his house before we let him take Eecha away. He agreed amiably enough, but as he left he said, you know, I really think you should just keep him. You clearly don't want to part with him.

We never heard from him again.

And that's when we stopped looking for a home for our cat.

Eecha went on to have many adventures: he was attacked by big tomcats, he was mauled by dogs and escaped narrowly with his life, he got stuck in a tree like a stereotypical cat, he travelled across the country in a train and met snakes and cows and goats in Chennai. He never stopped biting our ankles, though. Maybe that was his way of showing us his gratitude and affection for giving him a home.

Prayishchit

by Bhagwaticharan Verma
Translated by Sakshi Agarwal

If there was anyone in the whole house that Kabri the cat loved, it was Ramu's wife. And if there was anyone in the whole house that Ramu's wife hated, it was Kabri the cat. Ramu's wife, after spending two months at her parents', had come home to her in-laws' for the first time. Her dear husband's infatuation and her mother-in-law's figure of adulation, a girl of fourteen. The key to the storeroom now hung by the jewelled chain around her waist, the servants began working under her rule, and Ramu's wife oversaw everything. The mother-in-law took a string of beads and devoted herself to prayer and the scriptures.

But she was only a girl of fourteen after all. If one moment, the storeroom was alive with movement, the next, she had dozed off sitting in it. Kabri the cat seized the opportunity and began devouring the milk. Ramu's wife's life was in danger while Kabri the cat bared her claws in amusement. Ramu's wife was moving ghee into the great vessel when she nodded off, and the rest of the ghee went into Kabri the cat's belly. Ramu's wife covered the milk and just went off to give some to the cook, and the rest disappeared. If the situation had escalated until this point, it would have been harmless, but Ramu's wife became so unreservedly known to Kabri, that the mere act of eating became nearly impossible. A bowl brimming with rabri arrived in Ramu's wife's room, and by the time Ramu made an appearance, the bowl had been licked clean. Balai arrived from the market, and by the time Ramu's wife prepared a paan, it vanished.

Ramu's wife made up her mind. Either she would stay in the house or Kabri the cat. Both sides prepared for war and remained on alert. A trap for the cat was brought. Milk, cream, rats, and many different kinds of foods relished by the cat were put in. She didn't even spare them a look. But the cat did show a stirring too. Until now, she had been terrified of Ramu's wife, but now, she began playing the game. She still maintained a distance between the two of them, enough that Ramu's wife could never touch her.

With the cat in high spirits, Ramu's wife's life became even more prickly. She was gifted her mother-in-law's reproaches, and the husband received tasteless meals.

One day, Ramu's wife made kheer for Ramu. Pistachios, almonds, makhanas, and all sorts of dry fruits were decorated with gold flakes and mixed in the milk. And finally, a bowl filled to the brim with kheer was placed on a high shelf in the room, so the cat couldn't possibly reach it. Ramu's wife busied herself in the preparation of paan soon after.

Unknown to Ramu's wife, the cat emerged. Standing below the shelf, she looked up at the bowl, breathed in the aroma, judged the fare to be delectable, and estimated the height of the shelf. Ramu's wife, engrossed in her errand, was oblivious to it all. She finished her task and went off to give her mother-in-law the paan, and here, Kabri the cat leapt. Her paw hit the bowl and it fell on the floor with a clang.

When the sound reached Ramu's wife's ears, she tossed the paan before her mother-in-law and ran, only to appear and find the flowery bowl in pieces, the kheer spilt, and the cat flinging the kheer everywhere in the room. Upon seeing Ramu's wife, Kabri dashed off.

Ramu's wife's vision turned red.

Ramu's wife resolved to commit murder. She didn't sleep a wink the entire night. What strategy should she implement in her war against the cat so the creature doesn't come out of it alive? She lay there, pondering. When morning arrived, she saw Kabri sitting on the sill, gazing at her adoringly.

An idea meandered its way into Ramu's wife's mind, and she sat up smiling. As soon as Kabri saw her rise, she scurried off. Ramu's wife put a bowl of milk in her room's doorway and left. When she returned with a piece of wood, she discovered Kabri lapping up the milk. The cat had taken the bait and the time was right, she drew upon all her might and bashed the cat with the wood. Kabri didn't move, not an inch, she didn't cry, not a sound, she just flipped and fell on her back.

The clash caused the maid who left her broom, the cook who stepped out of the kitchen and the mother-in-law who interrupted her prayers to materialize at the site of the fatality. Ramu's wife stood there, her head bowed down like a criminal, listening as they began to talk.

The maid said, 'Arey Ram! The cat has breathed her last, Maaji. The cat has died because of the daughter-in-law, this is just tragic.'

The cook spoke, 'Maaji, the death of a cat is equal to that of a person. I won't work in the kitchen till this aura of guilt shrouds the daughter-in-law.'

The mother-in-law concurred, 'Yes, you're absolutely right. Until the daughter-in-law is liberated from her guilt, nobody can drink a drop of water or eat a morsel of food. Daughter-in-law, what have you done?'

The maid remarked, 'Now what has to be done? If you agree to it, I shall go fetch the priest.'

The mother-in-law felt her strength return, 'Yes, of course, run and call the priest.'

23

The news of the death spread like wildfire in the neighbourhood—there was a string of women constantly moving in and out of Ramu's house. They launched a barrage of questions, in the midst of which crouched the daughter-in-law.

When the message reached the priest, he was at prayer. The moment he heard, Pandit Paramsukh rose to his feet. Smiling at the priestess, he spoke, 'Don't cook today's meals. Lala Ghasiram's daughter-in-law took a cat's life. There shall be an atonement. We will be served a feast.'

Pandit Paramsukh Chaubey was a short and round man, four feet and ten inches long and fifty-eight inches around the waist. The face was rounded and chubby, with a giant moustache, of a light complexion, and his hair was tied in a traditional shikha that hung down his back.

It is said that when one seeks priests who have the appetite of five people, Pandit Paramsukh is given the primary position in that list of names.

Pandit Paramsukh arrived and the quorum was achieved. The Panchayat sat down: the mother-in-law, the maid, Kisnu's mother, Chhannu's grandma and Pandit Paramsukh. The rest of the women were manufacturing sympathy for the daughter-in-law.

Kisnu's mother commenced, 'Panditji, which circle of hell does the crime of killing a cat merit?'

Pandit Paramsukh glanced at his book, 'The circle of hell cannot be foretold merely from this information, we need the period of time when the cat was killed. Only then can we know which hell.'

'At about seven in the morning,' the maid of the house spoke.

The priest flipped through the pages, traced certain lines with his finger, touched his forehead and ruminated over it. His face became engulfed in a haze of confusion, he frowned in effort, his nose crinkled and his tone became grave, 'Hare Krishna! Hare Krishna! This is very unfortunate, the cat was killed in the early hours of the morning, in Brahma Muhurat! Ramu's wife's place is in the fifth circle of hell, in the torturous Kumbhipak! Ramu's mother, this is indeed very unfortunate.'

Ramu's mother teared up, 'So then Panditji, now what do we do? Only you can tell us!'

Pandit Paramsukh smiled, 'Ramu's mother, why are you worrying so much? When will priests like us come to your aid if not on days like these? There is a ritual for atonement in the scriptures, and so atonement will set everything right.'

Ramu's mother exclaimed, 'Panditji, this is the very reason we sent out for you. Do lead us on to what we must do now!'

'What has to be done? Just this, a cat of gold must be sculpted and then gifted by the daughter-in-law. Until the cat is given away, the house shall remain impure. After the cat is given away, we must begin a prayer of twenty-one days.'

Chhanu's grandma spoke, 'Of course, Panditji is absolutely right, we must give away the cat first and then start the prayers after.'

Ramu's mother enquired, 'Tell us, Panditji, the sculpture should weigh how many tolas?'

Pandit Paramsukh smiled. Stroking his paunch, he replied, 'How many tolas must the cat weigh? Arey Ramu's mother, the scriptures dictate that

25

the weight of the gold for the cat sculpture must be as much as the cat; but we are living in the perilous times of Kaliyug, religion and ritual have been degraded, reverence has been lost. So then, Ramu's mother, even if we make a cat weighing the cat, what will it weigh? Not more than twenty tolas or so. Well, so be it, make sure the cat weighs about twenty-one tolas and give it away. The rest is up to your faith!'

Ramu's mother looked at the priest with wide eyes, 'Oh god, twenty-one tolas of gold! Panditji, that is a lot of gold, can't we make do with a cat weighing about a tola?'

A chuckle escaped Pandit Paramsukh, 'Ramu's mother, a cat of a mere one tola! Is your attachment to your money overtaking your affection for your daughter-in-law? She has committed a grave wrong, it is not befitting that you choose such material attachments over her atonement.'

Negotiations began and both sides finally arrived at a compromise of eleven tolas.

And then came the matter of prayers. Pandit Paramsukh proclaimed, 'What is the difficulty there? What are we priests for? Ramu's mother, I shall recite the scriptures, all you have to do is send the paraphernalia to my home.'

'How much will it all cost?'

'Oh, we shall perform the prayers with the minimal amount of provisions. All we need for donations, ten maunds of wheat, one maund of rice, one maund of dal, one-whole maund of til, five maunds of jau and five maunds of channa, twenty seers ghee and one-whole maund of salt. That's all, and the matter will be resolved.'

'Oh god, so many things! Panditji, we'll have to spend a hundred or maybe a hundred and fifty rupees buying all this,' Ramu's mother sobbed.

'But this is the least we'll have to do. Killing a cat is such a serious crime, Ramu's mother! Stop looking at the costs, first look at your daughter's misdeed. It is a matter of atonement, it is not play—and more so, it is your own reputation! Every family has to atone for their wrongdoings. You are not some ordinary family. A hundred and fifty rupees or so is just the dirt of your hands.'

Pandit Paramsukh's words impacted the gathered five. Kisnu's mother spoke, 'Panditji is absolutely right in what he said, it's not as if taking a cat's life is some lowly misdeed. If you have committed a grave wrong, you must pay a high cost.'

Chhanu's grandmother affirmed, 'Of course, what else? It is only through gifts that we can right our misdeeds. There should be no frugality in such matters.'

The cook recited, 'And then, Maaji, you're big people. How will these costs even affect you in any way?'

Ramu's mother peered at the faces around her. All five were in agreement with the priest. Pandit Paramsukh was smiling from ear to ear, true to his name. He shot the final arrow, 'Listen to me, Ramu's mother! Your daughter is at the precipice of the fifth circle of hell, and it is your responsibility to save her. The cost is nothing. Don't turn away from her.'

Ramu's mother took a deep breath, 'We will have to dance on your palm as you tell us to, what else can we do now?'

Pandit Paamsukh's voice rose in anger, 'Ramu's mother! This is a matter of celebration! If you mind it even a bit, don't do it. I'm leaving.' The priest began collecting his things.

'Oh no, Panditji, Ramu's mother has no qualms. Understand her plight a little. Don't lose your temper like this!' the cook, Chhanu's grandma and Kisnu's mother sang in the same note.

Ramu's mother touched the priest's feet—and he sat down even more self-reassurance than before.

'What else must we do?'

'The twenty days prayer will be of twenty-one rupees and for twenty-one days, you must feed five Brahmins both times of the day,' Pandit Paramsukh paused. 'But don't worry about this, I shall alone manage eating both the meals, and in feeding me, you shall receive God's blessings for feeding five Brahmins.'

'Panditji is right in saying this. After all, look at his paunch!' the cook beamed, pulling the priest's leg.

'All right, make yourself busy with the preparations for the atonement. Ramu's mother, go and bring me eleven tolas of gold, I will go and get it sculpted. I will return in two hours. Make sure you have everything ready for the prayers by then. And listen, for the prayers...'

The priest hadn't been even completed his directions when the maid barged into the room, breathless. Everyone was taken by surprise. Ramu's mother asked worried, 'What is it, what happened?'

The maid spoke in a faltering voice, 'Maaji, the cat, it ran away!'

The Wet, The Fast, and Mao

by Anukrti Upadhyay

I – A City without Cats

There were no cats in the city I was born in. Or so it seemed to me. My home and neighbourhood otherwise abounded in all kinds of bird and animal life. There were cuckoos, bulbuls, bee-eaters, and sunbirds in the guava, pomegranate and custard apple trees in the garden, and whole colonies of noisy squirrels on the jamun and mulberry in the backyard. A family of chameleons lived in an old, gnarled champa beside the house-door. Troops of monkeys routinely whooped their way through the mango and neem and shirish trees lining the street, and peahens nested in the empty lot behind the house. Cows wandered down the street in the evenings and we fed them the first chapatis set aside at every meal. A bitch littered every year in a sandy patch at one end of the street and my mother cooked halwa for her, rich with ghee and spices meant for new mothers.

My nanny kept a couple of goats for milk at the back of our house. I was allowed to caress their large-eyed, soft-eared kids. My father, a bird-fancier, kept budgerigars and assorted song-birds in a large cage. I helped him put out bird-seed, fill earthen pots with water and break bits of cuttle-fish bones to scatter around the cage.

But cats were entirely absent from this parade of birds and animals. No one mentioned them, or kept them as pets. The only cats I had seen were in my colouring books. They looked up from the printed pages, gambolling with colourful balls of yarn, so impossibly round-eyed and furry that I knew they couldn't be real. To me they were imaginary creatures or, at least, creatures who lived in other places, where children, unaccompanied by adults, picnicked on hills overgrown with heather and ate pies and drank ginger-beer, that is to say, charming beings found only in story-books.

It was my mother who told me the story of the young woman who kept a cat despite the opposition of her entire family. Why did no one want the cat, I asked, was it because she ate the cream off the milk? By then my views about cats were coloured by a story I had read—'Prayashchit' by Bhagwaticharan Verma. The story in Hindi, written sometime in the early twentieth-century and an all-time favourite of every children's anthologist, was about a naughty cat and a harassed daughter-in-law. In the story, the cat regularly licked the cream off the milk and caused trouble for the young daughter-in-law of the household.

No, this cat did not steal milk-cream, my mother answered, but cats are considered inauspicious, people do not keep them in their homes. I was puzzled. Are animals inauspicious, I asked? Of course not, my mother replied, we worship all nature, and that includes animals. You know that Durga ji rides a lion and Ganesh a mouse and we pray to the lion and mouse when we pray to the gods. We even give sweetmeats to crows which feed on garbage and to tiny ants which crawl everywhere. It is only cats that are considered bad omen. My confusion mounted. If every creature, from rats to lions, was worshipped, even plain crows and ants were fed ritual meals, why then was there no place for cats? Why were cats alone considered inauspicious?

My mother sighed. Don't you want to hear the rest of the story, she asked?

This cat was a model pet, she continued, she ate whatever scraps the young woman gave to her, crept quietly under her bed at night, never soiled the house and even pressed the woman's limbs as she slept. The cat always kept out of the way of the men-folk when they left for work, as if she knew she shouldn't fall in their path. My mother's large eyes softened as she spoke. I was awed by the cat's numerous perfections and felt sure that everyone must have eventually come around to loving her. Did everyone love her when they saw how nice she was, I asked? No, my mother shook her head, no, only I loved her, she said softly.

I puzzled over the story of the virtuous and yet unloved cat for a long time. What more could she have done to be loved by all?

II - The Catman of Bombay

I found the answer many years later one afternoon in one of the many small alleys leading to the tank of Banganga in Bombay and it surprised me. Banganga is an incongruity in the heart of the mega-city, reminiscent of the narrow streets of Banaras rather than the leafy lanes of South Bombay. The tank, fed by an underground spring, is ringed with temples and a cluster of dwelling-houses. There are shops and food-stalls and hawkers selling bangles and knick-knacks. The narrow lanes are always filled with people —temple-goers, washer-men carrying loads of washing, vegetable vendors, sellers of fried goodies. Men and women go about their chores, groups of transgenders pass by talking loudly, bands of monks sing hymns. Children swim in the tank's green waters and old women sit on the stone steps oiling and braiding the hair of young girls.

As I walked down a lane one late morning, I noticed an unusual number of cats. They lay about in the dusty street and on stoops, prowled along the low walls and peeped through the rusty gates of a municipal school. They seemed too purposeful to be a random congregation of strays. There was a strange, expectant air about them. A man wheeling a bicycle entered the lane and a ripple went through the assembled cats. Ears pricked, tails gently swaying, they watched his every movement keenly. Whistling, he leaned his bicycle against a wall and undid the bundles tied to its carrier. A strong smell of fish filled the lane. The man threw pieces of fish to the waiting cats who caught them neatly in their mouths. It appeared to be a well-drilled routine, all was as orderly as can be. There was no jostling or pushing or mewling or swarming. As he moved amongst them, giving bits to the smaller ones, occasionally he reached down to stroke a bent head or a raised back. When the food was over, the cats dispersed. They did not cluster around the man or rub against his legs, they simply licked their mouths, sniffed at the few fallen fish-scales and went their way. The entire operation, from start to finish, took no more than fifteen minutes. I couldn't contain my curiosity. 'You feed the cats every day?' I asked. The man nodded. 'On your own or someone helps you with buying the fish?'

He looked at me. 'I am a tailor, I have my shop up the lane. I make enough money to be able to buy a handful of fish for the cats.'

'Of course,' I said hastily, embarrassed at my tactlessness, 'but why do you feed them?'

'Why? Because they need the food. Why else?' He retrieved his cycle and wheeled it away. At the head of the lane, he stopped and turned. 'Sometimes there is no particular reason for doing something, the act itself is its own reason, I feed the cats, that is my dharma, the cats eat the food, that's theirs.' I marvelled at his giving the ancient Gita a new shake.

I have, since, witnessed cats performing their cat-dharma with elan across the world. Draped on roof-tops in Hong Kong and resting in the doorways in London's inner city, I have seen them watch the swarms of rushing office-goers without judgement, curled up in dim cosy shops on the peaceful islands in Greece, and in old houses in Spain's white villages they have been aloof but tolerant of caresses, outside spotless restaurants in Tokyo and Kyoto, they have crouched with politely averted eyes, cleaning their paws assiduously. Sometimes as I look up at the full moon, I have a strange conviction that the markings in its brilliant disc are actually a cat watching the sleeping world, watching endlessly.

III - Mao

I came across Mao in the cavernous underground parking-lot of an office building in Nariman Point. She was cowering in a corner, her stringy tail aloft, her thin body trembling. There was no sign of a mother cat or siblings. The place smelt of hot metal, petrol fumes and staleness. Sounds of footsteps, slamming doors, revving engines bounced off the concrete walls and echoed all around. I picked her up. She fitted in my two hands and had enormous, leaf-shaped ears. Her tilted eyes glowed golden in the gloom and when she mewed, her tiny face wrinkled and her eyes closed. I could feel her heart beat inside her fragile chest. Leaving her there wasn't an option. I brought her home.

I wondered what she made of the transition from the noisy parking lot to the quiet apartment, I wondered how she managed to nestle in the hands which, with the slightest pressure, could crush her tiny skull, I wondered how she could look at me unflinchingly, close her eyes and fall asleep. I wondered at her ability to forget, to trust and accept.

At the vet's, she remained still as the young doctor probed and prodded her with gentle fingers, opening her mouth, peering into her ears. But when I picked her up, she buried her needle-like claws into my sleeve and clung to me. In the car, she crouched in my lap and evacuated her bowels, her heart hammering in her chest. I felt her fear, held her, and soothed her.

At home, I watched her and marvelled at the gradual assertion of her personality. She climbed into my lap to peep at the laptop and paw at my books. She tore holes in the blanket I fluffed up for her and slept on my knee instead. She trailed behind everyone and mewed loudly to remind us of her presence. She had clear preferences—she did not like kitten food, she liked bits of bread moistened with watered milk, she loved eggs.

It was always clear that Mao was going to be an outdoor cat. She adamantly refused to use her litter tray for anything but to sit and gaze around and relieved herself discreetly in corners. She preferred the garden and freedom of the yard downstairs. She liked climbing up into the champa tree and then mewing till someone helped her down. She chased after bugs and squirrels, lost count of time and forgot to return home for meals. Neighbours called to say they saw her in the back-garden or sitting in a window opening or stalking the croton borders. Once someone found her in the lane behind the building and brought her back.

There were other cats in the building—a couple of hulking toms and an often-pregnant calico. Mao had had her ear chewed by one of them and hid for two days in a shoe cabinet kept outside the gym in our building. When I finally found her, she had made a nest among the shoes and was fast asleep. As I moved the shoes to retrieve her, she came awake, twitching all over and taut, ready to flee. She did not resist being carried and did not wince when I cleaned her ear with alcohol. When I put her down though, she immediately retreated to the shoe-cabinet. After her ear healed, she accepted the boundaries and ventured no further than the large, spreading rain-tree in the driveway. She learnt to not be tempted to follow the bigger cats. Often, as evening light faded, I found her perched on the compound wall contemplating the lane behind the building where the street-cats played and fought. She made no attempt to join them and was satisfied with watching.

IV - What I think Mao thinks

Mao sits on the grey mat in the abbreviated lobby of our building, her limbs elegantly together, tail held aloft at an angle. Her white and orange fur lies smooth and she lifts the small triangle of her face towards the sun over which clouds are now streaming.

She watches the world, curious but not eager. The gaze of her yellow eyes, the colour of summer sun, seems inscrutable and detached.

An insect flits by, its green body iridescent in the sun. A roosting bat shuffles among the ashoka trees. Kicked by a careless foot, a pebble rolls. Her ears twitch. She is aware and unafraid. She chooses not to engage. She sits still and fulfilled like a Buddha.

Someone bends and scratches her under the chin. She stretches out and accepts the pleasure unabashedly. She is inviting and independent. The scratcher rises to leave. Work waits or an errand, banal urgencies of everyday life. She watches the person leave, silent and unmoving. When they return, she won't be here. She knows the futility of waiting. She knows how to want without being weighed down.

Someone passes by gingerly, avoiding even the shadow of her sleek, furry body. She surveys the avoider with wide-open eyes. She does not move or shrink. She occupies her space, easeful and assured.

She contemplates the trees through the curtain of fast-falling rain. When it stops raining, she rises and stretches her limbs, the lines of her body flow and compact. She steps out daintily and sniffs the sweet-smelling air. Gold coin-like leaves are falling from the rain-tree and bulbuls are singing. Children returning from school cluster around her. She pauses among them for a few moments and then saunters off. She is not indifferent; she is not attached. She is present and composed.

She has attained equipoise.

V - What Mao Actually Thinks

The Big Warm is hiding. It is nice when the Big Warm is looking at me.

Wet has arrived. It was hovering above in the dark just before light and I knew it wouldn't wait there for long. The Wet is not-friend, it is greedy, it wants everything, it won't stop till it has covered everything.

I look out at the Wet and wait.

Soon the Fast comes as well, howling and lashing at the Big Greens. 'Hello!' I call out to the Fast, 'It isn't their fault, they haven't done anything!' And they hadn't, till the Fast began to thrash them. Then they hit back of course, throwing their shaggy heads about and whipping the Fast with their long arms. The Fast yowls and chases after the Wet. I know it will never catch the Wet. The way to catch the Wet is to sit still, absolutely still and let it come to you, I have explained to the Fast often.

The Fast is friend, it makes leaves turn round and round and the buzzing things spin and the flying things tumble and flutter. But it can't be still and it can't let the Wet be. It is difficult to be the Fast.

I am happy to be Mao. I don't want to be the Fast or the Wet. I can sit here and watch them and the others. I don't want to run after them. I don't want them to run after me. The Wet should stay out, the Fast should slow down. I can then go and see if there is something in the holes I found right where the mud lies banked up along the path.

A door opens. I know the foot-steps. It is Food-mother.

No, I don't want to sit on the soft thing the Food-mother has brought. It smells of strange smells, not of Food-mother or mud or crushed snails or dry leaves. When the Wet goes away, I will take the soft thing outside and roll it about in the mud and the moving things that live in the mud. Then I will sit on it. Till then I will sit right here, it is hard and cold here and I cannot roll about but it will do.

The Fast has come yelling back and is among the Big Greens again but the Wet is retreating. There are patches of light in the dark. Soon the Wet will be gone.

I must lick and clean the places where the Wet has touched me.

Flying things are coming out of the Big Greens. The Wet is lying outside on the ground. It is quite done and tired.

'Be still,' I scold the Fast, 'be still now.'

The Fast is crying. It is difficult to be friend of the Fast.

The flying things are chattering everywhere. It is light and the smells are just right.

There are moving things all around, they are slipping and slithering and skittering.

There are many sounds of dripping and trickling and gurgling. The furry things are clicking and calling and chattering. The Wet is leaving.

It is the Small One. It is friend but this is no time for scratching or patting. I don't want to stop here anymore. The Wet has left. I need to find out where the hopping thing has disappeared. There is something peeping from under the leaves. There are sounds—crunching, ticking, rustling. I need to check them. Ok, just one last time, here, below my chin. It is difficult to be friend of the Small One.

I must go and look for the Big Warm now. I know he is out there some-where.

The Cat That Got My Tongue

by Gayathri Sankar

The campus Cat's entry to our college was innocuous, foretelling none of the chaos that would follow her soft, padded steps. No one could pinpoint precisely when it was that she had appeared in our college. Some suspected her of being an ageless deity, born long before our humble institution. That nonsense probably stemmed from Team Pawsitive; they revered the little runt like she was God Herself. They seemed to think that our college was built around her—the specific plot chosen *for* the Cat, whether consciously or not. To rid the campus of the Cat was unthinkable. We wouldn't be evicting the Cat from our home, we would be evicting her from *her* own home, which she had so graciously lent to us.

Despite Team Pawsitive's passionate propaganda, something about the Cat seemed sinister to me. This wasn't based on my general dislike of cats, although that may have influenced my opinion somewhat. I definitely thought it was unhygienic to let her roam around the area we ate in. But more than that, I sensed some kind of ancient, evil power lurking in the four-legged furball, though I struggled to articulate exactly what. There was something overly assured about her gait. Something unnerving about her cold, calculating yellow eyes. Something entitled about the way she purred at me while I was eating, looking at my plate expectantly. 'Shoo,' I said to her unsympathetically when she approached me in the mess once. She let out a single, plaintive 'meow' and I felt a chill run up my back. For a second my hands moved of their own accord, like I was a puppet on a string. I tore off a piece of my samosa, tempted to throw a morsel at her. There was something compelling about her short, frank plea. But I fought against the urge. Regaining control of my hands, I insolently stuffed the doughy crust into my own mouth. She blinked coldly at me and walked away. I spat it out when she had left—the mess really needs to work on their samosas.

As if dealing with her in the mess wasn't irritating enough, next the Cat began to appear in my classes. She seemed to especially enjoy philosophy. I'd find her lounging in the front row of my lectures, teacher's pet that she was. She rarely made a sound in class but the professors would straighten up on the days she appeared, looking alert and almost jittery. They'd address half the lectures to her, making more eye contact with her than anyone else. She appeared on the Dean's List at the end of the semester although her class participation was minimal. It was maddening to compete with such a smug, silent spectre. Any protests I made would be met with an argument about how everyone has a right to education. It became a tedious debate that erupted constantly around campus. I grew tired of the self-righteous magnanimity of the Cat's Followers. I understand compassion for all creatures, but shouldn't a line be drawn somewhere? What if the fleas traversing her fur wanted to be economics majors next? The world just doesn't need more economics majors.

More people finally started siding with me when a rumour began that the Cat was going to be appointed as a professor. It was a mystery how she could have acquired the necessary qualifications. The rumour had started in April so I initially dismissed it as an April Fool's joke blown out of proportion. Then one of my friends insisted they had seen her being escorted to the Pro Vice Chancellor's office (carried by four students while seated on a cushion). An uneasy feeling stirred in the pit of my stomach, aided only partially by the mess's latest attempt at paapdi chaat.

The rumours were confirmed at the end of my second semester. Well, they weren't *fully* true—she would only be teaching a co-curricular—but a line was obviously still being crossed. An article was even published about her on Buzzfeed. I tried not to think about the Cat over the holidays, but she popped up in conversation like a whack-a-mole. At a family gathering, one of my cousins asked me which college I was attending. Generally, when I answer this question, my response is received with a curl of the lip. Over the years I've grown accustomed, even attached, to our university's unfavourable reputation. It makes for rousing conversation. However, this time her face lit up. 'Oh, the college where a cat is going to be teaching a course!' she said. 'How quirky.'

I winced. The Cat seemed to overshadow everything; I couldn't even be insulted in peace anymore.

There was obviously great speculation around her course over the summer —she was to teach 'feline dialect' (not even registered as an official language in India). Despite everyone's reservations, the seats ended up filling rapidly during registration. Friends who had declared the course to be overhyped wept when they didn't land seats, which infuriated but didn't surprise me. College is a three-year performance in hypocrisy, where everyone's a method actor.

Only one of my fur-brained friends managed to get into the class. Despite my probing, for the first few weeks she didn't say much, revealing only that her teacher's methods were unconventional and that she was having some trouble keeping up. But by the second month she'd speak about it with a glow in her cheeks and a distant, glazed look in her eyes, claiming it had changed her life. The Cat, I was convinced, had been given the actual means to start a cult.

'Shut up,' said Tanya, when I insinuated this. 'You're coming from a place of bias. Just attend a few classes with me, you'll change your mind.'

I was so absolutely certain that this wouldn't be the case that I complied. I resented the accusation that I was biased. I was just a critical thinker, clear-headed enough to not be seduced by a feline's wily charms. Besides, this wasn't just for *my* own good. If *Animal Farm* had taught me anything, it was that animals who mingle too much with humans inevitably become alcoholics.

'So what do you do, meow at each other?' I asked Tanya as we entered the classroom. This was apparently a totally absurd idea, making her burst into laughter. 'You'll see,' she said enigmatically. 'You just need to see.'

I saw nothing. The first half of the class was just the Cat sitting on the desk, lazily sweeping its surface with her tail and surveying the class with bored, yellow eyes. Sometimes she moved around a little and the students around me took notes furiously. I played along for a while, then my eyelids began to feel heavy. 'Tanya, is the entire class going to be like this?' I whispered, wondering if everyone was involved in a scheme to mess with me. Maybe the Cat was getting revenge for that one time in the mess I refused to share my food?

One of the students, Rishi, raised his hand. 'Uh, could you repeat the last thing you said?' he asked. 'I was having trouble following.' The kid next to him nodded in agreement. I looked at him with bulging eyes and turned to look back at the cat. It yawned and stretched, twitching an ear.

'Hey, um, what's going on?' I asked.

Rishi looked at me and one of his eyes twitched. The kid next to him arched her back. The cat made a low growly noise, more of a vibration than a sound. I shrank back into my chair.

'The teacher's asking you to raise your hand and not talk amongst each other,' Tanya whispered to me, looking embarrassed.

What an *elaborate* hoax, I'd had enough. 'This is honestly a lazy prank,' I announced, getting up to leave. 'You guys could at least meow at each other to make it appear more realistic.'

Peals of laughter rang through the class. Tanya raised her hand. 'Permission to speak in English?' she asked the Cat, who looked at her indifferently. 'She's new here—I should have explained beforehand. The first rule of class is that you can't meow.' Tanya said. 'Adult cats don't meow to each other or to other animals, it's something they developed to communicate with humans. Because humans are too stupid to understand non-vocal communication.'

'So you guys are communicating with each other... non-verbally?' I asked.

'Yeah!' she said. 'It's such a rich language, it allows so much more to be conveyed.'

'Okay, you know what?' I said testily. 'I'm going to whisper something in your ear, and I want you to non-verbally communicate it to the student opposite you.'

'I'll try,' said Tanya uncomfortably. 'I'm not that good yet, maybe you should whisper it to the teacher.'

'Fine!' I snapped. The Cat was now regally perched on the windowsill, not even paying me attention. She was eyeing a bird on the other side of the glass. I strode up to her and she fixed her yellow gaze on me, somehow expectant and disinterested at the same time. I leaned down, feeling slightly silly now, and whispered into her ear.

The Cat looked at me and then looked at the class. Her tail flicked almost imperceptibly. She yawned.

Rishi raised his hand again, eagerly. 'You whispered in her ear that you're sorry you didn't share any of your food with her that one time in the mess. And that your fear of cats arises from this one time that you tried to cuddle with a kitten called Kitty Perry and it scratched you. She apologises for your bad experience with Kitty, but also wants to remind you that cats, like humans, need to be asked before having their personal space invaded. And that one bad experience shouldn't determine your opinion of an entire species.'

I opened my mouth and closed it again. I could suddenly see Kitty Perry clearly in my head. A soft white snowball of a kitten with black button eyes. I could see my small grubby nine-year-old hands reaching out to grab him. The sound of Kitty hissing and the silver flash of claws. My eyes welling up with tears—not from the pain, but from a feeling I didn't know to name then, that I now recognize as my first taste of rejection.

The Cat sneezed.

'She also said that the cat was probably bitter because Kitty Perry is a pretty undignified name. What happens when it grows up? Does it become Catty Perry? That just sounds like a bad mispronunciation.'

'I-I just said the first part,' I spluttered. 'About being sorry for not feeding her. How did she... even know about Kitty Perry?'

'Cat language enriches your ability to listen, not just to speak,' said Tanya sagely.

'Also, she wasn't asking you to feed her that day. She was warning you that the samosa would give you food poisoning,' Rishi added.

I looked into the Cat's eyes properly, for the first time. I suddenly noticed the flecks of gold, like piercing sun-rays, or streaks of lightning. Had those always been there? The black slits she had for pupils expanded and contracted rhythmically, moving to the beat of a song that had begun to play inside my head. Maybe it had *always* been playing inside my head and I just hadn't paid attention. I understood then that all human language is a translation —an inadequate translation of our thoughts into words. But this language, awakening something visceral in me, was a step ahead. It didn't fall into the trap of using words at all.

I slumped my shoulders and pouted slightly, trying to communicate that I was sorry. The class collectively groaned. 'That's deeply offensive,' someone yelled. 'No profanity please.'

'Hey, this is just my first class,' I grumbled as I sat back down. 'Give me a break.'

Rahat
by Natasha Badhwar

One of the hardest things I have done in my life so far is waking my children up on a misty March morning in 2021 to tell them that Rahat had died. Rahat is the name of our beloved cat, the first born animal in our family.

Rahat was an adventure-seeking tomcat. He was also the most vulnerable in our family. He was small, but he lived expansively. In that moment of breaking the news to our children, I was learning a life lesson. I had to keep moving despite blinding grief and brace myself to hold the distress of others. The pain was physical. The luxury of being able to break down would have to wait.

We used to spend a lot of our time with Rahat; searching for him in the grassy plots around our house, to bring him back home. Once we found him trapped high on a thorny tree. The girls and I managed to extricate him with the help of a step-ladder. For days afterwards, I admired the cuts and scratches on the back of my hands with pride.

Rahat's name served a dual purpose in those moments of looking for him. 'Rahat, Rahat...' we would call out in various tones, almost as if it were a chant. Rahat means solace, and it always reminded us to stay calm. He was okay. He would return. He was obedient that way. He loved us.

Rahat's short life was the site of many miracles. He had a pronounced limp from a spinal injury he had recovered from at six months of age. He had been rescued as a palm-sized, abandoned kitten by a schoolgirl who brought him home in a cardboard box. He was fostered by a multi-talented artist, who took him to work with her as she nursed him to health and instilled cat-confidence in him. He was put up for adoption by a close-knit group of animal champions who expend time, energy and love trying to make sure that as many street-animals get safe, protective homes as they can manage.

Rahat came to us when he was three months old. Our youngest daughter had just turned eleven. She reminded us that we had said we would adopt pets when she was ready to care for them. 'I'm ready,' she announced a few months before her birthday.

We brought our cat home in a blue-green cat carrier, talking to him on the long car ride home. We watched as he explored the house and found safe corners. We celebrated when he chose to sleep next to my head in my bed. We felt accepted. We were jubilant.

Two weeks later, we brought Scarlet, a rescued puppy, to add to our family. Both of them were the same age. My phone is full of videos of Scarlet and Rahat chasing each other, Rahat swatting Scarlet from a safe height, the two of them sleeping cosily on the same mat when winter came, and other moments of our cat and dog bonding with each other.

Rahat used to call out incessantly from behind the wire mesh door when we went out for a walk with Scarlet. Friends warned us not to let him out. But Rahat wanted to be out in the world. He was not smart about it. Or timid. I wish I could describe the joy he exuded as he ran out with his peculiar gait and turned in the loose mud to feel the earth on his back.

'Rahat!' I would call out to him from the first floor balcony. He would respond in cat-speak from the spinach patch below.

By the time we finally lost Rahat, I had managed to convince myself to

47

trust him and the universe to keep him safe. Despite our fretting and fears, he would come back to us each time he went out.

Rahat was at home with us. He is now in another home without us. Our grief is doing the thing it does, coming in waves. Transforming into guilt and shame. Making it hard to sleep. Making waking up difficult. We hold it close, we let our tears roll.

Rahat's presence gave us joy every day. Now Rahat's memory is what we have. What would Rahat want us to do?

Rahat was generous. When a pair of new cats began visiting our home during the weeks of lockdown, he would let them eat from his bowl. When one of them moved in and gave birth to two kittens, Rahat made space for them too. This is what we must do too. The human heart has infinite space. We must extend ourselves. Be capacious.

For months I was not able to speak to anyone about the death of Rahat. Temporarily, the silence felt protective. What use is a voice when it has lost the power to call out to a loved one and make them appear? I have no capacity to have a conversation about what has gripped my heart and drenched it in pain. I go about my everyday life looking okay on the outside. Yet, when I began to write here, dear reader, there was nothing else I could write about.

I hope reading about Rahat evokes memories of your own deep loves and losses. I hope you are reminded of the unexpected grace we discover as we unwrap the folds of grief, one petal at a time.

First published in The Tribune *on 14 March, 2021.*

The Writer And Her Cat

by Meenakshi Reddy Madhavan

I was twenty-five when I left Delhi for the first time and moved with a suitcase and an idea of a Different Life to Bombay. This Different Life would include but not be limited to: suddenly meeting the man of my dreams and enjoying both heady romance and comfortable co-habiting; becoming the kind of ace journalist the magazine that hired me couldn't do without; becoming the sort of cosmopolitan, world-weary young person that my one Friend From Delhi Who Moved To Bombay had already accomplished, and finally, having the space and bandwidth to finish the first draft of my first novel.

My book had been commissioned on nothing more than the fact that I had a very popular blog. When it was first put to me that I might be able to publish something, I took this very calmly and in my stride, much more than I would've if the same thing had happened to me today, for example. At twenty-five, I was both the most confident person in the world and also a person who you could turn inside out and watch all her stuffing blow away in the wind.

So, I wasn't prepared for the tremendous bout of homesickness I got just one month into my move. I don't know if I can explain being homesick to someone who never has been—it is an almost internal *caving*, some part of you untethers and floats off in the sea of your mind, looking for a place to anchor itself to, and that place no longer exists. Being homesick is a lot like being lovesick, only you torture yourself with Could Have Beens about a specific time of day, you sitting in your room, your phone going off with a message, one of your many friends who you made over a *lifetime* in one city. How arrogant, how full of hubris for you to assume you could blithely leave anything behind—books, clothes, people you haven't spoken to in over two years, now you yearn for them all equally and you writhe in remembrance. Everything about Bombay reminded me that it was *Not Delhi*, something Bombay people held up as a virtue, but which made me miss my original city more and more. I rattled through the streets in a *rick-shaw*, not an *auto*, I said kanda for *pyaaz*, I went to Pali Naka instead of GK1, and I made friends I hadn't known for years and years and years, friends who accepted me as this person, this Bombay Person, instead of projecting upon me years of our shared memories.

But in all this, I was also having a great time. I loved living in Bombay, loved the newness of it, and the independence of it, and the new friends who thought of me in this new way instead of, well, *projecting upon me years of our shared memories*. I needed an anchor though, I needed something to tie me to the city, otherwise I just drifted through my days. My colleagues at my new job assured me that it was okay to work from home since the office was so far away, so I sat at home all day trying to do journalism. In the evenings, I met the friends I had just made—my resolution was just to accept all invi-tations—so I went out with the sort of hectic energy I have never been able to summon up since. Every night, I drank and smoked and laughed, every morning I woke up and lay in my bed, listening to the crows, and seeing that particular Bombay sunshine wash across the walls of my room. And still I felt apart, like my life was happening to me.

So: a kitten. It was, honestly, the last thing I needed. A pet! If I was giving myself advice now, so many hundreds of years later, I would say it was a terrible idea. 'You can barely look after yourself!' I'd say, making the adult expression of condescension mixed with amusement and disapproval that I feel on my face from time to time, whenever I encounter a young person do-ing something foolhardy and stupid. And my younger self would stare back at me and shrug and say, 'I'll figure it out' because that's how I dealt with the world then, I figured it out eventually.

A friend of a friend had a mother who kept cats. She had a large rambling bungalow with a garden and the sound of the sea just over the wall—a rarity for this city, but I was still so new to Bombay, and so used to my friends' large Delhi houses, I took it as a matter of course and was not at all amazed by the real estate I found myself in. I remember the (human) mother introducing me to the (cat) mother, I had asked for the grey tabby kitten, but, said the lady, the grey was sadly dead, killed by a dog just yesterday. 'The only one I can catch is the orange one,' she said. 'A little girl. She's the tamest.' We poured the unsuspecting kitten into my pink plastic picnic basket, she yowled, my friend's friend's mother looked emotional. 'You must feel free to give her back if you find you can't handle her,' she said. This offer was repeated a few times over the next few months, and I found myself rejecting it like I did the training wheels on my bicycle when I was five: with indignation and vehemence. We were in this together now, my little kitty and I.

A writer and her cat has a better ring to it than crazy cat lady. Mark Twain had Bambino, his black cat. Ernest Hemingway's familiar was Snowball, white, prone to fornicating. Samuel Johnson's Hodge has a statue dedicated to his catness in London. Doris Lessing wrote a little book all about her cats. (Have you read it? It's very good.) Ursula K. Le Guin had Pard, who she blogged about sometimes. Who else, who else? Angela Carter, Charles Dickens, H.G. Wells (whose cat, much like a put-upon host, made a loud noise whenever guests stayed too long), Isaac Newton—not a writer-writer, but then he invented the cat flap, so he gets a special mention, Byron's Beppo who drank milk out of a skull, a poet's pretension perhaps, but milk is milk no matter what you serve it out of, says the cat. (Note: cats are lactose intolerant, I have learned over my many years of living with them, so no milk, skulls optional.) Sylvia Plath, cat's name: Daddy. And me, with my little kitten, who I thought I'd call Noor, it was such a perfect cat name, but when it came to it, her little testicles descended and Noor turned definitively into a boy, called, forevermore, TC. (I made this mistake again, with one of my current cats. Suzie turned into a Bruno. It's very hard to tell when they're so small.)

TC for The Cat, because he thought he was the only cat in the world. Did he? I certainly did. TC also after my favourite Delhi haunt, Turquoise Cottage, a smoky bar that played retro music and let regulars have happy hours all night. My novel had a bar like TC, but I was polishing it up in Bombay, so I watched TC, my kitten, instead, and pretended we were both somewhere else.

I want to say I loved him, because of course I loved him, but in a way that will not be recognisable to anyone who hasn't lived with a cat. Dog people have a simpler love for their pets, it's more like a parents' love for their child, if we're comparing. Dogs require so much of us, we have to be affectionate and stern and disciplined about walking them and not leaving them alone, and cuddling them when they need it, and in return, they give us absolute loyalty. With a cat... well. That transactional relationship isn't there. It isn't even in the original contract. I feed my cats, take them to the vet when they need it, clean up piss and puke and poop, and occasionally, in return, they will stretch across my lap and purr like someone's turned their motors on. Occasionally they'll let me bury my hands in the soft fur of their bellies for more than five seconds. Occasionally, they'll sit across from me, just out of reach, very straight, like Egyptian statues of the goddess Bastet, tails wound around their feet, eyes half-closed, and they'll allow me to admire them. If I say their name, one transparent suede-like ear triangle will rotate towards me, a way of showing they hear me. I respect their boundaries. They do not often respect mine—standing on my chest, one uncomfortable questing paw right in the middle of my breast, winding in and out of my feet, almost trip-ping me over when I'm in a particular hurry, not giving me any warning of a sudden scratch that leaves a raised welt across my arm.

So, I loved TC, even when he peed right on my pillow while I was asleep on it, as a way of marking his territory, when his claw caught on the skin of my little finger when he was playing under the sheets as I was changing them, when he sat just across from me, and waited for me to notice him and then sauntered away. I caught him a lot, I caught him and I held him to me in affection, but he was not a physically affectionate cat. He liked to be stroked while he was standing just in front of you, tip of nose to tip of tail. He liked the underside of his chin to be scratched. He was so much clearer in his rules than the various men who peopled my life then, coming in and out, TC in the bedroom or out of it, depending. We were a team, and then he died, but by the time he died, I had moved cities and homes, and I had a Person, and this person and I had two other cats together, bio-cats instead of step-cats, you understand, and so while I grieved for him, I grieve for him, present tense, I have all these other loved ones—not to take his place but to keep me from seeing how empty it could be without him.

The nature of loving pets is to know that you're going to lose them. Their short little lives will intersect with yours briefly and absolutely, and then there will be a time when you are still living and they are dead. We don't confront this very often—when you bring a brand-new kitten to your home, you don't watch its quicksilver moves and imagine it dead the very next second, but that's the way it is. What is fifteen years to me after all? Fifteen years of my life, a whole lifetime to my cat, if he or she is lucky. TC died when he was eight, not so very old for a cat. If he was human, he'd have been in his forties. A kitten we fostered died almost immediately. Beloved family dogs have come and gone, and still I go on. It seems so strange to acknowledge this, and it's such a *private* sorrow. Who can understand how I mourn for my pets unless they have mourned for a pet? Who can understand how I find it hard to write this, how I still stutter over the words, unless I equate it to loving a human, as though that's the only kind of love there is. And yet, my cats see me every day, all day. I interact with them more than I interact with any other human, save one. I love them *because* they are not human not despite it.

Because I loved him, I had to kill him. He was suffering, a call to the vet, stroking his little ears, looking away while she injected him, a start, a stop. 'He was a cat,' I thought, half-stunned. 'Take him for all in all. I shall not look upon him again.' In the time between the previous paragraph and this one, I have taken off for three weeks. I couldn't—can't—write about his death without the sudden sharp sorrow. The guilt, even though it was a kind-ness, even though he was suffering, lives with me still. I would have done it again, I might have to do it again, take a call for a beloved pet, put them out of their misery as I hope someone will do for me when my time comes, but still: taking a life, a short little life, a life you love... it's *really hard*.

Because I loved Bombay, I had to leave it. I'd seen the best of the city; I wasn't ready to see the worst of it. I was brought down low by heartbreak, a prolonged break-up that felt like it would never end, like I would be sixty, seventy, eighty years old, and yet breaking up with this man, who I could barely remember being in love with in the first place. I felt tired and old, weary of constantly struggling, of being independent and trying to remem-ber why I wanted this free-wheeling lifestyle. Things that I loved about Bombay started to sour: why did the whole city feel so *proud* of its hustle and grit? Didn't they realise that only made it harsher? Why was there so much traffic? Why were the houses so small and so expensive? Why did everyone I like have to move away?

So: back home to Delhi. Since Delhi and I were tied up to each other, like siblings, like a birthmark, I didn't have to pretend to love it, or even *like* it very much. I had nothing to prove, I was from Delhi, so back I returned. It was the right decision, a few months in a small flat in the centre of the city, which cost half of what it would've in Bombay, and I felt my soul returning a bit. If TC, a Bombay feline, felt any regret at leaving the city of his birth, he did not say. I have thousands of photographs of him from that time, lying in patches of sun—winter was new to him—his sandy fur soft, his pupils little lines across his leaf-green eyes.

Not long after this, I met and moved in with the man I'm married to. TC was his first cat, he was so charmed by the species, we got a 'collective' kitten. And then another one. And then a third when the second one died of a stomach ailment. TC did not like the kittens, but once they had each other, they mostly avoided him. Sometimes I'd catch his eye, and he'd give me this look, 'My god, woman, what have you done?' but mostly, they stayed in separate parts of the house. He died not long after, of kidney failure, which the vet said a lot of cats got, I shouldn't blame myself, it was common, and sadly, usually fatal.

I've lost so many pets in my life, I feel like if I believed in a god, in an afterlife, in the idea of a rainbow bridge, I would be swarmed when I got there: dogs, cats, countless fish, a squirrel baby once, all running up to me, tugging at my clothes, placing their heads under my hands for me to pet (well, maybe not the fish) and I would feel so happy, because here at last, we'd live together forever, not one life over in fifteen years or less, and another life, having to go on and on without them.

I don't want you to think I spend all my time thinking about how my pets are going to die or anything. I get a lot of pleasure from them, and sometimes they are a pain in the ass, especially when they pee on things and scratch the furniture or yowl at each other in the middle of the night. But the fact is, when you have a pet, you think about death. Every passing year reminds you that you're living on borrowed time. My kittens are six-and-a-half-year-old cats now, maybe I'll get lucky and have them for another ten years, but maybe it'll only be six. I must be prepared for everything. We have three cats—maybe we'll beat the odds, and all three will live till twenty. I love them so much and yet, because of TC, I am prepared for their deaths in a way I never was before.

Other pets have come and gone in my life, but TC was the first one who only belonged to me. I owe him so much, and ultimately he was the greatest gift Bombay gave to me.

Seventy Per Cent Cat

by Vangmayi Parakala

Are you a dog person? You might be a cat.

I may be most unsuited to be a part of this anthology. I have never had a cat and have never sought the company of one. I can also safely say I don't quite like cat company.

However, my first foray into writing, mere days after bringing home a dog—the pet that I had begged for, for months—was a short story about a family of cats.

Let me explain. Spark, a black Labrador-Coon Hound cross, was barely a few months old, when Amma drove him home from a friend's house in her blue Maruti van. He was little and scared, confused in new surroundings, and burrowed himself under the back seat. He refused to come prancing out into his new 'forever home', as I had expected he would.

We whistled, petted, *tchtched*, offered treats. A few minutes later, it seemed as though a whole army of us had assembled to coax the cute little mutt with liquid gold eyes, into the house.

All of this within just an hour of bringing Spark home. This had to be the red-flag that I, seven years old and sibling-less, should've seen. I hadn't.

Over the next few months, I slowly but surely felt a slow erosion of my rights and privileges as the Only Child. Amma and Paatti were changing too. They were falling in love with him! I almost never saw Amma. If it wasn't work, she was busy taking Spark for walks, feeding him, toilet-training him, and keeping up with his doctors' appointments. Paatti was still reserved in her affection—her routine with him was a rough pat-pat-'okay enough, go now', but the glee on her face, when his tail whipped against the folds of her almost-uniform of Sungudi saris, was unmistakable.

I was feeling neglected, petulant, and jealous.

In a not-very-thought-out passive aggressive move, I wrote a 'short story' about a family of cats. (The real reason I suppose was I'd recently learnt how to draw a cartoon cat from someone at school: two ovals, one big and one small; two triangles for the ears; three dots, for the eyes and nose; a free flow of lines for whiskers and the tail.)

I then did a fair copy onto quartered-and-cut A4 size sheets of paper. The topmost page, the book cover, carried the illustration. I self-published this by stapling these sheets together, and presenting it to my family. I was sure I'd made some sort of a statement.

Whatever this act of defiance meant, two things were certain: one, I had begun warming up to Spark as he sat by my side, snout on his paw, as I angrily wrote my first literary tome. And two, that I owe my fictional family of felines an indescribable debt: to date, it's one of my earliest memories, if not one of the very few over all from my childhood, of the one thing that I have wanted to keep doing since—writing.

Regardless, something about cats has disconcerted me and mostly everyone with whom I am close.

The insincere protagonist

I have spent more than two decades being not very interested in cats due to this same reason. Cats are, in a vague sense, unreachable. You'd never know them. They never show themselves to you as dogs do.

Given the cultural and generational unease with keeping a pet at home, the immediate family on Amma's side never had any. Yet Paatti, who was touching seventy by the time we got Spark, had her own weirdly expressed love for him. Could I fathom her with a cat in the room we shared till she passed away when I was sixteen?

No. But irrelevant, because when, with my incessant pleas, I had initiated the discussion on the possibility of a pet in the house, there was never a doubt in my mind that the pet needed to be a dog. This was, after all, a few years after the whole country saw that shrill little Pomeranian, Tuffy, in *Hum Aapke Hai Koun..!* (1994)

I'd had the *Spot* series of books by Eric Hill, which Amma had bought for my bedtime reading, influence me deeply too—for days I'd want her to read me nothing but Spot in the Garden.

There was, however, just the one story about a cat that Nanna had told me. He'd made it up on the fly, as I suspect many fathers do when it's their turn with bedtime stories. It had no beginning or end.

'Once upon a time, there was a cat. He was playing cricket with his other cat friends. The first ball that the cat got was a blue one. He hit it successfully.'

'And then?'

'Next, he got a green-coloured one, he hit that too.'

'And then?'

'Then, he got a red-coloured ball. *Aa ball ni kooda gheettiiiga kottedu.*' (He hit that ball too, reeeealllly hard.)

And on and on it went till he started to repeat colours, or I fell asleep. My father had, I suspect, strongly banked on the latter.

There is many a positive mention of dogs in our epics and sacred texts. The most famous is in the 'Mahaprasthanika Parva' of The Mahabharata. After his wife Draupadi and the rest of the Pandavas have died, Yudhisthira continues his journey on to Mount Meru with only a dog for company. Soon, Indra appears on his chariot, telling Yudhishthira to hop on, that he needn't walk the rest of the way. Yudhisthira refuses to get on without his beloved friend, the dog.

But there were no such inseparable cat-friends, were there?

Recently, Amma stumbled upon a mention of a cat, when reading Volume 8 of The Mahabharata as translated by Bibek Debroy. This is in the 'Apad Dharma Parva', the chapter on guidelines for desperate and dangerous times. Bhishma tells Yudhisthira about Palita, a wise rat, who initiates friendship with Lomasha, a cat who is otherwise out to eat him.

One night, Palita calculates that Lomasha too would need to escape a net that a Chandala had cast. They join forces, but the next morning, once the danger of the night has passed, Lomasha calls out to Palita, hoping they can be friends. Lomasha also promises not to harm the rat. But Palita is wiser than that, gives Lomasha a sassy earful of wisdom—how one may join forces with an enemy to defeat a common foe, but that you ought to be wise and not trust them once your mutual goal is achieved—and goes on his way.

Such cat-wary tales are also popular at tourist sites.

When on a trip to Chennai for a wedding a few years ago, my history-loving great-uncle N Mama wanted to use the opportunity to drive me to Mahabalipuram. It wasn't for the Shore Temple, as much as it was to spend time viewing the details of the impressive bas-relief of *Bhageeratha's Penance*.

As dusk turned to night, so did our excitement to cranky disappointment—how would we see its details in the dark? But thanks to an ingenious cab driver who spotlighted the rock with the car's headlights, I had a hurried, DIY sound-and-light-show in the two-and-a-half minutes before traffic picked back up.

In that time, N Mama had drawn my attention to a specific detail in the bas relief—it was a cat standing with his palms joined in a namaste over his head, as the Ganga flowed nearby, brought to Earth thanks to Bhageeratha's penance.

As Mahabalipuram receded into the night, N Mama recalled the story: a deceptive cat, pretending to be an ascetic, gains the trust of the mice around him. He tells them that strict asceticism has made him weak, and that to get to the river's bank every day, he needs their help. The mice, duped, agree to carry him over. Every day at the other banks, he made a meal of the group that brought him there. One day, a wise mouse quietly followed the cat to uncover the truth about the missing mice. Seeing the cat is no ascetic, he goes back home, and informs the rest of the mice of this horrible truth.

The end. The message was clear. The only cat I was going near was the cat-pose in yoga, which, when effectively coupled with the cow-pose (!), eased my lower back that was imprisoned in a chair all day long at work.

A distrust of independence

I have often thought about these stories. In the earlier story of Palita and Lomasha from The Mahabharata, is the rat's the lesser evil than what the cat would have committed because the former is upfront and the latter *could have been* sneaky, like the ascetic from the rock at Mahabalipuram?

Maybe what we see as deception isn't that at all in cats' dictionaries; maybe, through history, cats were only trying to look out for themselves, just as the rat Palita had done. It just seems that cats didn't think they owed anyone much of their truth… it's also possible they didn't figure it out enough themselves to be able to lay it out.

It is a dog-eat-dog world after all… hold on—where was that highly regarded loyalty when this expression was coined?

Loyalty. This very righteous quality forms the bedrock of how and why we've domesticated dogs for as long as we can remember. Much research has been done on this: humans brought canines into their lives to fulfil specific purposes—hunting, keeping their sheep together, guarding their settlements, or their person on journeys. There was a contractual undercurrent to the relationship, which has now evolved into dogs loving us unconditionally if we give them some bit of love and a whole lot of food.

Cats however, a cat-keeping friend theorised, seem to have domesticated themselves.

It makes me want to say they're the pinnacle of petdom—because cats have, in the evolution of friendly relations between man and beast, skipped the 'domestication' stage altogether. Their pet-status is the beginning and end of their relationship with humans. Some also choose to be absent from pet duties when they please. We don't expect a cat to alert us when a stranger is at our door. They'd only entered our settlements to eat the rats that came for our scraps.

In an essay in the *New Yorker* from October 2015, author Ferris Jabr cites a study by Wesley Warren, a geneticist at Washington University in St Louis: 'cats have diverged much less from their wildcat ancestors than dogs have from wolves and that the cat genome has much more modest signatures of artificial selection.'

Meaning that cats—who humans haven't domesticated like they have dogs —retain more of their wild traits, like a hunch for hunting, and are largely more self-reliant in their instincts than a pet dog is.

I've come to believe that this feral quality is to blame for words like 'sly', 'deceitful', 'not loyal', being tagged to cats. The most you'd hear against a dog—but only say from the last decade and a little more—is that it'll be too much work or that its shedding coat will get the house messy.

Things have obviously changed, and it's less taboo to have cats as pets now. In my generation, particularly. I think I saw the discourse expanding in the mid-2000s, when the sound of dial-up internet started to screech into our homes.

A lot of us, who felt we were misfits in our social circles, whether with our middle- and high-school crowds or with our band of cousins, had managed to forge deep friendships on Internet forums. Friendships thrived especially in the writing and art communities or blogging platforms.

With our Internet experience then still blissfully free of trolls and bots, we had owned our otherwise dubious labels—geeky, awkward, klutzy—and flaunted them with a humorous ease. In such spaces, the 'crazy' was dropped from 'cat lady', and it was alright, sometimes celebratory even, to identify as an introvert. It was on such forums that cute cat videos and gifs started becoming popular (alongside dog videos too, but who didn't love dogs already), and then later, cat memes too originated.

So, you see, it is almost tempting to armchair-hypothesise that it is the people who gave more to the world than they got, kind of like dogs did, and those who started to feel slightly ill-at-ease with their immediate world and its rules—even those who seemed gregarious and extroverted while inhabiting it—who turned to cats for company. Yet, there may be some truth in it.

Why and how else would a few similar women, who grew up way before this Internet age, and belonged to orthodox, traditional South Indian families, have also taken to them?

Low-maintenance love

It was this question, and my faint recollection of the Telugu writer, late Abburi Chayadevi garu having cats, that led me to agree to this essay. My parents knew her and her late husband, the writer Abburi Varada Rajeswara Rao garu well. I was very young when we'd go over to her place in Bagh Lingampally in Hyderabad. As is the practice between families in Andhra, we would exchange little jaadis of *avakaya* and *magaya* every summer.

It's a shame that I remember close to nothing of those visits, except three things. One: I recall Chayadevi garu's soft, slightly raspy voice that felt like the salted and sun-drying mangoes that we made magaya with. Two: her crafty doll-making. And three: her cats and her cat-themed sofa covers.

Chayadevi garu wasn't a prolific writer, but when she did write, she pricked you into being aware. She was *woke* before 'being woke' was even a thing.

So far, everything I've read by her has been a comment on domesticity, a woman's place in the society that she was born in, and fictionalised versions of her and her family's lives. She was born in 1933 in Rajahmundry to a strict writer-father who was vocal about having expected a son instead; the family's older daughter had inspired this younger one to write her most popular work, *Bonsai Brathuku* (1974), translated into English as *Bonsai Lives*—a comment on how women aren't given the opportunity to grow into their own selves; they're carefully brought up only to occupy the limited space of domesticity.

For a woman of such vision, being the wife of the fastidious Rajeswara Rao garu—he expected only full, fresh, hot meals each time he ate, no tiffin or snack business for him; he was even particular about how much tempering there ought to be in a dish—couldn't have been easy.

In March 2006, the Sahitya Akademi had published a 'Meet The Author' with her, soon after she received their award for *Tanamargam* (Her Way), a collection of stories. Some anecdotes from this interview show how, despite the limitations of the times, she'd carved a niche for herself as a feminist writer. She lived in the system but had her own subtle ways of subverting it.

For instance, in the interview she recalls how her unfulfilled yearning to have children of her own, prompted her to write the story *Gaddu Nela* (A Bad Month). 'When I mentioned the theme to my husband, he uttered the word "chi!" considering it ridiculous,' she said in the interview. But she never stopped writing what she wanted and needed to. She also went on to recall how the poet and translator Srinivas Rayaprol had omitted a line from one of her stories, 'Srimati Udyogini', when he translated it in 1975: '...perhaps, considering it anti-traditional. [In the story] [t]he interviewer at the end of the interview, asks the housewife if she would marry the same man given another chance. She replies emphatically, saying "Yes," but says to herself, "It's supposed to be the duty of the Indian woman to say so!" I found the omission of this sentence after the book came out,' the interview quotes her as having said.

On paper, Chayadevi garu wasn't bound by the usual traditional shackles that limited women. Because her father had wanted a son, he treated her like one, sent her to school in short-pants as opposed to a *parikini* (long skirt) till a teacher suggested one day that it was perhaps time to make the switch. She earned an MA in Political Science, went on to study Library Sciences and ended up doing a ten-year-stint at the Jawaharlal Nehru University in New Delhi as Deputy Librarian. A major contrast even to her own older sister, let alone many girls, and later, women her age, she was appreciated and respected by her male peers. But somehow I get the sense they weren't ready for all that it might really entail.

Yet, Rajeswara Rao garu never thwarted her. She continued to be a wonderful cook, catering to her husband's exacting tastes, but she also spoke her mind with a graceful nuance, always with a little smile playing on her face. She advocated for feminism to be armed with a sense of humour. I've heard my parents recall on occasion, how she often punned on the words *pillilu* (cats) and *pillalu* (children), when people asked after her family's well-being.

When she wasn't split between her wifely duties and her writerly life—in addition to writing numerous short stories, she had columns in Telugu magazines like *Bhumika*, edited *Vanita*, and also translated German fiction into Telugu—she found solace in doll-making and spending time with the cats who were always in and out of the house.

I can't imagine a dog in their place—another demanding commitment in a life such as hers, already filled with caring for others while forging her own path.

Her feline friendships started in 1982. When they first moved into their Bagh Lingampally home, their yard was infested with rats. Her mother-in-law, who lived with them then had asked Chayadevi to coax some cats in to tackle this problem.

'I brought a cat home by offering it milk. Slowly it became my pet,' she recalled in an interview recorded in the book *Sweeping the Front Yard*, published by SPARROW. Her story 'Brahmastram' (Brahma's Weapon) is about this. Soon, Chayadevi and the cat got so close that her mother-in-law got jealous, she recalled in the interview.

Rajeswara Rao garu too. 'My husband used to get annoyed at all these cats and ask me to choose between the cats and him,' she said. When they realised that he was allergic to them because of his asthma, she put their then-cat in a bag and tried leaving it far away from the house. The trick didn't work—ten days later, it found its way back home, skinny and sad.

There was no looking back since. 'Cats filled my entire life,' she'd said.

The no-pets rule

Thirty years before Chayadevi garu first befriended a cat with a glass of milk, Amma's older cousin and my Perima, V, did the same.

It was the early 1950's. In Tiruchirapalli in Tamil Nadu, in the cowshed of a middle-class, conservative family's home, a cat gave birth to five kittens.

Ordinarily, a house like this would not have a pet—especially not in the way that I, a child of post-liberalisation India, have come to think of keeping pets. Many households across India kept domesticated cows, but only in a shed in their backyards—not sitting by the feet of your writing desk or climbing into bed with you!—as they provided for the family's daily dairy needs and were also seen as holy.

V Perima's family, like many such families, would leave out grains and water for visiting birds and squirrels. If a dog decided to walk by the verandah or *tinnai*, it would've been fed with whatever was available at hand, or given some milk; it would keep coming back, out of habit, and become a part of their lives. Some would even be given generic names—there's a family joke about Kuppuswamy, a regular stray-dog visitor, who usually ate everything given to him, except the one time he famously refused the terrible chapatis an aunt had tried to make.

Every day, V Perima's family would also leave balls of rice out for crows—they were after all the avian avatars of the family's ancestors, who were being remembered and fed everyday. Such animal-friendships were commonplace, but none crossed the threshold of the *tinnai* to come into the house.

But one day, a cat decided to give birth in the cow shed adjoining V Perima's house. Days later, it continued to stay there. My aunt, only twelve years old then, had taken over some milk to feed the new mother; and once she did, the cat gradually began following her around, one day crossing over to the inside.

It was the beginning of a lifelong friendship. After this, V Perima was almost never pet-less. Later, when they lived in Bengaluru for a while, her children would bring home a dog—which would learn to co-exist with the cat they already had at home.

Amma recalls that V Perima, already very soft-spoken, quiet, and reserved, was even quieter with her cats. But her communication with them, over her conversations with people, flowed easier—between a melodious mutter and a meow, it was like a secret language between Tamil and Cat.

The first time I spoke to V Perima and her husband N, was during the initial days of the COVID-lockdown in 2020. The couple has long since moved out of Tamil Nadu, and now spend their retired years in a small pilgrimage town in Andhra Pradesh.

Five minutes in, I realised that recollections of her soft, almost hesitant and reluctant way of speaking, were not exaggerated. Perhaps to mitigate any possible awkwardness with a newly acquainted relative, N Perippa would step in and answer many of my questions for her. She would venture a whispered, almost dream-like sentence when she found a wedge between his words.

'No one said anything if it didn't create any problem,' she said when I asked her if her family objected to her growing friendship with the cat from the cowshed. 'Also, the cat would just go hide under the bed during the day, so mostly no one noticed it. But once, it brought home a dead mouse from somewhere. I chased it out,' she recalled. From then on, the cat knew to go out, eat what it wanted outside, and to come back home later.

Becoming a Cat Lady

Almost a decade younger than V Perima is K Aunty, my friend S's mother. She too had a similar upbringing vis-a-vis official pets coming indoors.

'The reason they didn't let us have pets in our homes,' she said, indicating a vegetarian household, socio-culturally similar to V Perima's, but in this case in Swarna, in Prakasm district of Andhra Pradesh, 'is the factor of cleanliness.' Not only would the cats bring dead mice and other prey indoors, they would also quietly come into kitchens through many a backdoor, 'put their mouths into' open containers, and drink up any milk in the vicinity, before sneaking out.

Based in the U.S. for a long time now, K Aunty had hesitated initially when her son brought home a cat a few years ago. He had adopted Gandalf, his black-and-white pet cat when he was away at medical school. But soon, odd and long hours working at the hospital meant that Gandalf needed a stable home. When he brought the cat to his parents' place, he had assured his mother that Gandalf wouldn't behave like the strays she'd grown up seeing.

They'd struck a deal. Gandalf had a week to prove himself. If not, they'd give him away at a shelter nearby.

That week, with her husband and kids mostly away at work, it was just Gandalf and Aunty.

'I became comfortable with him very suddenly. I don't know how that happened,' she says, trying to recall that first and important week. But S interrupts: 'Gandalf chose her.'

The family remembers how Gandalf would sit next to her when she did her daily prayers. Soon, Aunty was looking up videos on Youtube on how to clip Gandalf's claws, and starting grooming him all by herself when time came. She's now even fluent in Gandalf's love languages: 'He blinks when he wants to say he loves us... did you know cats do that?!' Aunty now speaks Cat thanks to specialised cat-related channels online, like that of 'cat whisperer' Jackson Galaxy.

If there's one thing she doesn't do for him, it's to change his litter box, because she's allergic. However, Gandalf is very aware of cleanliness, she stresses. Her son had already potty-trained him by putting his paws in the sand inside the litter box to show him where he was to relieve himself.

'But I think it's also an innate thing, that what you do has to be buried in the sand,' S says. 'There are a lot of things he knows by himself.' She says this especially since Gandalf did not grow up around cats. This only confirms what Ferris Jabr had written in his article. 'My brother got him when he was two weeks old. But things like sharpening his claws, cleaning himself, hunting, he just knows.'

Gandalf even hunted and brought home a dragonfly once, as a gift for his human family. These sharp feral instincts even if used to express love and belonging, would have been rejected by an older, more conservative generation. Not only on grounds of hygiene, but also because these were strictly vegetarian households that didn't want the impurity of unattended dead animals anywhere near their living quarters.

This is us

I want to come back to this strong sense of self and self-reliance in cats. They know their way around the world. They quite literally land on their feet when they fall.

Are we scared of those that can be this way?

Humans favour communal cohesion. Our tendency to glorify loyalty perhaps is a subset of this. Appreciating and respecting, let alone understanding, stronger shades of individualism is a still-new and evolving thought. It is especially something that women, often associated in common metaphor with cats, have had to fight long and hard for. They still do.

On paper, everyone wants their children to be self-reliant. Presumably, that's why they send them to boarding school, to summer camp, to different cities for college. We want our siblings and partners to all be able to stand up for themselves, to have their own interests and their own full lives, separate from our relationships with them.

I get the sense that while we all want to believe this, the true strength of our convictions here might be wanting.

We want dogs because they're easier to understand and don't stroll out by themselves when they feel like they need something else. Dogs shower us with their joy, they make obvious their pain, they mourn with us by never leaving our side if they sense we are grieving, and they wake us up with the bounce of energy that many of us lack on a Monday morning.

We also want dogs before we have babies, because it's a shorter-term test of how much we can care for a dependent and loving creature, before we have a moody one that's going to need us even when it turns thirty and has three degrees on her resumé.

But cats? Cats remind us of ourselves. They do everything that we want to do but don't, can't, or won't.

It's not like we are all deceiving or sly or sneaky, and neither are all cats. We only, maybe always, want to put ourselves first, with no consequences or questions asked.

We want to be loved only when we want to, and we need a partner who understands our love language and learns to speak it like it's their mother tongue.

We want to show love, but will they get it when we say 'I love you and did this for you' with the weird and awkward equivalent of bringing back a dead dragonfly home to a human?

We want to be by their sides when they're sick or grieving, but could we also take a quick stroll out in between to celebrate the things happening in our own lives and heads, when it might not be appropriate to do so publicly?

In that sense, I am, without doubt, at least 70% cat.

It's no wonder then that I'll always be a dog person. No wonder then, that I don't like cat company. I mean, would I REALLY want to live with myself?

Nine Lives

by Aneela Babar

(Epilogue by Arhaan Babar Ray)

'And this mess is so big
And so deep and so tall,
We cannot pick it up.
There is no way at all!'
— Dr Seuss, The Cat in the Hat

As a people, we are guilty of repeating our stories. But what if this is not because we have run out of stories to tell? What if we have cornered ourselves in a time loop and now just relive the same anecdotes we are so fond of sharing? My cats are the nine lives I have lived. I may have been trying to write down the story of my life with felines for a while, but here, now, while writing this, I realize that they, in turn, are chronicling all the Aneelas I am—and will be in the coming days. And though all these years I have struggled with change and disruption (and fears, if it results with a homebody cat walking off into the sunset)—what if each episode was actually drawing me closer to the very version of my life I have aspired to?

Part I: Rawalpindi, 1988

I am walking down the street—and there is a cat in the bag. It will take me some years to usher in all the bad puns and references to Schrödinger. Until the cat is out of the bag, for a brief period I can be considered simultaneously a child with a pet or not, both linked to a random event.

The cat escaping.

Suffocating.

Gulp! The mind wanders.

However, in the very same moment, I am self-aware that I have become the worst kind of cliché for my community. A Pashtun walking down a street, with a bag containing something (someone?) that is visibly squirming. I am beside myself just then. For how could it be that despite all the efforts previous generations of Babars may have made, I am walking down the street, an epitome of the *Pashtun jo bori mai bacho ko utha kar le jaate hain*, a Pashtun that steals your children and puts them in a sack?

Later, much later, years to this afternoon in Rawalpindi, my sister and I will have an exchange where I will ask her:
'Hey Have You Been Kidnapping Little Children?'

'Umm, no.'

'Well, neither have I. This makes two out of three Pashtuns. Who could this third child-snatching Pashtun be then?'

But there, just then, I am a young person, nervous and ultimately thrilled of being simultaneously a cliché and a Schrödinger away from a cat as a pet.

And not just any cat.

This is a cat that has been rescued and fostered by the most glamorous family in Rawalpindi, which, by the way, is simultaneously small-town Pakistan and the power-centre for the country, General Head Quarters, cough cough.

Unless the denizens of the cantonment are readying themselves for another coup, Rawalpindi is every afternoon in Maycomb (Great Depression and rabid-dog-slowing-down-the-town, optional). Until the day a fast bowler will run up to the crease, and the long-haired son of my cat's foster family will Dil Dil his town onto the map of Pakistan, *until then* Pindi is small-town, the Army Museum is 'culture', and Karachi is abroad. Until then, our years in Rawalpindi are marked by a gardener painting the flowerpots fire-engine red, with a white border, every spring, the flowerbeds prepared and lined with brick that has been carefully whitewashed.

One day I actually look up whether there is a cardinal rule out there some-where, for the support staff to salute everything that moves and whitewash anything that is stationary. The results of this search remain uncertain. How-ever, I *do* know for certain that there are clear, if unwritten, rules that gov-ern the turning-on or switching-off of room-heaters and geysers, based on precise dates on the Gregorian calendar. It could very well be that this is a date our grandmothers and General Head Quarters, Rawalpindi, had agreed upon one year. Say it was 1950. Since that year, neither the Rawalpindi grandmothers nor the GHQ have relented. There are no accommodating weather gods or climate change. And so, we shiver under a cold tap on a particularly cruel day in autumn, and wonder at the blazing room-heater in offices on a freak warm winter day.

On this Rawalpindi afternoon, not unseasonably warm or cold, with the cat in the bag, I am walking down a street with gardens similar to mine, lined by trees with identical tree-trunks, whitewashed in the regulation military white. I may not be able to spell social capital. But in a town so provincial, and being a young person so inconsequential, I am hoping to build myself some capital adopting this particular cat. Could aura and charm be passed on if you were a cat-beat away from a charismatic family?

I hope that it is.

Naming my cat in a town like Rawalpindi should be an interesting exer-cise—should I go with Karnail-ia? Dhol Sipahiya? Jarnail-ia? Captaan Sa-hib? Askari Meow? But I have read the Bible of Rawalpindi bookshelves: the Reader's Digest. 'Try hollering your child's name out of your kitchen-door twice a day, asking him to get home,' one of the contributors counselled new parents. As a new cat-parent, I think this over, and consider the prospect of calling out for a *Lucifer* every afternoon quite attractive. Lucifer. (When the animated rendition of *Cinderella* came out on VHS, my peers started day-dreaming of a flesh-and-blood incarnation of Prince Charming while I lost my heart to the Tremaine family cat, Lucifer.) This wily black cat is my first encounter with charming antagonists with complicated origin stories. Long before the Hindi films *Darr* and *Baazigar*—and a very likeable Shahrukh Khan—made us pledge our troth to anti-heroes.

Unfortunately, I know my surroundings are not yet ready for any of my latent anti-establishment tendencies, so I tell everyone that I am naming him Lucifer after the Lucifer match-sticks, as he will grow up to strike every-where and anything. Sadly, the moniker Lucifer is bastardised as Mausoofa by the help. So Mausoofa he is, until he is christened Miao ji (out of respect) when Chica-the-kitten joins our household.

Before I set out to leave their house with my Lucifer, the matriarch *familia glamarosa* of the foster-family advises me to rub butter on the cat's paws once I get home. She explains there is something to the act of licking off the butter from her paws that assures a cat she is finally home.

Aunty does not tell *me* anything though about what could cure me of being born with a mole under the foot. In a town where spending summer break with grandparents is the most a Rawalpindi child can aspire to, the wander-lust it brought was positively dangerous.

Part II: Melbourne, 2007

My husband has arranged to adopt a kitten while I am away in Rawalpindi. I now live in Melbourne.

Back home, I walk around the kitchen one evening, trying to dodge an extremely active kitten, who darts from under the table to pounce on my toes, as is true to her curriculum vitae. While we have started to share how we are feeling on Facebook these days, we still get our news from the TV and the papers; and so, I hear about Benazir Bhutto's assassination from the news channels. It is after an election rally in Rawalpindi.

Twenty-eight years ago her father had been led to the gallows from a jail cell in the same town. There are urban legends of how he would stand in the window, looking out towards the Prime Minister House, until I realise that the raconteur may just be confusing him with a certain Shah Jehan, looking out at the Taj Mahal. The old Pindi jail was brought down one year, all except the lone cell that had housed this former premier—the Pakistan People Party is still hoping to build a memorial. One summer, I walked around the site and tried photographing it, but the photo studio returned the film-reel saying it had been exposed to light. I am convinced the jail cell is sacred-land and like capturing poltergeists on film, it is impossible to photograph.[01]

Upon hearing of the assassination, I alternate between our shared kitten-care duties and crying for our loss. Ours is a generation that has been scarred by General Zia, and though we had learnt that our dreams for Benazir Bhutto were flawed, the Benazir Bhutto years are as close to Camelot as one can get. And now, between the embers of the bomb blast and the roses on her grave, it seems that these dreams are finally being laid to rest. I am a Bhutto acolyte, yes, but the year before her death saw me critical of her Machiavellian politics.

But this Melbourne morning it seems she is having the last laugh as she becomes immortalized as our slain democrat. In death, she is becoming the elusive Salome of the seven veils of popular imagination, with her obituaries giving tantalizing hints to her real self. From a flighty young woman who

---

[01] I am less convinced of this now, as I go through a constant photo stream of teenagers pouting for selfies at the cinema complex and McDonalds set up at the site of the jail cell and gallows now.

consumed paperback romances and sped past us in her yellow MG, searching for the closest Baskin Robbins, she turns into a thorn in the side of a military dictator, a serious foe, indulging in a decade-long struggle to keep her father's name and political legacy alive. She is at times the workaholic, campaigning long hours through pregnancies, a diligent politician surviving on four hours' sleep, and then a much-maligned name with corruption and nepotism cases brought against her and her coterie.

I promptly name the kitten Pesho Bibi. (Pesho is Pushto for Cat. Bibi, or lady, sounded a lot like BB.)

Months later, there is an evening when my husband walks past an abandoned microwave in the kitchen—we have read an article about the perils of microwaved food. The cat now uses it as a vantage point to perch upon and play staring matches with the tabby from next door. I am watching a film on SBS in the living room, waiting for dinner.

The man sets two plates while lounge music plays on a laptop in the kitchen. The cat, from its corner, twitches its ears. So much cordiality and joviality does not bode well. Follow the two, she tells herself.

And so she does, from the kitchen to the living room, curling between legs, wondering why no one is paying attention to the TV any more. The humans are getting moony-eyed, her cat-radar catching signals that soon there might be mischief afoot. Must not let them get out of my cat-sight, must follow the humans. And so she follows the one who is getting a bottle of fragrant oil, while the other potters around the house putting dishes and glasses away. The humans make their way to the room on the landing; however, she too is quick; right on their non-tails in hot pursuit. No, no! They are closing the door now. Must. Not. Let. Them. Do. That.

The cat can hear one of them whispering inside now, and starts scratching the door.

'Do something, I don't think Pesho is going to go away.'

'Ignore her.'

My own memories of that evening include looking up from the bed at one point, to the sight of a cat's paw wedged under the door, furiously trying to wrest it open.

I burst out laughing.

People might say that getting a cat may help anxious couples in getting pregnant. Let us just say I got lucky despite all its efforts to hijack the project.

Motherhood—and being mother to Pesho and the Baby-in-the-Pram is not easy. There are days when I watch the baby and the cat stretched out on a blanket in the sun and get homesick for Rawalpindi winter afternoons, when the sun is out, but someone will complain, 'This is not a good winter sun to sit out in, *garmee nahee hai is mey*!' I coax the cat to come down from the wall, and the baby to release the grass blades in his fist, reminiscing of other winter afternoons like this, when I played with a cat, all the while my heart sinking that the day is ending and there is so much homework to do.

On other days, the leaves turning red in Melbourne bring to mind memories of a cat diving under a canopy of red and purple leaves. And so I live and walk the lanes of a town that is now becoming familiar, even if I miss the streetscape of another. And, before long, my mind starts playing tricks with me—coaxing me that if I follow Pesho's lead and escape behind the fence, I will emerge into a Rawalpindi afternoon and frequent the streets I crave.

I go back to these mind-games over and over, using the cats I meet as a portal to other streets, other timelines. I speak to these cats in Pushto.

Eventually, I have to move countries. Again. And am losing Pesho Bibi to quarantine rules. She is a fair dinkum Aussie and like generations of Brahmins who were at the danger of losing their faith once they crossed the kaala pani, she too is facing the risk of being excommunicated if she follows my gypsy stead.

I had planned to only be away for a year, but this year has now stretched to a decade.

Over the coming years, I visit Pesho Bibi each Christmas with my boy, and for a while he tells people that he has a sister who we have left behind in Australia.

I am living now in cities with my house-door locked to the outside world, telling myself it will be great to pretend it is the 1950s. For me, the 50s were the decade for good Hindi cinema, and so I too can be happy if I channel those years. Oh, the places I can go. But I have parked myself in the 'The Waiting Place', waiting, waiting, waiting for something (or someone) to happen, to break me out of my vigil. Later, I will read Marie Popova and how 'happiness comes at us unbidden and elemental, there is almost a terror to its coming—to the totality of it, to the way it submerges and saturates and supinates us with something vast and uncontrollable and sublime, thrusting us past the limits of our longing' and see myself in her words.

I decide never to keep cats again, spare the toddler—a child of diaspora—the heart ache I carry.

And so, to that end, I have installed the Japanese mobile game *Neko Atsume* on our gadgets; we busy ourselves trying to lure rare cats to the yard. We subscribe to cat-memes and create folders on our laptop. I have outsourced the cat-shaped hole in our hearts to cat-cafes. I plan school holidays around the desirability and access to cat-cafes and take photographs every summer with a rainbow bouquet of haughty cats. We sanitize our hands and put on carpet slippers, promise the staff that we will not touch any of the cats, we buy treats for them and are thrilled when they stoop to play with us.

My family takes a look at the photographs of us ensconced on sofas, trying to get as many cats in the camera frame. They remember the cat lady who had parked herself in front of the National Defence College in Rawalpindi. An old woman had fashioned herself a residence from wooden crates and tarpaulin, and spent her day plying skeins of wool and string, surrounded by her beloved cats. Every afternoon, she would hoist a bag on her shoulders, and walk the bazaar, crossing the photo studio around the corner with the framed photographs of long-haired US Marines in *shalwar kamiz*, posing with Darra Adamkhel guns. A local newspaper once did a feature on this cat lady of Lalkurti, Rawalpindi. But for the most, she was left to her own devices. When our love affair with the Americans waned, there were rumours that The Cats and Her were American spies clandestinely conducting surveillance of the National Defence College.

(I step away from my laptop to jot down a WhatsApp message to my mother, asking her when we last saw the woman with the many cats. My mother writes back: *'She sat opp building which I think was national assembly. But what was it before that? Building has changed so many hands.'*
    I reply, *'Im talking about the Lalkurti woman. Was the NDC building ever the National Assembly????'*
    doing a quick search online
    'Yes. It was Ayub Hall.'
    Damn.)

The building, which hosted Pakistan's national legislature while they waited out the shift of capital from Karachi to Islamabad, was the National Defence College of my childhood and later, it became the Pakistani-army run National University of Science and Technology. It is now the Garrison Human Resource Development Centre, a fun fact which tells you more of my country's tryst with militarism than anything else.

I am back on the phone with my mother and she insists that those were kinder years—a woman could live on the streets if she was white-haired and didn't mean anyone harm. Little boys didn't throw stones though clearly she was struggling with emotional health. It could very well be that, around the same time, when the old lady with the cats was asked to move because Colonel/Brigadier/General *sahib*'s car is on the way, men started violating women's bodies. Cats, buildings, women: there is Rushdie's Salim Sinai-esque being mysteriously shackled to history, our destinies and fates 'indissolubly chained to those of (our) country'.

Part III: Delhi, 2020

It was the best of times, it was the worst of times,
it was the age of wisdom, it was the age of foolishness, it was the epoch of belief,
it was the epoch of incredulity, it was the season of light, it was the season of darkness,
it was the spring of hope, it was the winter of despair.
—Charles Dickens, *A Tale of Two Cities*

The world wakes up to sourdough starters and banana bread, Dalgona coffees and Zoom parties. My son and I bring home two cats. Maybe I am tired of saying *Oh But I Have Always Had Cats* or that my perfectly planned world and calendar has been so shook up that I am ready for what heartache may come.

Two cats.
Thing One and Thing Two.

Twiddle Dee Twiddle Dum.

Oh, no, no, no Dipankar, you haven't got it at all—the primeval texture of Indian philosophy is that of Duality... yes, Duality...

The warp and weft of our ancient garment, the sari itself—a single length of cloth which yet swathes our Indian womanhood—the warp and weft of the universe itself, the tension between Being and Non-Being—yes, indubitably it is Duality alone that reigns over us here in our ancient land.
—Vikram Seth, *A Suitable Boy*

Some say, compar'd to Bononcini
That Mynheer Handel's but a Ninny
Others aver, that he to Handel
Is scarcely fit to hold a Candle
Strange all this Difference should be
'Twixt Tweedle-dum and Tweedle-dee
—John Byrom, *Tweedle-dum and Tweedle-dee*

I see my cats and begin drawing parallels with Saleem and Shiva from *Midnight's Children*. If one is a meticulous planner, the other rushes into adventures that involves us defying the lockdown and walking in the street in the middle of the night, calling out plaintively. If one is emotionally needy, the other watches us from a distance, biding time until we have won his approval.

We take our time naming them. Wait till their personalities develop, we tell each other. If I have ensured that our boy has a name that accommodates the duality of his Pakistan and India lives, why deprive the kittens of theirs?

Should their name be a requiem to all the cats I have ever loved? Should it be a hat tip to my love for Hindi popular culture: Chor and Sipahi? Karan and Arjun? Jai and Veeru? Lata and Noor Jehan? Ganga and Indus? Lahore and Benares? Sachin and Shahid?

A friend suggests that we name them 14 and 15 (August). Numerical names are greatly underestimated, it seems. The two fight and make up enough to live up to those names.

I hum, *Muhabbat men nahi hai farq jeene aur marne ka/ Usi ko dekh kar jiite hain jis kafir pe dam nikle.*
(When it comes to love there is not much difference between life and death.
We draw a breath each time we catch a glimpse of our assassin.)

It soon transpires that I should name them Marie and Kondo as they proceed to demolish all that sparked joy in my life. Crockery, curtains, sofas, books, the newspaper, treats, a copper *attar dan* that had survived Partition and my moves across continents to return to India. (It is a clean break and I dub it 'Breaking India' and tell my boy that even Radcliffe was kinder.)

Well-wishers despair at our home and marvel at our courage to persevere. I quote the 'Eastern beloved' theory to explain my relationship with the cats. Just as in days of yore, a lovelorn poet would tell the world: no, no, my beloved is not snooty and cold-hearted, why do you assume so? I lament the intermediaries instead who will not deliver this missive to my beloved. Truth be told, my beloved would willingly reciprocate my love, but if only.

My cats are not that bad, I say. They can be really sweet and kind, it is just the times that are cruel and disorienting. We just have to wait.

One afternoon, I watch my cats who, depending on the time of the day, usually station themselves in a window, a balcony, by an open door, to watch what is happening in the streetscape below. Shades of *Bazeecha-e-itfal hai duniya mere aage/ Hota hai shab-o-roz tamasha mere aage… The world is but a*

85

child's playground before me, night and day a playhouse hosts performances before me. One of the cats stretches on his hind legs, preparing to claw his way up the bamboo fence that forms our balcony wall, all so he can enter into a staring competition with the cows that have parked themselves downstairs.

There is something however to how the cat peers across the fence that takes me back to my street in Rawalpindi and the deposed dictator who was placed under house arrest four houses down from us. After the initial excitement, the man became part of the street topography. No more so when he would clamber up a wooden crate to look at the world from the gap in the hedge bordering his compound. Some chapters are yet to be whitewashed from Rawalpindi's history, the flailing energies of the constant gardeners notwithstanding.

Other afternoons, I look at my notebooks, my words interspersed with lines which read like a Ouija Board to me when I re-read them, steering me one way or the other. This is what I finally distill.

1) We cannot consign to history what is so much part of our present;

2) You should never move back to where you came from, because that's where everything went wrong, the place you've been trying to escape from was inside your head your whole life.

Epilogue
Delhi, 2021

Hi, I'm the Baby mentioned earlier. My name is Arhaan Babar Ray.

I am a proud owner of two cats. Jude and Bibigul. Frankly, Bibigul is a sweetheart. Jude is a true foodie. In fact, I think Jude would sell our organs for a bowl of dry food—we feed him every three minutes. Bibigul actually walks up to me and begs for pets and scratches.

I remember the day we got them, the first thing they did was poop in the cat litter. Now it's not always that way.

These cats are quite naughty too. My grandmother did give us a fair warning though. In her words: '*Agar ye Dilli ke ladke intne gande hain, to billi kaise honge?!*' If Delhi boys are so terrible, what would you expect of their cats. And of course, she was right.

Like mentioned earlier, they have done their fair share of damage. My mother has been telling me that every morning Bibi slaps her with her paw for food, and then bites her toes. I have experienced the toe-biting myself but the slaps, I don't know. Jude likes Mama though. And Bibi loves me.

Fun fact: Bibigul is a girl's name but he's a boy. Apparently, this is not the first time my mother accidentally named a boy-cat as a girl. My mother's cat in Rawalpindi was a Chico, not the 'Chica' she named him.

Another fun fact: When my mother was writing her part of the chapter, the cats kept coming close to her and sleeping on the table. Now they're coming next to me. I feel that they know what we are doing and want to contribute too!

I always wanted cats when I was younger. I feel they're much more civilized than dogs or other animals. But now, when I got these cats, I feel that these *dilli ke bacchae* are just as naughty.

Anyway, it's time to feed them.

(Otherwise, Jude will end my free trial of life.)

Weather Forecast
by Aditi Sriram

Monday

Today is the start of Saras' solo, internet-free work trip. Which sounds fancy until she has to drive herself from Bombay to her family's farm in rural Maharashtra. Simultaneously navigating and steering, meekly waiting for massive trucks to give her way, Saras spends six hours completing what is usually a four-hour journey. Highways, village roads, two-wheeler traffic, four-legged traffic, it's all the classic juxtapositions of an emerging economy, which Saras has always enjoyed—until now, when they attain the higher levels of a video game, out to distract and kill her. After she reaches the farm and turns off the vehicle, relieving her ears of the engine's buzz, she exhales the sigh she has been holding on to for the last hour of the drive, a mix of prayers and road rage. It is only much later, barefoot and lounging in the verandah with a glass of wine, that she feels her fingers fully exorcise their steering wheel grip and lie limp on the arms of the chair.

It's dark already, but it isn't late. Hardly eight o'clock. Sitting under the night sky, in its studded silence, Saras contemplates sleep. She loves this about being so far away from the city and its wiring. Out here, in the middle of nowhere, deprived of panoramic electricity, her body magically activates its caveman instincts. Saras yawns, which makes her chuckle. The sound is strange and hollow compared to the frog chorus performing a few feet away. That has got to be the longest running musical in history, she jokes, not for the first time. *Sorry, Phantom.*

She takes exaggerated steps back to her room, grateful that her feet remain un-slimed by snails and other nocturnal commuters. Leaving the light off, Saras flicks on the fan, which rouses with a rickety rumble. The curtains come to life as well, dancing in the flimsy breeze, pressing up against the window panes and backing away, as if unsure how to proceed. Shapes and silhouettes form in their coquetry, blobs that merge into each other, fall upon each other, draw back and try again. It looks like some kind of alien sex. Saras stares at the images until her eyes blur and the curtains lose their solidity. Maybe give them some privacy, she scolds herself, squeezing her eyes shut.

She wonders if she should stay awake, do some sketching in the dark. This is a work trip after all, although her parents laughed each time she said the farm was the perfect place for her research. She could sketch some insects and send them a photo, explain why she's out here, for the inspiration of it all. But her brain, half-asleep, dismisses the idea. First, it's not about drawing; she wants to show them a story. Second, no internet, so no messages. But she has time. They're only arriving on Saturday. *I will have had a few brainstorms by then.*

The curtains continue to heave and blush. Beyond them, the night is a massive, open-mouthed yawn. It radiates a furry black sheen. Tomorrow then, Saras tells herself. She checks the time on her phone as she climbs under the covers and her last thought is of an army of frogs croaking "The Music of the Night."

Tuesday

Saras wakes to a sky the color of wet paper and knows it will rain. She heads to the kitchen to see if there is anything left over from the family's previous trip, at least some tea leaves she can dunk in hot water. Her mind is already preoccupied with what fruit and vegetables she should stock up on, and how much she will embarrass herself as the only person in the market who doesn't know what is currently in season, so when she spots a kitten asleep in a corner, she thinks she has made it up. But she hasn't. It is tiny and grey, and at first Saras can't tell if it is asleep, or squinting – or scowling; aren't cats always scowling? Her first instinct is to walk past it and hope it eventually disappears: that is how one deals with the insect- and wild-life on a farm. Lizards inevitably crawl back into rooftops; monkeys bound away into far-off trees; cockroaches vanish when the sun comes back out; moths end up dead inside lamps. Surely this kitten will leave, at some point or another. Its mother will find it, some villager will claim it. Saras isn't bothered.

Rather, she is in luck: there is not only loose leaf-tea, but coffee powder as well. And two unopened cartons of tetra pack milk, which means she can have a proper morning beverage without journeying in search of fresh milk. Saras brings her chai to the verandah and sinks into a low-rising chair. This is her favorite spot on the property: sitting here, she can see most of the fields, the baby stream running alongside, and the mountains in the distance. Behind her is the kitchen, sunlit and ergonomic, and to her left are three brick-walled rooms connected by stone pathways. Their roofs slope up and down, one after the other, their own little mountain range.

Recently, Saras had been sent on an assignment to a primary school in Bandra. She was to observe a group of children constructing toy houses with different materials—Lego, wooden blocks, kitchenware, books—and see what they came up with. If you want to draw for kids, her boss had told her, study how they draw. Only then can you find your edge. One little girl had created this very impressive cordillera of rooftops by leaning books against each other, and she had copied it in her sketchbook because she loved the strong, clean lines. Now sitting in her verandah, she appreciates the symmetrical setup all over again. Sometimes the most effective structures are also the most aesthetic.

The sun climbs higher in the sky but doesn't add any colour to it. Unaffected by rain or by glare, Saras reads a novel, trying not to hear her mother's voice asking, from six hours away, whether her "work trip" will involve doing actual work. Her mother loves the word work, loves partnering it with different prepositions: work on this some more! Don't get worked up! Why don't you work out! Each pairing rattles against the inside of Saras' head, trying to escape, and her coping mechanism is to replace it with another w-word she can think of, which makes the instruction much funnier. Whisk more; you're getting wobbled up; shall we whine out together?

But the jokes don't change what happened at her previous job. Or what a worm her boss, turned out to be.

Not at first, though. Rajesh had hired her into her first job after college, and been the ideal boss, mentor, colleague. His company designed graphics for all kinds of publications, from science textbooks to literary magazines, from museum catalogues to restaurant menus. As all these establishments dealt with increasing overheads and diminishing profits, it had become cheaper for them to outsource their creative work. For Saras, with a bachelors in design, a small firm sounded like the right mix of relevance, self-expression, and idealism. When one of her professors had introduced her to Rajesh, she approved of his vision and his handshake. He had offered her the job shortly before she graduated and she couldn't believe her luck. It never occurred to her to look for other jobs before accepting this one.

The work was hard, the hours were long, the technology was dizzying. Rajesh had assembled an energetic team, mostly fresh out of college, whose opinions and egos fueled their motivation. Comparatively, Saras was more quiescent. It was Rajesh who noticed that her designs regularly inspired the team's final creations, even though she wasn't the loudest person in the room. He ensured that her images, even some of her original sketches, were prominent all over the company website, and she appreciated his subtle, but persistent, support. Her mother approved. "Work hard," she advised, not for the first time. And Saras chuckled, because her brain had heard "wiggle hard."

But it was just a few months later that a story broke that linked Rajesh's team to an underground software that used reams of copyrighted images to support causes that were illegal, and often criminal. Apparently, Rajesh had been contributing their designs to this software, for sinful sums of money, and Saras' images were all over this scandal. Without her knowledge. Everyone's work, and salaries came under scrutiny, even though nobody except for Rajesh had been involved, but it was too late. Her reputation, her art, her future, all of it was wrecked.

Equal parts embarrassed and terrified, Saras hid in her room for months, waiting to stop being a cliche. She was the "wrongfully accused," the "naive junior associate," the "opportunistic millennial," and in the slimiest reports, she was "Rajesh's confidante," whatever that was supposed to mean. When it was all over, nearly a year later, Saras felt able to look for jobs again, but swore that she would only draw for someone she completely trusted. Then she met Nirupama, a woman who published children's books, wore clips in her short grey hair, and used her eyeliner to draw the perfect winged eye, and also to doodle on a napkin. Saras sensed that they could have a professional future together. They became a two-person team that commissioned original children's literature and created the illustrations. Saras laughed more than she had in a year.

When Nirupama asked her to create her own book—text and art, both— Saras felt it was too soon. Hadn't they just started working together? 'You're ready,'Nirupama had said, her eyeliner undulating as she smiled. 'This project will do you good!' her mother agreed. 'Give you some time to work off all that stress.' *Write off all that stress*, Saras's mind translated, and because it made sense, in more ways than one, she packed a bag and drove to the farm.

Occasionally she glances up to see if the kitten is still there. It is. As late morning turns into late afternoon, and no one turns up at the property gate, human or feline, to collect this measly thing. Saras tries to discern if its stomach is rising and falling. Maybe it isn't hungry, just extremely tired. This little patch of hueless sky that has descended into her world and rearranged itself into a mammal with four legs and a tail. She hopes it isn't dying.

Trying to ignore these lazily urgent thoughts, Saras keeps reading. She still has the sandwiches she had brought from home, which will last her the rest of the day. She is relieved that she can postpone food shopping until tomorrow, and basks in her hard-earned solitude. New roommate notwithstanding. Today seems like the kind of day when nothing will happen.

As if on cue, it begins to rain. Something ruptures in the greyness above, and now there is noise and moisture. And movement. Crabs slink out of their water-logged holes and the earth resounds with what sounds like applause. The rain drums on the verandah's roof tiles and drips through where it can. *All this thunder and lightning, and for what? Some water droplets?* A Bombay girl, Saras has always thought of the rain as pure melodrama.

The cat doesn't react to the onslaught, but now appears to be breathing quite rapidly. She needs to act now. Feed it or leave it alone? Even though she is still holding her book and staring at it, her mind has wandered off, wondering about the feline ability to haunt those who have neglected them. *Ok, a cup of milk then.* She puts her book down. But you don't want it to hang around, do you? Saras picks her book back up. *Milk isn't a meal.* She flips it over to hold her page. *But it might attract more animals into the property, and Ma will have a fit.* Saras does the yes-or-no, this-or-that dance all the time at home, but here too? *Just leave a katori of milk near the damn thing.*

Saras places a cup of milk near the kitten, adjusting it a few times before determining the appropriate proximity to the animal's face. *Get out of your*

head! For a moment, she waits, in case the kitten wishes to choose this moment to wake up, take a drink, and deem Saras its savior. Nothing. It sleeps on. The frogs cackle in the background, encouraged by the twilight rain. Saras heads to her bedroom, to read some more. An hour later, she bundles up her blanket in her arms and returns to her chair in the verandah. She has decided to sleep here tonight. *And I won't change my mind!* As the rain hollers on, Saras dreams of her mother yelling bloody murder for sharing their kitchenware with a filthy stray.

Wednesday

Sleeping across a chair and a foot stool has left her feeling stiff and fidgety. Yesterday it had felt exciting to sleep outdoors, the novelty of rural independence goosebumping across her skin. But those goosebumps have swollen into mosquito bites. Saras remembers the cat. If only I had a tail to keep the damn insects away, she chuckles.

The tail-possessing creature from the night before is no longer in the corner; the cup sits empty and unaccompanied. Saras decides to wash it later; *sorry Ma, chai comes first*. By the time she returns to the verandah with her mug, the world above her is fluorescing from blue to yellow. The mountains obstruct her view of the horizon, but she can imagine the sun as a long rim of light, glowing and rising before it spills over.

Saras' limbs re-awaken, this time in a much better mood. Saras plans her day. To make it as a children's book illustrator I have to find my *edge*, she reminds herself, quoting Nirupama's favorite word. And if my *edge* is contemporary rural life, then I need to get out there and look at it. The dairy is only a few kilometers away, and I can see how the cattle is actually, properly milked. The neighbors' roosters will announce themselves at some point. And if I'm lucky, I can catch a fisherman's wife setting up her husband's catch on the side of the road. Saras has always pondered these women's piscatorial displays. Sometimes the catch is arranged by size, sometimes by freshness, she can never tell. *And that is the very definition of a lack of edge.*

Half an hour later, she has breakfasted and dressed and is ready to step out. That is when she sees it again: the cat. Or is it? This time it is awake, and wears a coat of orange and yellow stripes. Saras stares, trying to make sense of this new creature. Its eyes are flecked with the same amber shade as its coat, and they flicker like a candle flame. For a moment, Saras wants to recreate these colors in her sketchbook, but she changes her mind. *These cats are unreal.* And she wants to reach the dairy before the last cow is milked.

The cat licks the ground, as if searching for leftovers from the previous day's milk.

Saras shakes her head. 'Sorry, I have to run, but if you're here later, I'll have something for you.'

In the car, she admits how absurd that sounded. *I was talking to a cat.* But she doesn't have time to dwell. Saras spends the rest of the day in multiple locations, observing, sketching, chatting, eating. When she returns home later that evening, her mind crowded with images, her pencils blunt and shorter, there is no cat to be found.

She settles back into her chair in the verandah, satisfied with her day and excited for the wine that will follow, when the sunset makes her catch her breath. The sky, light pink just a moment ago, has deepened into orange. Streaked through this marmalade is its partner, honey. Saras is struck by the orange and yellow. Hasn't she seen this before? Yellow and orange. Doesn't it look just like—

That's it, bedtime, Saras thinks, cutting off the thought before it fully materialises.

Thursday

Saras wakes up with her sketchbook next to her. Animals in various poses stare back, but somehow they feel lackluster. Children's book illustrations are most alluring, most successful when they are bright and bold and vivid. Think *Hungry Caterpillar*. *Karadi Tales* books. Any *Tinkle* magazine cover. Cows don't have to be black-and-white. Dogs don't have to be brown. Fish don't have to be grey.

In fact, marine life is so much fun to work with, there are so many techniques to create a fish's shimmering scales, or a coral reef's rainbow. Saras's mind starts racing. The ocean. The beach is ten minutes from here. She could focus on contemporary rural coastal life: fisher families and their daily expeditions. *Maybe that's my edge*. Why do farm animals all over again? That is every children's book all over the world.

The idea is thrilling. There are so many components. The men off on their early morning catches—or the late-night ones. Their wives waiting with their empty baskets. The tides, the sand, the boats, the net. All the different materials and tools. The risks, the weather. The scale of it all. Saras jots down some words as she thinks. She knows where she'll be spending the rest of her day.

She avoids the kitchen completely—there is a small shop near the beach where she can order breakfast—and drives straight to the nearest beach. She prays that it doesn't rain, so that she can photograph and draw undisturbed. The weather gods acquiesce.

The fishermen's boats are not completely made of wood, as she expected. Styrofoam cubes cover the entire surface and form an additional floatation layer between boat and sea. The wood is worn and weathered, and matches the fishermen's faces.

There are no women on the beach. They could be in the market, but Saras is too bashful to clarify this with the fishermen. One takes her on a short trip into the water, and she is impressed by his strength to row against the current. The boat seems much larger once she is sitting in it. He rarely fishes during the monsoon, the man says, but he can show her a little bit of the sea. It is too murky to see anything below the surface; Saras thinks she has spotted a jellyfish, but it is just a plastic bag. Hearing the water slapping against the Styrofoam and thirst scratching at her throat, she is unsettled by how endless, bottomless and relentless the sea is. After a couple of hours in the blazing sun, Saras feels fully desiccated. Her morning omelette is also long digested and now she is hungry.

Back at home Saras prepares an elaborate lunch. She half-expects feline company when she brings her plate to the verandah to eat. Will it be the grey one or the sunset one today?

So when she does hear a meow, she doesn't do what her mother does and blame it on exposure to the sun. *I've been expecting you, I think?* A head sticks out from around the corner: triangular ears and whiskers and unblinking eyes. Then a body and legs and a tail. And a cat walks up to her, confident and grand, and sits by her chair as if this is what the two of them do together every day. This visitor is lustrous, its fur a glossy steel that is almost navy. Saras remembers a set of colour pencils her parents gifted her one year, 74 distinct shades, each pencil the exact same height and pointiness, with the colour names printed along the side of each pencil. This cat's coat is in that set, she can recall it instantly: "Russian Blue."

Russian Blue's gaze doesn't leave Saras' plate for even an instant. Saras doesn't take her eyes off the cat either—partly a professional habit, partly because she has to keep reminding herself that these cats are corporeal. She soaks up the daal and subji in her roti and chews slowly. She sits up, adopting her own regal posture. She waits.

The cat scrunches its eyes closed and reopens them, and Saras notices that the right eye is blue, the left one green. Or is it the other way around? Each time Russian Blue blinks, its eyes seem to switch colours, the aquamarine flowing back and forth. First grey, then striped, now tidal. *Have I been alone too long?*

She makes no attempt to touch the cat, and as her plate empties, the animal's interest wanes. Eventually Russian Blue recedes into the trees behind the kitchen. But Saras leaves a cup of milk on the stairs before she turns in for the night.

Friday

Saras hears music outside her window and recognizes Manju's old radio squawking from the kitchen. Manju used to be the caretaker when Saras was much younger, and would look after her, too; apparently Saras could converse with Manju in fluent Marathi back then. Now she thinks—and draws? —in English, and her Marathi has reduced to a few words here and there. Manju has moved on, too, and tends to other properties. She drops in once a week to keep an eye on things and Saras is always happy to see her. Plus, she won't have to make her own tea this morning.

Manju is humming along to the song when Saras joins her in the kitchen.

'Ah, Saroo, I guessed that you have come alone! Your mother wouldn't allow such a mess to pile up, hmm?' Manju's Hindi is inflected with Marathi.

Saras is a little embarrassed and a little annoyed. But mostly she is grateful that all the empty wine bottles and glasses are in her room, and that she can put them away after Manju has left.

'Good morning, Manju tai, nice to see you too,' she says in an English-Hindi mix. 'Hahn ji, I've come on my own. Need to get some work done and Ma will just keep bothering me!'

'And she'll bother you even more when she lands up tomorrow and sees the kitchen in this state. You're lucky I dropped in today.'

Saras ignores the friendly jibe and changes the subject. 'Do you have a cat, Manju tai?'

'No, of course not!'

'What do you mean, of course not?'

'Well, you can't keep a cat, everyone knows that. If a cat wants a home, it chooses where to go, and who will look after it. Only dogs are stupid enough for leashes. Cats live their own lives.'

'But I know lots of dogs who aren't forced to wear—anyway, what I'm asking is, have you seen a cat around here, when you come to the farm?'

'No, I don't think so. What colour?'

Saras hesitates. 'Well, it depends on the time of day. The—the color is sometimes—well, it's always different.' Stammering in Hindi makes Saras sound even more unsure of herself.

'Chh! You haven't been eating enough while you've been here, have you. Too much tea and eggs, it will affect your brain. Let me make you some poha, nice and fresh, and you can focus on your work. Tell me, what are you drawing nowadays? Your mother said you're working with a nice old lady now.'

99

Saras pictures winged-eyes arching at those words. *Old? Nice?* Her stomach grumbles at the mention of poha. 'Ok, thank you, yes, I'll have some breakfast!'

A few minutes elapse as Manju chops, stirs, seasons. 'Hahn, so, your work?' she prompts.

'Actually, I've come here looking for things to draw that kids will like. Any ideas?' Saras idly pops a piece of raw onion in her mouth.

'You are surrounded by a million things and you don't know what to draw? Chh, Saroo, what is this!' They giggle together.

'Of course, there's lots to see here, but I don't know what to choose—animals on land, or in the sea, or the farmers at work. Plus, it was raining cats and dogs a few days ago. I just get too distracted.'

'It's Shravan Maas, nearly the end of the monsoons. The rains that come now are especially lucky. If it rains, the world is trying to tell you something, show you something, Saroo. So keep a lookout.'

Saras sits at the table blowing on her plate of poha—in signature Manju style, it will be too hot to eat for several more minutes.

Relishing her teaching moment, Manju continues. 'Have you been watching the moon as it has been growing, from a slice into a full onion?' She gestures at some neglected purple crescents on the cutting board. 'The moon has been so bright these past few nights, probably since the rain clouds have all emptied out. Tomorrow is Purnima—'

Saras looks up.

'The full moon, Saroo, you should know that! Narali Purnima is tomorrow, the moon will be stronger than a tube light, glowing like a bride in her most expensive sari. You won't be able to sleep.'

The poha sits warm in Saras' stomach; if this was a children's book, she'd have drawn steam coming out of her ears. She is enjoying Manju's oration, even as it grows more ridiculous with every metaphor. 'I hadn't noticed—'

'You will. The moon will come to you, just like the rain has. Now go, get to work. You've eaten so you can focus properly. I'll make some parathas for your lunch, gol-gol like the moon. After I've done some cleaning, that is. And I'll get more milk. How have you managed to go through two cartons already? How much chai do you drink, girl?'

The rest of the day is quiet, dry, and, indeed, focused. Saras has forgotten marine biology and animal husbandry. Thanks to her parents' fondness for encyclopaedias, which used to collect dust in Bombay and now breathe fresh air here, she is reading about lunar cycles and all the mysterious phenomena that occur at the whim of this moody satellite. Like a good mythical creature, the moon is tethered to its master, but exerts its own influence. It keeps changing its form: at times it is grey and obscured, other times it is more blinding than the sun. Its very nature is to come and go, wax and wane, ebb and flow, rise and set. *Leave me alone*, Saras interprets, *but don't stop looking for me.*

Hours pass and Saras is unaware. Her stomach is fuller today, and so is her sketchbook. What am I looking for, she wonders as she scribbles.

Maybe my edge is a crescent, Saras muses, before she nods off to sleep.

Saturday

Saras is up early; she needs to replenish her groceries before her parents arrive, and the market is always more crowded on weekends.

The verandah is gleaming and Saras knows any traces of milk or cat fur will have been scrubbed clean. *Thank you, Manju.* But as she walks around to the driver's side of the car, Sars nearly trips over the biggest cat that has appeared so far. It is pitch black and splayed out on the ground. Not in your usual corner this time, Saras thinks. Must be important. She stands there, waiting. Something is going to happen. Something has to. She wouldn't be surprised if the damn thing opened its mouth and spoke, and proclaimed that it was God. *Definitely no leashes for this species.*

But the cat doesn't meow again. Instead, it rolls over. Slowly, deliberately, onto its back and then again onto its front. Its charcoal fur is interrupted by a burst of white on its belly, which is completely hidden again when the cat resumes its sitting position. It rolls again.

The cat rolls over a third time. Black mutates into white. Then it walks away, it's tail an inky letter S.

In the car, Saras rumbles over potholes and puddles to the market. It is abuzz today and there are coconuts everywhere. The women are discussing Narali Purnima and Saras thanks Manju again. Some eavesdropping, and she learns that everyone will be on the beach in the evening, offering coconuts. The senior fishermen will dispatch the juniors into the sea for their first catch in the new fishing season. Since the rains are almost over—and what a season it's been.

'The only problem is the sky,' one vegetable vendor complains to Saras. 'Why, what does the sky have to do with it?'

'Today is supposed to be a full moon day, but we'll only see the moon if the sky is clear. And look at it, just look. Completely cloudy.'

'Those will clear out, surely,' Saras attempts a rebuttal forecast, ignoring how discordant her voice sounds amongst these locals. *Chh, Saroo!* 'If the monsoon is ending, isn't there less chance of rain?'

'That's how it usually is, but these clouds are different. They'll get darker and bigger throughout the day, and be heavy with rain by the time we reach the beach.'

Saras is internalising the woman's worried expression, the sweat in the folds of her neck, the large red bindi sitting perfectly between her eyebrows. Gol-gol and bridal-red. Something clicks. Saras smiles.

'You don't need to worry, mausi,' she says. 'The moon will be absolutely bright and visible in the sky today. I guarantee it.'

'That's sweet of you, beta, but how do you know? They say the moon will be hidden for much of tonight.'

'No, I am sure of it. When the clouds hide it, the moon will reappear. The clouds will try three times, and the moon will come back out every time. You just wait and see, mausi, the moon will be just where it should be.'

'Beta, don't say such things! It will only make the moon even more shy. Here, take your subzi and carry on! Let's not disrespect the clouds any further.'

Saras smiles and takes her bag of vegetables. 'Three times, mausi. Pakka. The clouds will roll away and the moon will show itself to you three times tonight.'

Along Came Billo

by Maneesha Taneja

A Cat-Story that Also Involves Dogs in a Starring Role

My name is Maneesha Taneja. I live in Noida, a suburb of Delhi. I share my house with my husband Ashutosh whom I met in college, and two dogs and a cat. I was not an animal person. This is the story of how that happened.

In the July of 1988 I left Lucknow, where my parents lived, and went to Jawaharlal Nehru University, New Delhi, for my undergraduate studies in Spanish. In August, my sister acquired a dog. It did seem that she was waiting for me to leave to fulfill a long-cherished desire She was the animal-crazy creature in our house. And to a large extent, my baby brother was too. The dog had belonged to a family in the neighbourhood, a Pomeranian or a Spitz. They had had a baby and were unable to care for the dog along with the baby. My sister was only too happy to take in the dog.

I went home that October, and Bruno and I did not become friends. We lived in a duplex and that was rather convenient for me. If he was upstairs, I was downstairs. Or the other way around. The highlight of the holiday, I remember, was that a stray cat came in, scratched Bruno on the nose rather badly, and there was much hysteria and panic. A rushed visit to the vet and an injection is what I remember. And of course, laughing no end at this reversal of roles... a cat getting the better of a dog! Little did I know how this scene would be repeated in my life many years later.

In December, the family went for a holiday to Jodhpur, and then to Delhi for my cousin's wedding. My sister had stayed on at home as she had board exams that year, and, of course, for Bruno. Sadly, for my sister, during that very break, Bruno fell ill and died. My siblings were heartbroken. I felt sad for them but personally it didn't really affect me. I wasn't a "pet person". (Pets at home, from there-on, were limited to a snail, a tortoise, a couple of stray dogs fed outside and taken care of.)

Years went by. I finished my studies, got married and got a job. My in-laws were in Lucknow and I went visiting. My sister too was in Lucknow, married there. She came to meet me, and with her came this tiny bundle of fur. A Lhasa Terrier puppy. My indifference to dogs melted away instantly. The pup was adorable, had this floppy mop of hair that covered his eyes. His name was Mowgli.

Five years after I met Mowgli, he came to live with us. My sister's marriage did not work out, and she shifted to Noida. All she brought with her was her dog. This turned out to be a dream come true for my husband. He had always wanted a dog but at home his mother wouldn't let him keep one, and then I wasn't too keen. I was not averse to them *per se*, but I was doing a PhD and a job; finances were tight, and a pet involved a lot of work and commitment. I wasn't ready for that. Hell, this was the same reason I wasn't prepared to have a child!

Of course, the situation was such that I could neither protest or voice any objections. My sister's well-being mattered more than my rather selfish objections. Mowgli settled into our lives and the gentle soul brought us immense happiness for the next five years, when he fell ill and passed away in June 2006.

With the loss of an animal, we begin to remember. We remember the padding of soft paws, afternoons spent playing fetch, bird calls. We remember friendship. In animals, we not only find a friend, but also a confidant;

someone with whom we can share our deepest longings and our deepest fears.

In July 2006 we got Poco Loco home. An American Cocker Spaniel he was all energy, and all he wanted to do was play. I remember being in tears many a times because he wouldn't let me be. The considerate spouse insisted we get another dog. Apparently, he would get company, the two could play together, and I would be spared. It seemed *so* logical that I fell for it. Chhotu, a Lhasa Apso came home a year and half after Poco Loco. Turns out, the big dog was a cowardy-custard, who took three months to let the small dog even come near him. There was of course no respite for me! In fact, I was now dealing with two demanding dogs and wondering how I had landed up in such a situation.

Over the years however, they settled down into companionship, though they have not played together. Chhotu copies Poco Loco at every step—how to eat, sleep, walk, everything; Chhotu will not go for a walk without him, nor eat if Poco isn't eating. Poco Loco cares for him in his own way but isn't as attached. All he cares about is my husband. That is the axis in life.

Life has a way of throwing many a curve ball. Ashutosh gave up journalism and ventured into politics. He contested the Parliamentary elections on 2014 and the day the results came, and he lost, I remember that when he came home, Poco Loco had somehow gleaned that we were all disappointed. He just snuggled up to Ashutosh and stayed there. This was in such contrast to his usual welcome where he would dance, jump and bark and lick him thoroughly.

Life with the dogs was interesting. Before Poco Loco came home, I had laid down my terms. I did not walk them or bathe them. I gave them their food, and when they were unwell, they would come cling to me for all the love and affection they had for Ashutosh. I guess it must be an instinct to look for the maternal figure in times of distress. Friends and family knew well enough to not refer to them as dogs for they were our children. Friends who were petrified of pets learnt to walk in and not scream or run in fear. And as far as my siblings were concerned, these two were as much their pets as ours.

And now for the twist in the tale.

In December 2017, I went to Bhopal to spend time with my maternal aunt, my Maasi. This, for me, is always a rejuvenating holiday, even when only 4–5 days. I got back to Delhi late at night as the fog had delayed trains by hours. Early next morning, the doorbell rang. Still half-asleep, I went to answer it and found a neighbour's school-going son standing there with a basket.

"Aunty, can you keep her for a couple of days? I have school and my parents are not allowing me to leave her at home when I'm not there. Vacations start from the day after and I will take her back then."

I was stupefied. This child was a kind soul who went about rescuing animals all over, and providing first aid to all manner of injured pigeons, squirrels, sparrows, dogs, in the apartment block. And mostly the treatment involved knocking at our door and asking what should be done and if I can provide any ointment, medicines etc. etc. What he held in the basket was a kitten, so tiny that it set you going aww. But: a kitten with two dogs in the house? And who was going to look after it?

As is wont in such situations, the husband's antennae shot up and he materialised there instantly.

'Of course, child, we shall see to this.' And that was that.

Sukanti lives with us and looks after our house and cooks the most amazing food for us. She too ooh-ed and aah-d. It was then that I was filled in on the backstory. Apparently, four days ago the child had found this little kitten on the staircase, hurt and bleeding. The first port of call had obviously been our house and Ashutosh had promptly taken the boy and the kitten to the vet. It was about 2 months old, if not younger, and had fallen off from one of the higher floors. It was given first aid, and floating on a hope and a prayer, they came home. School was closed for the next four days, so the boy decided to keep the kitten at home and look after it, for our house was a death trap of sorts, with two dogs, one of whom was a rather snappy Apso, ready to bite off legs and heads and anything he didn't like.

Some time ago, my husband and sister-in-law had rescued a cat in our apartment block, when it was being attacked by a dog. We had given it first aid—the poor thing had had its tail bitten—and we kept it in our service balcony, with food and water, for a couple of days. The moment it felt better, it took off on its own. We live on the first floor and it is an open balcony. I'm sure it too was no fan of the dogs living right there! Taking my cue from this, I suggested we make this kitten comfortable there, till such time as the kid took it back, which was, of course, a couple of days.

Sukanti, taken in by the helpless gnome look of the kitten, offered to keep it in her room as it was winter, and the balcony would be too cold. The kid never did come back. When I went to check on him three days later, I learnt that the family had gone off for a holiday, and we were now left holding the kitten. In another couple of days, Sukanti went off for her annual pilgrimage home, and so began the fun and games.

Ashutosh's sister had, for many years, a cat, as did my cousin. The two of them were our advisers now. We were told to get a litter box and get the kitten to use it. A litter box was got. Now where to install it? We chose our bath. It is large enough and attached to our room. The kitten would be close by but, with the door closed, it would also be safe from any eager-beaver dog. She had been christened Billo. Billo is a Punjabi word that is derived from the Hindi word "*billi* (Cat)" but usually the word *billo* is used for a girl who has eyes that aren't black.

Ashutosh is great with kids and pets, and wins their confidence very easily. He was home a lot, and took it on himself to make sure that the three creatures would cohabit peacefully. At the time, he was disillusioned with politics, after having spent the last few years actively involved in it. He was locked in, reassessing his choices, confronting the collapse of his ideals. He would bring the kitten out and let the dogs smell her, whilst he held her to him. Poco Loco was of course not really interested; in fact, he was scared. He is petrified of all things that move, other than humans. I remember him meeting one of his progenies at one time and running in reverse gear to get away! All the rats of the world would wander into our house because our dog sat on the bed while they rampaged around, chased by me wielding a broom!

Billo very soon adjusted to the dogs. She realised they came as a package with the human that she doted on most. She was a regular Indian cat, grey in colour, with maybe a rust shadow, and her hind paws were white, as though she was wearing socks. Her liquid eyes seemed to peer into your very soul. Billo would jump, skid and goof around.

Billo soon joined the dogs in their morning medicine-ritual. Every morning, Ashutosh would sit the dogs down and give them their vitamins. Poco Loco had eye problems and had to be administered eye drops. He would sit through the ministrations patiently. Chhotu on the other hand could not be fed any medicine unless of course you wanted your hand bitten off. So, if he felt like it, he would have the vitamin, otherwise you just let him be. Billo too started coming to this daily ritual and would drink her vitamin syrup from the bottle cap, happily enough. I really wondered how, for that syrup smelled vile, as liver tonics do. It was a sight to behold. The two dogs and the cat waiting their turns for the medicine, and their favourite human administering the doses lovingly.

Billo loved to play with water, which was a surprise for us because traditionally it is believed that cats don't like water. She would stare at a dripping tap as looong as it dripped. She would stare with fascination at the water falling from a shower. We have a small terrace—our house is on the first floor of a three-floor building. Every morning, Ashutosh would water the plants, and she would sunbathe and enjoy the open air. If it rained, she would chase rain drops. Of course, from the terrace she would jump off to the neighbour's ledge or one of our window ledges. There she would sit and stare at the world, often not knowing how to jump back to the terrace. Then would begin the operation Rescue Billo. Either Ashutosh or the driver would jump, slide and maneuver to the ledge, catch her and hand her over and come back.

Nothing deterred her and soon it became a game for her to do this all the time. In the night she would sleep with us, curled up inside the quilt. The first night she went in, she started purring. I was only used to dogs. They slept next to us but only snored. This sound that seemed like the revving of a motor was rather unnerving. It took some time to understand that this was purring. I had always imagined a cat's purring to be gentle and melodious. This really was a motor going vroom vroom! Well, you live and learn. In no time it was rather comforting to have this purring ball sleeping next to us.

Soon enough, she went on heat. This meant all night of meowing loudly, crying soulfully to all the stray cats outside—and we have quite a few of those. The nights were spent calling her and keeping her in our room, which had her quiet on the meowing-front but busy on the let's-scratch-this-door-open front. So, we eventually put her in the bathroom, so that some semblance of sleep could be had. She would quiet down after a while but the next morning was like walking into a tornado hit zone. Everything thrown around, the wiper bitten and clawed through. A couple of cycles of this and we took the proffered advice to get her spayed.

Our veterinarian had treated our dogs forever, so we merrily went there. Date and time were fixed and we were assured that it was a simple procedure and she would recover in a couple of days. D-day dawned and off we went.

The surgery took longer than anticipated and she apparently had resisted the anesthesia a lot and fought a lot. "A feisty one," the doc called her. We came home with our groggy baby who looked rather the worse for wear. By evening she started to move around. We were supposed to take her for her dressing on the third day. She hadn't been eating so we put it down to a loss of appetite. She would sit near the water bowl and stare at it. We wondered what was happening. Ashutosh realised that she was unable to drink the water. She wanted to but was unable to move her jaw. It was a dash to the clinic and we realised her jaw was clenched tight. The doctor assured her she would be fine, and this was sometimes a side effect of the anesthesia.

Things did not improve. We ended up grinding her food in a mixer and feeding her with a syringe. Every few hours water too was given with a syringe to hydrate her. She didn't improve. One evening, she suddenly seemed very listless. We realised her stitches had opened. Sunday evenings are terrible for pet owners. Doctors aren't available and hospitals for emergencies are few and far between. It took us a lot of calls and much internet search to find a vet, but one look, and she was unwilling to take any proactive action. The very next morning we rushed to a vet 30 kms away who had been treating Poco Loco for his eye issues for some time and had really gained our trust. He took blood samples and started treatment right away.

The next day, Ashutosh had a commitment in Varanasi. With a very heavy heart he went when I told him it was alright, I would manage. We would manage. Billo was a fighter who didn't give up. She had fought injury and survived a close call with death earlier and she would do so again. The next day we went to the vet, and Ashutosh went off to the airport from there. The blood reports were in. She had tick fever. What was crazy was that she had a tick fever that was prevalent in dogs. The chances of a cross-species infection are one in a million. She was the one in a million.

The doctor was hopeful. Billo too was fighting; she didn't give up. But that night she seemed to just tire. Of the ordeal, the battle. I could see her sinking. It was heartbreaking to see that tiny thing suffering, in pain, and looking at me with eyes that asked for help. Early morning, I called a friend and we drove to the vet. Billo was critical. Her temperature was dropping, she was giving up. Despite all efforts, the little one did not survive. She left.

I thought cats had nine lives. This one just had two. She died in my arms and there was nothing I could do to save her. Ashutosh came home that morning to see his little kitten gone. We buried her in a park near the house. And every morning when we go for our walk, I wish her a good morning. She lies there under a tree, free from pain.

Billo came into our lives, especially Ashutosh's life, at a time when he was at crossroads. She provided the calm and the distraction he had required. She brought joy when things seemed chaotic. At a time when he was grappling with his disappointments and the way forward, she provided succor. He decided to end his foray into politics and get back to his first love, journalism. I strongly believe that it was serendipity that Billo came into our lives at that point. This was the universe helping out in tough times. She came, she comforted, and she went away.

I remember how Billo would look at me with pure mischief dancing in her billo-eyes, standing next to a vase, or anything fragile for that matter, and then, while looking me in the eye, just kick it off the table. Chhotu, once on his evening walk, just stopped in the middle of the road and barked madly at a stray cat that sat atop a tree (who looked a lot like Billo), wondering why it wasn't coming home! Sukanti took Billo's death very hard. One day, she would one day want another cat; the next day swear that never would she have another one at home. Could anyone replace Billo?

Three months later, Sukanti came to me and said plaintively, 'Didi, bring another Billo.'

At the end of September, Billo 2.0 came home. A two-month-old kitten, a spotted Indian with white paws, white underbelly, and a white smudge upon her nose. A gentle kitten that had originally been named Signorina. My colleague Tanya rescues cats and, at any time, has 10-12 of them at her house. She is the one I had turned to, and she gave me this little lady.

I got her home and then began the usual job of acquainting her with Poco Loco and Chhotu. She was scared, as is but natural, but Chhotu could not understand why she was not playing with them and joining in, in the morning ritual of medicine eating! He would bark at her as if scolding her! It took some time, but she made friends with them.

A couple of months after she came home, she played in water, got wet, and climbed onto the bed to wipe herself dry as Poco Loco and Chhotu tend to do. It was a while before she figured out her grooming skills and innate catness. She eats chicken for that is what they eat. Fish is completely rejected —that is another thing I thought I knew. Cats were supposed to eat fish and this cat was only interested in chicken. She eats the dogs' food and they eat hers. When I figured they were crazy about cat food, I got them dog food packets. Well, she ate those, and they ate the cat food.

She is truly a lovely lady who keeps us entertained and has brought us much joy. She sits near the door that opens into the terrace, and knowing that Ashutosh is the only one who takes her out for her regular fresh air outings, cajoles him with the sweetest meows and big eyes. Then when that does not help, she starts to attack him, scratching, jumping, anything that will get the door open. Of course, all this punctuated with trying to slide the door open herself. When the doorbell rings, she runs with Chhotu to the front door and waits there for us. Poco Loco no longer pays heed to the doorbell and ignores it completely. She doesn't break things and has only scratched all couches to bare threads. (I have made peace with it.) You can either have elegant couches or adorable cats. I have chosen adorable cat. She sleeps next to my head, and I have to move my pillow to make space for her. Then place a cushion a little lower, so Chhotu doesn't come and sleep on top of her because he insists on sleeping with me too.

For a long time. I would wake up at four in the morning to Billo nibbling my finger. I would open my eyes and she would touch me on the cheek with the gentlest paw touch ever. She wanted food. You could keep as many bowls you liked but she wouldn't eat the food. I had to get up and give her a fresh handful. Every night. She spent the whole day on Ashutosh's shoulder, his lap, playing with him, and following him around like Mary's little lamb, but when it came to asking for food in the middle of the night, she would wake me. Many times, he would go and give her the food, but she would come right back and try and wake me up. This had to be somebody from a previous birth, taking revenge on me for all on behalf of all those who have learnt the hard way how grouchy I am when I wake up, whatever the time. I made my peace with this too. I just have to negotiate the sleeping Chhotu when I get off the bed and back onto it, because for all his love for me, he is still a snappy Apso.

I have a sweet tooth so there has always been a jar of candy in the house. Billo darling has been swiping my toffees and playing football with them. It is mesmerizing to see her play with that. The way she dribbles with that candy would give Messi a run for his money. She doesn't play with cat toys like ropes, but prefers balls. We have a huge collection of tennis balls in the house thanks to Poco Loco. Till a year ago, he would find some ball or the other in the hedges, when he went for his walks. Balls that cricket-playing kids had lost there. They were all brought home and we now have a basketful. Billo has seen Poco Loco and Chhotu playing with those, and she too has learnt. I will not be surprised if the meowing soon turns to barking.

Billo has found her safe corners and happy places. In the morning, she sleeps in the guest room, on top of the wooden cupboard there. Afternoons are spent wherever Ashutosh is in the house. A point is chosen from where she can keep an eye on him and snooze. One movement, and she is up and tangled in his feet. In fact, every time we sit down for a meal, she goes to her bowl and eats the food kept in that. Our mealtimes are now synchronized. Her bowls are kept on a height so that the dogs don't get to them and polish everything off as they tend to do at the first chance they get. Some days she insists on eating with them, and you have to put her bowl where they are eating. She hugs Poco Loco at every possible opportunity. Hangs on to him like a monkey and licks his nose. She dangles from his ear or holds on to his hind leg and just lets herself be dragged around like a little mop. With Chhotu, the relationship is different. She stalks him, then hits him on the nose and runs away while he growls, snaps and chases after her. A genuine cat and dog game: who would have thought? Everytime she jumps onto the ledge from the terrace and is brought back, Billo 1.0-style, Chhotu seems to give her an earful. He barks at her and it really seems as if he is admonishing her.

My younger brother has recently adopted a dog. Betty, a young Pitbull, was rescued from a dog-fighting ring. She came visiting recently. Betty is calm and gentle usually but apparently hates cats. Poco Loco ignored her, Chhotu had amorous intentions on her which she nipped in the bud with one snap, and Billo was petrified. She hid under the bed till we pulled her out and let her climb into the cupboard and stay on the topmost shelf where she hid like a baby. It took her three days to recover from Betty's visit of a couple of hours. And this when the door to our room had been closed and Betty had not been allowed to go in there. That now is our next adventure: to make sure they can co-exist and be friends. It's not going to be easy but then this is my family and other animals.

I did not realise when, despite my early reservations, I fell in love with my creatures. They became my life. The joy they greet you with when you come home. The unconditional love they offer. Friends of mine say they are like children who never grow up—and are therefore a more difficult proposition. I disagree. There are times, perhaps when they are unwell, that they might require extra attention, but their love is a lot less complicated, and utterly unconditional. Yes, they require us to feed them all their lives but then they just eat what they get. Pets love you no matter what: they don't care about your success, if you have had a bad hair day, or you failed to build a healthy relationship with your partner. They love you unconditionally. And what can be better than having a live-in life booster?

Of course, don't go believing everything you hear about pets. Cats are said to be solitary creatures. Billo isn't. She snuggles and wants to play. She has a special meow for when she wants hide and seek. They say cats don't like water—well, that's another myth broken. And everybody told me there would be no rats or mice coming in looking for food and shelter once we had a cat. Suffice it to say that I am trying to motivate Billo to at least scare the one I saw running around the house. She hasn't been obliging, so I ended up ordering a mouse trap. In hindsight, that was a rather stupid thing to do. She can get in wherever I set the trap. And I really don't want to have her catch her paw or nose investigating that trap. This was when I learnt that there are no rules and no boundaries. One just has to play along and find the best fit.

And that, dear readers, is my story. Did I ever think I would be comfort-able with pets in the house? No. But then again, once they came home, they

117

were no longer pets. They became the masters. They became our family. And there can be no better.

Billo is now two years old and we have not had the heart or the courage to get her spayed. We have learnt to live with the all-night meowing when she is on heat.

Rest of the year, she remains part-cat, part-dog, part-human, full master.

Stray Cat Blues

by Nilanjana Roy

We didn't choose the cats; they came to us, one by one, drawn by some mysterious thread.

I will never understand what makes animals trust, and risk, approaching humans. A friend and I discussed this once and she said, laughing, "Just like people leaping into their romances."

But it isn't the same thing at all. There is a look you see in the eyes of animals who have been hurt by humans, of baffled dread and acceptance. It is common to maimed kittens, beagle pups still bandaged from research experiments, chickens waiting for their turn under the butcher's knife, an elephant recovering from bullet wounds in a Sri Lankan orphanage, tonga horses whipped down to the bone. If the human question in the face of suffering is 'why me?', the animal question is: 'Why did they do this to me?' The risk for strays who trust the wrong person is that they might lose a limb, or their freedom, or their lives.

Tiglath was about seven months old when he made his decision, though we had known him almost from the time he was born. His mother, a delicate beauty with impressive spitting skills, brought him along to join the conga line of the strays we used to feed on the balcony. She was a firm believer in bringing up kittens by smacking them soundly. If Tiggy was dawdling, she would whack him across his bottom so that he shot in like a startled, striped ginger ball, sometimes collapsing the conga line like a row of dominoes.

He watched our cat, Mara, who held herself aloof from the balcony cats, for many weeks before he made up his mind. Tiggy is by nature a bouncing, bounding, friendly fellow, but in those days, his expression was often solemn, his whiskers raised in a petition that we pretended not to understand.

Until the day he stepped firmly across the threshold that divided the balcony from the house and explained to us that he was now our cat. Mara was not pleased, but Tiggy craftily employed a Buddhist approach, surrendering abjectly to her, lying at her paws with his belly exposed until she acquiesced.

A week after he had come to us, Tiggy changed his mind. He scratched in such desperation at the door that we let him go. He shot out, joyously, making for a familiar roof, and I thought he'd never return. A day later, he shot back in, bedraggled, his ginger fur sticking up in punk spikes. He let it be known that he was never going out again, thank you very much, and that was that.

In his cheerful, accommodating company, Mara became more of a cat than she had ever been; she had come to us as a kitten and been perhaps too strongly inflected by human behaviour. In Tiggy's company, she could bound at sparrows and pigeons, and they could sharpen their claws on the furniture together. These were areas where we were sadly deficient, and after one or two polite invitations, Mara accepted that we were neither bounders nor sharpeners.

The night she died, Tiggy kept vigil in the bedroom along with me and my partner. He had been steadily more gentle with Mara as her illness progressed. On that night, he didn't nuzzle her—any touch hurt her by then—but he sat where they could see each other, closed his thoughtful green eyes and breathed in tandem with her until she shifted slightly in my arms and let out her last breath. He was quieter than usual for the next few days, but accepting of her death, as animals tend to be.

Bathsheba adopted us some years after Mara's death, by which time Tiggy was a senior citizen. She had been found in a car-wash bucket by a neighbour's driver in urgent need of a bath, which prompted the name we gave her. She tried to fight the bucket, the car and the driver, swaggered into our house when he brought her upstairs, and successfully fought a table leg, my toes and the watering can.

Bathsheba was tiny for her age, but she didn't seem to realise that she was a very small creature. We took her to Friendicoes SECA (an animal hospital and rescue centre in New Delhi) since we weren't intending to adopt more cats, but the vets explained that she was too young to have much chance of survival in a shelter. I prevented her from trying to fight the vet, the shelter dog and a grim monkey, and took her back home. In the car, she attacked my ear and my wrist, habits that have unfortunately lasted.

'She's a classic beauty,' said my besotted partner.

'Mmm,' I said, eyeing the puncture marks she'd left. This has more or less set the template for our relationship—equal parts love and love bites, both delivered by a furiously independent creature.

Two years later, when I'd just finished writing *The Hundred Names Of Darkness*, Lolakitty arrived, startling us with her resemblance to the black-and-gold tortoiseshell from the book. She was starving and injured, but she radiated a rare sweetness. She had all the signs of a cat who had been accustomed to people and then been abandoned, for whatever reasons, and she charmed everybody from the neighbourhood children to our vets.

Bathsheba has now spent years trying to fight Lola in an attempt to persuade The Other Cat to leave. Then she confuses all of us by following Lola around obsessively, wailing if Lola refuses to play with her, sleep with her, cuddle her, or otherwise be Bathsheba's toy.

Three strays, three companions: they couldn't be more different from each other.

The differences between individuals from any species are probably much wider than the distinctions between one kind of mammal and another, including humans.

We had both quit our jobs to work from home somewhere in between Tiglath and Bathsheba, so we had ample opportunity to study the cats (and vice-versa). I often watch Tiglath, wanting to trace what's going on in his mind when he jerks his head to follow the movement of black kites, or allows the two lady cats to use him as a large pliable playground.

One day, when a friend dropped by, I saw Tiggy settle down in a corner of the room. For the rest of the afternoon, Tiggy tracked our friend's movements and conversation with immense fascination, as though he were spending a very pleasant day at the zoo. He is a people-watcher; Lola is a people-pleaser; and Bathsheba, predictably, is mixed up.

She loves visitors; but she is wary of them. She runs growling from the room when strangers arrive; but she laments when they leave. She can't retract her claws, so she doesn't understand why people cry out when she affectionately kneads their knees into ribbons.

I don't treat cats as children. Cats are cats, companions if you're lucky, but very much their own selves, not to be used as child-substitutes. But on one occasion, I understood a little how a parent must feel when their child suffers rejection. Friends had come over, and Tiggy and Lola, always sociable, had strolled across to be cuddled and petted. I noticed Bathsheba sitting quietly at the door, and called to her, but she growled and would not come.

The other two lay around in the living room all afternoon, basking in the chin-scratching and admiration. Some hours later, I got up to make coffee and realised that Bathsheba was still there. There was longing in her eyes— animal longing, which is completely unconcealed, openly displayed—and she was making soft, barely audible distress calls.

This is where the barrier between humans and a creature, however beloved, from another species is erected. At first, I assumed Bathsheba was sad because she would have liked to have been cuddled, but was prevented by fear. But perhaps, in her feline mind, she saw her friends being taken hostage by strangers. Or, more simply, it might be that she smelled outsiders in her territory, and didn't like the intrusion.

Over the years, the other three cats—Mara, Tiglath and Lola—had shown us how easy it is to cross the divide between animal and human. Attentiveness and empathy bridges most communication gaps. This turned out to be applicable to many other species, from elephants and stray dogs to dolphins, frogs and mongooses.

But Bathsheba teaches me respect for the distance between humans and other animals. Spending time with her, I have understood that she has her own particular, intense loves, joys and sorrows. She went exploring once and was lost for three days; when we found her, she was shivering and terrified, curled up on a neighbour's roof. For months afterwards, she yelped in her sleep, cycling her paws frantically, but I cannot know for sure what shapes stalked her nightmares. You may be privileged to share part of your world with animals, but their interior lives are just as unknowable, and sacred, as our own.

First published in Mint Lounge *on 5 June 2015.*

The Trouble with a Cat

by Sandip Roy

There were two things that Soham knew as immutable truths.

He hated cats.

And he hated fish.

Everything else he thought was subject to change. Like how as a child the yolk of eggs repulsed him. Now he loved it, scooping out the dense golden center of a hardboiled egg like crumbly sunshine. 'Sunny side up,' he told the waiter at the diner on the corner of Church and 15th Street. Two eggs any style with bacon or sausage it said on the menu. Breakfast served 24 hours.

'That's what you always get,' said Derek, laughing gently. 'Sunny side up.'

Soham smiled sheepishly. It was true. He was a creature of habit, gently blurring into his father. The diner buzzed with noise and laughter, and the walls plastered with old posters seemed to sweat coffee and fried eggs. Someone had fed coins in the jukebox and it was playing the Supremes. Derek ordered a spinach and cheese omelette. Soham was content. The universe was spinning in a very orderly fashion.

At that precise moment, Derek turned to him and said, apropos of nothing, 'think we should get a cat.'

The universe braked to a halt around him. He imagined omelettes and pancakes and ketchup bottles sliding off the tables and crashing to the floor.

'Why do you think we should get a umm—that?' Soham asked cautiously, as if even saying the word would make it materialise between them. In the forests of the Sundarbans, near Calcutta where he was from, the villagers never took the name of the tiger, afraid it would summon the beast.

Derek just looked at him. Soham recognised the look. It meant he had again committed some cultural transgression like falling asleep at the opera or not realizing Derek had made the pasta sauce from scratch. Derek picked up his fork and struck the bottle of ketchup with it. Then he said, 'Because now that we have a house we need a cat to make it a home.'

It was spring in San Francisco, the spring they bought a house together. It was the first house he had ever owned in America. The little two-bedroom two-bath house, the colour of lemon cream, clung precariously to the San Francisco hillside, as though an extra-strong gust of wind would send it tumbling. It was advertised as needing some TLC. That was the only reason they could afford it. Soham could hardly believe he owned a house in San Francisco. For years he had lived out of suitcases, very proud that his entire life fit into his Honda hatchback.

Derek called it his commitment issue. 'You can't even commit to a piece of furniture,' he'd said once. 'I'm always afraid I'll wake up one morning and find you have gone back to India.'

They had been dating for almost four years. On a foggy April morning Soham had signed his name to a piece of paper that tied him to 1090 square feet in San Francisco. The first time they sat in the empty living room, eating cold fried rice and chicken with black bean sauce from the cheap Chinese takeaway, Soham realised there was no going back. Derek was talking about where to place the couch. Soham was wondering how he would tell

125

his mother he had bought a house in San Francisco and was moving in with his boyfriend.

That night after they got home from the diner, Soham called his mother. She knew about Derek but they'd never quite acknowledged it. She listened silently while he nervously rambled on about mortgage interest tax breaks and investment values. Then when he had run out of steam, she asked, 'Does that mean you are settling in America?'

Soham froze. He watched Derek carefully arranging spices in alphabetical order in the kitchen cabinet. Once, all his spices lived in plastic bags and empty yogurt containers while Derek's were in spice jars. No longer. Cumin. Oregano. Panchphoran. Poppyseed. Rosemary. Turmeric. Their lives had merged into identical matching clear spice jars with white lids. He changed the subject to his mother's health but her question hung in the air until as if by some unspoken agreement they both turned their backs to it.

In bed that night Soham pulled Derek close to him and buried his face in his hair. He kissed his earlobe and then said, 'What about a dog?'

'Cats are low maintenance,' said Derek. 'With our jobs, it's not fair on a dog.'

Soham sighed, 'Why do you like cats so much?'

'I've always grown up with cats,' Derek replied. 'It's nice to come home and see your cat sitting at the window staring out. Why do you hate cats so much?'

Soham could visualise the cat at the window in a Hallmark card sort of way. But he sighed and said, 'I don't like cats, just as I don't like fish. There's no reason. It just is.' In the dark he could sense Derek smiling at him.

The next day Derek took him to Hamano Sushi. 'But I don't eat sushi,' he protested as they walked to the restaurant.

'You can eat teriyaki if you must,' Derek said, pushing him along. It started with just trying a little bit of the California roll. Then he got more adventurous and reached for the Philadelphia roll with its tangy cream cheese and smoked salmon. Then in a giant leap of faith he tried raw fatty tuna. To his amazement he quite liked it.

'It's not fishy with that icky black oily skin like fish curries back home,' he said in a tone of wonder. As a little boy he would pout over his dinner if there was fish. 'Too fishy' he'd whine, his nose crinkled up in distaste at a rohu curry. 'Too oily' he'd complain about the koi that had his aunts breathless in anticipation. 'Too many bones.' The litany of complaints was endless.

His mother was flabbergasted. How on earth had a fish fanatic like her produced a boy like Soham? Especially in a place like Bengal, where you could barely eat anything without being impaled on a fish bone. Innocuous green leafy vegetables would get jazzed up with leftover fish skin and bones. The dal might have a fish head swimming in it for special occasions.

As he smeared pungent green wasabi on his tuna roll, and garnished it with a shell-pink sliver of pickled ginger, Soham felt that in the middle of San Francisco he had miraculously regained his cultural heritage. He was no more a fish outcaste.

'I might be able to actually sit down and eat fish with my mother if she ever comes to San Francisco,' he told Derek dipping his tuna roll into the soy sauce.

Derek smiled at him and Soham knew that he was going to demand payment for breaking the fish curse.

'Meow,' said Derek.

'At least let's get a short haired one,' Soham mumbled, trying to assert some modicum of control over the situation. 'And it has to be black. To match the couch.'

The cat Derek chose was a short-haired jet-black kitten with golden saucer eyes.

'Isn't he cute?' Derek stuck his finger out at the kitten.

Soham shrugged and quoted Ogden Nash.

The trouble with a kitten is that

It grows into a cat.

'You always say that,' Derek said, rolling his eyes. The little thing inched forward tentatively and sniffed at the finger.

'Whatever,' Soham said grumpily. But watching Derek's face light up as he scratched the kitten's chin, he knew he was going to give in. He would do anything to see his face light up like that. He'd never told him that of course. It seemed too flowery. He couldn't imagine his father ever saying that to his mother.

They named the cat Dumbledore. Harry Potter was one of the few books they both managed to read and enjoy. Soham had bought the book for his niece before one of his annual trips to India. Derek had stayed up till two in the morning to finish the book before he left.

'You have to read it,' he told him, tucking the book into his carry-on bag.

Soham had been dismissive. His choice of fiction tended to be more from the Booker prize shortlist. But he'd tried Harry Potter on the airplane on the long journey. 'You were right,' he'd said when he called from India. 'It was a great read.' He could tell Derek had been pleased. It made Soham smile but he never told Derek that.

For the first few weeks he kept his distance from the cat. The cat, he made clear, was Derek's. He needed to get it cat food, change its litter and make sure it got its shots. Soham felt that by tolerating it in the house he had come more than half-way. In the morning, if he was up before Derek, it would come padding up to its food bowl and mew piteously. Soham would turn on his electric toothbrush and try to block out its accusing little cries. Once it coughed up a little hair ball. Soham couldn't bring himself to touch it.

'It grosses me out,' he complained later.

'What would you do if we had a baby and it soiled its diapers?' Derek demanded.

About to protest, Soham stopped himself. It was just about a cat he told himself, let's not make it a training course for having a baby.

The next day when he woke up the cat was sitting on the comforter at the foot of the bed. It looked at him and stretched. He wagged his finger at it. 'Not on the bed,' he said. It swatted his hand with its little paw. As he stood in the bathroom, his eyes still half-closed, brushing his teeth, it came up and offered its head to be scratched.

One day when he came home from the gym on a warm Sunday afternoon, he found Derek napping in bed. The open copy of Time magazine lay on the pillow next to him. The sunflowers he had picked up at the farmers market were in a vase above the bed. And Dumbledore sat on his chest, curled into a little ball, purring gently. He stood at the door watching the little tableau. A lock of his chestnut hair trailed across Derek's face. The warm buttery sunshine streamed across the bed and his belly. The cat looked at him out of those round golden eyes and twitched its tail. He never forgot that moment. That was the moment he made peace with Dumbledore.

One day he noticed he was talking to Derek through Dumbledore.

'Hey,' he told the cat. 'Go tell your daddy to get ready.'

In August, his mother announced she was coming to visit. It would be the first time she met either Derek or Dumbledore. She knew about Derek but had not been warned about Dumbledore.

'She's going to hate me,' Derek said flatly.

'Of course not. Why would she?' Soham said defensively.

'Because I am a man. I'm not Indian. And I have a piercing. Should I go on?' Derek retorted. 'Perhaps I should move out while she is here.'

'Don't be silly,' Soham said. But a part of him knew life would be easier for all concerned if he did.

On the day his mother arrived, Derek got some calla lilies for her room. He placed the vase in the bedroom and went back to cooking chicken. Soham said he was sure she would have eaten on the plane. 'Just in case, anyway,' said Derek, his lips pursed over a copy of Madhur Jaffrey's *Quick and Easy Indian Cooking* that he'd had express delivered.

In the end his mother had said nothing about the lilies though she managed to thank Derek for the chicken. Most of it she packed for Soham's lunch the next day.

The rest of her trip she took over the kitchen and had already cooked three dishes by the time either he or Derek came home from work. Madhur Jaffrey languished on the counter.

But while she managed to compliment Derek on her chicken curry, the cat was a different matter.

'My goodness, I didn't know you had a cat,' she screamed as she watched Dumbledore amble up the stairs. The cat, froze.

'Oh my god, look how it stares at me,' she said.

'Ma, it's just a cat,' Soham said placatingly.

'Just a cat? You know how I am around cats,' she said sharply. 'Where did you pick up such bad habits from?' He noticed she was looking at Derek as she spoke.

'Come here, kitty,' said Derek evenly. He poured his dry food into a bowl.

'My goodness,' said his mother. 'Its own special food. At least cats in India just ate what they could find—fish bones and mice.'

If Soham had hoped the cat would grow on her just like it had on him, he was mistaken.

His mother would try not to show her hostility in front of Derek and accepted it as a grim peculiar fact of life in America—on par with toilet paper, fat-free milk, seat belts and Derek. But when Derek was out of sight, Soham would hear a few choice Bengali expletives flung at the cat and an emphatic

131

'Shoo, shoo,' followed by a fake kick. Fake, because the last thing she wanted to do was physically touch the cat. Unlike cats in India, Dumbledore had never encountered someone like this hissing spitting woman before. He appeared flabbergasted.

'Why don't you do something before she kills the cat?' demanded Derek.

Soham tried to explain cats in India were regarded as dirty scavenging beasts, mangy creatures that prowled along walls sneaking up to snatch a fish head when the cook wasn't looking.

'You won't understand,' he finally said wearily. How could he take him to his childhood, he wondered. There would be yappy white Spitzes with names like Fluffy, and Alsatians as big as wolves, fat-bellied orange goldfish, a bright green parrot that loved to eat red chillis. But cats just prowled the neighbourhood like thieves in the night, yowling and mating, scattering chicken feathers and fish bones on the terrace, hiding their little blind naked kittens in the coal bin.

It was the first time he felt a gulf between them that he could not bridge with a story. It was too many oceans apart, in languages that made no sense to him.

Two days later he was woken by his mother screaming. He rushed out of the bedroom to find her standing in the middle of her room clutching her housecoat around her. In the middle of the floor, between the door and her bed, lay a small dead mouse its little legs frozen in mid-air.

'Ohh,' she screamed. 'Look what I see the first thing in the morning. I am going to be sick.'

'It's a peace offering,' said Derek who had come up behind Soham.

'Peace?' spluttered his mother in indignation. 'Soham, get rid of this mouse at once. And the cat.'

'This is pretty gross,' said Soham as he tried to find something to pick up the mouse with. 'Also you didn't have to call it a peace offering.'

'It's not the cat your mother dislikes, Soham,' said Derek. 'Don't you get that? Here. Move. Let me get rid of the mouse.'

When he came home that evening, he found Derek sitting in the garage with the cat on his lap.

'Is something the matter?' he said. Derek just looked at him but didn't answer. The cat stared at him as well and meowed. Then he noticed its food bowl filled with salmon kibbles in the corner.

'Oh, you moved the food bowl down from the kitchen,' he said. 'Probably a good idea, to get it out of my mom's hair.'

'I didn't move the food bowl,' said Derek, his voice taut, while he stroked the cat's head.

'Oh,' Soham said, unsure what to do. Upstairs he could smell the frying onions as his mother cooked dinner. 'It's just a little while longer,' he said placatingly. 'Her cooking dinner is her own peace offering.'

'She's cooking your favourite things. For you,' said Derek with a shrug.

'Well I can't ask her to not cook for me,' replied Soham. 'I mean I didn't want her to make it.'

'That's the problem isn't it, Soham? What do you want?' Derek said and looked away.

It was time, Soham thought, to unleash the sushi.

His mother was skeptical.

'Ma,' Soham said proudly. 'You must. I am sure you'll love it—it's fish and rice after all. Derek's the one who taught me to enjoy it.'

'You won't eat my fish curry and you'll eat fish sliced by some Japanese stranger!' protested his mother.

At the restaurant, he expansively asked Derek to do all the ordering. Derek looked at his mother questioningly.

'Oh, I don't know,' she said, nervously looking at the chopsticks. 'You choose. I don't know these fish.'

Derek asked for forks when he did the ordering and then poured out the green tea.

'Green tea,' she said gingerly taking a sip. 'It's different but very light. Not bad.' Soham exhaled and smiled reassuringly at Derek. When the sushi arrived festooned with bits of avocado and sprinkled with glowing orange fish roe, Romola looked at it approvingly. 'It's pretty,' she said smiling at Derek.

But as soon as she took her first bite of fatty tuna Soham knew it had all been a dreadful mistake. She gulped it down with water and put her fork down.

'Are you okay?' said Derek worriedly.

'Yes,' said Romola miserably. 'I am just not so hungry. It's so cold and clammy.'

'Well, you don't want warm raw fish,' said Derek.

Soham saw the color drain from his mother's face.

'Raw fish?' she said weakly. 'Like raw raw? Doesn't it make you sick?'

'It doesn't taste fishy,' mumbled Soham.

'You didn't explain to your mother it was raw?' Derek's voice had a sharp edge.

Trapped in between them, Soham looked from one to the other, paralysed, unable to say anything. He wanted to say that he just wanted to please them both. But nothing came out.

Finally, Derek said, 'Let me order some tempura. It's fried vegetables and shrimp.'

'It's alright,' his mother said. 'I have some leftover dal and rice at home anyway. Don't worry about me.' Then she turned to Soham and said in Bengali, 'Raw fish? What am I—a cat?'

As they got into the car Derek turned to Soham and hissed, 'I can't believe you didn't tell her and just left it all to me. It was your big idea.'

That night in bed he reached out to Derek but he curled away from him. The cat was purring at his feet. Soham poked at it with his toe but it wouldn't budge. He lay awake for awhile. From his breathing, he knew Derek was awake too. He wanted to tell him things, he wanted to explain things, but he just lay there letting the inky silence grow between them. He imagined it rising like water in a dammed river, slowly filling up the space between them, the clock radio with its phosphorescent digital numbers floating away like a little tugboat. When the sun on his face jerked him awake, he felt he had been awake all night.

When he took his mother to see an Indian music concert at Stanford University he didn't ask Derek if he wanted to go. 'I knew you'd be bored,' he told him. Derek nodded as if he understood. Halfway through the concert Soham noticed his mother's eyes were closed as her lips silently formed the words to the song. She opened her eyes and saw Soham looking at her. She smiled and gently shook her head.

'It was your father's favourite song. We didn't often go to concerts but I'd hear him singing it in the bathroom when he took his shower.'

Soham felt a pang as sharp as the sting of wasabi. Tears pricked the corners of his eyes but he blinked them away. My parents didn't have that much in common he thought and yet somehow they made it work.

When they came home Derek was watching a sit-com on television, a half empty can of Diet Coke and a pizza box in front of him.

'How was your concert?' he said without taking his eyes or ears from the TV.

Four and a half months after his mother left, Derek moved out. Soham wanted to try counseling but Derek said it was too late. He had met an architect from Massachusetts. Like him, he had summered on the Cape as a kid. 'We like the same things,' he said. 'It's so much easier, you know.'

'No, I don't know,' Soham thought. 'My parents didn't like the same things. But they built a life together.' But as he watched Derek pack his things he realised even after almost five years together their lives remained tightly separated into individual compartments. There was never any question which book belonged to whom.

To his surprise, Derek left him the cat. The apartment he was moving into didn't allow pets. 'Plus, he's used to this house, going in and out of the backyard,' Derek said. 'I don't want him cooped up in a small apartment. I hope to buy a house in a few months. Then if you don't want him, I can take Dumbledore.'

Soham shrugged. He felt tired and his head hurt.

Derek embraced him before he left and kissed him on the forehead. He picked up the cat and stroked its head. 'Look after Soham,' he told Dumbledore. 'Make sure he gets up and goes to work and changes your litter.'

'Don't go,' Soham wanted to say. 'Stay here with me and the cat.' But he just hugged him back woodenly and helped carry his bag down. When he got into the U-Haul van Derek's eyes were smudged with tears.

'Shut the door,' Derek said. 'The cat will get out.'

The first night after he left, Soham slept curled up on Derek's side of the bed. Derek's pillow still smelled of him. In the morning, he rolled over and felt a soft furry warmth engulf him. Spluttering, he opened his eyes and saw Dumbledore sitting by the pillow. He wondered if the cat missed Derek. But he seemed perfectly content as long as Soham poured him a heaping bowl of food.

'Why didn't he take that awful cat?' his mother asked over the phone. 'If anything, he should have taken that.' Soham, busy making one cup of tea with one tea bag, did not answer.

'Well, what's over is over,' said his mother soothingly. 'How are you managing all alone?'

Outside it was raining, the gray wintry drizzle rolling down the hillside and spattering against the kitchen window. Soham could see the pine tree in the yard shivering in the wind. It was chilly. They needed to get double-paned glass for the windows he thought. That was on the long to-do list he and Derek had once drawn up.

'Should I come back and stay with you for a little while?' asked his mother.

He had a vision of his mother landing in San Francisco armed with folders bulging with resumes of suitable young women with post-graduate degrees and wheatish complexions. At the same time, there was a sudden rush of comfort at the thought of her standing in the kitchen, chopping onions, cooking a pot of chicken curry and humming some old Bengali song. 'But by the time I come next time you need to get rid of that terrible thing,' she continued. 'It just makes me shudder to even think of it.' Soham didn't answer. The cat looked back at him out of those unblinking golden saucer eyes and gently flicked its tail. Soham quietly scratched Dumbledore's chin and smiled at him.

Real, Imaginary and In-Between Or A Short History of My Life in Cats

by Shreemayee Das

The doorbell rings, and we stiffen.

It's a regular morning at our home in Mumbai. I'm getting ready for work, R has already started tapping at his laptop, and we're discussing how we're going to coordinate our schedule to reach the venue where we're producing a comedy show that night, by 7 PM. When we hear the bell, we give each other a 'Did you order anything?' look. No, we hadn't. So, who was ringing the bell at 8 AM?

R and I had moved in together a couple of months back. We'd found a tiny apartment in a calm and peaceful locality and were paying more rent than the flat deserved. That sounds like every Bombay story, I know. What also sounds like every Bombay story is that we had really struggled to get a flat. We weren't married, and we had freelance jobs. We were on a pretty tight budget. We had exactly a month to figure everything out, or at least one of us would be homeless. We'd somehow convinced R's ex-landlord to give us one of his flats—he liked to think he was progressive and hadn't batted an eye at the "live-in" situation.

The building society secretary, however, didn't like the word progressive. Somehow, we had convinced him that the wedding was in December that year (*shubh mahurat* and all that) and got the house. But we still felt anxious every time the doorbell rang. Was the music too loud? Had they seen our friend leave at 4 AM? Were they checking how the wedding prep was going?

I opened the door. Building uncle was standing, twirling his white moustache, frown so permanent that the creases were a part of his face.

'*Aap log billi ko khilate ho?*' he growled.

Good morning to you, too, Uncle. And what *billi*?

'*Yahaan billi kyu aata hai? Aap khilate ho?*' he asked again.

I peeped outside. There was no billi. Sure, one cat sunbathed in the society garden often and did love to rub himself against R—but no, it wasn't anywhere near our door, and no, we hadn't fed it, had we?

'*Hum kabhi kabhi paani dete hai*,' R conceded. I glared at him—why would he admit it, ugh? In my head, which deals only in extremities, we will be thrown out of the house now. This very moment, in fact. Building uncle had probably rung the bell because this was all one big conspiracy, and he had definitely got police for backup. While I spiral in my imagination, R glares back. The Mumbai summers have been atrociously hot, and he's been thoughtful enough to leave water out for the cat every day. R is empathetic like that and very kind. I'm the one with the self-preservation instinct in this relationship.

Uncle isn't impressed, either. Clearly, kindness is not something he looks for in young men or potential tenants. He's more concerned with how much these young men earn and how much they'd be willing to donate to the Building Ganpati Puja Fund. R is kind there too. I don't want trouble there either.

'*Paani mat do*,' he finally says. '*Billi roz aayega. Woh potty karega toh kaun saaf karega?*' he asks before he storms off, grumbling under his breath.

The cat literally lives in the small garden within the building society! I'm assuming some families feed him, and some pet him, and if he does potty in the society grounds, someone cleans it. Why do only we have to bear the brunt of Building Uncle's wrath?

But we don't leave water outside for the cat again. It's not a battle we can afford to fight at the moment.

Living as an unmarried couple has made us compromise on all sorts of things. Living in building societies that don't encourage (or are plain unkind to) animals is just one.

That's what you get for not following conventional norms in this country.

This is not to say that I've always loved cats and wanted one ever since I was a child, or had lots of cats growing up. In fact, far from it. A regular lover of Enid Blyton stories, my fondness for dogs grew with every story I read of Timmy and Scamper and Buster and my favourite, Loony. Kiki even made me consider getting birds, and Bill and Clarissa's love for horses had made me go through some awkward phase of horse appreciation as well, but not cats. The only cats I ever loved were Macavity and Gus and that too, at the ripe old age of sixteen, when I first discovered Eliot. In my childhood fantasies, I envisioned growing up, having lots of friends and lots of dogs. Cats were noticeably absent. A bit weird, really, since my first friend was a cat.

One of my earliest memories of childhood, one I can picture perfectly in my head, maybe because it was repeated so often as I grew up, was of a stray cat who appeared every day during lunch. Moturam was what the help at home, Mashi, called it—it was either a reference to its size, which I don't remember, or it was a reference to the way it waited while I sat in my high-chair being fed rice and fish. The leftovers, and the fish bones, would go to Moturam. I was a lonely child—there were no kids of my age in the neighbourhood, and Moturam was my first friend, friends in a way only people who share food are. Mashi, who had a vivid imagination, spun tales describing the life of Moturam, as I ate—a new adventure every day. Moturam in search of food, Moturam with his friends, Moturam defeating all the thuggish dogs on the street through his sheer courage and grace. At night if we heard cats wailing, Mashi would say *See, Moturam is fighting again* or *See, Moturam has come to say goodnight*, if she desperately needed me to go to sleep.

Moturam had a charmed life; years later, when I read *Old Possum's Book of Cats*, so many reminded me of the stories of Moturam. Moturam taught me to share food; Moturam's was one of the first stories I fell in love with. Yet as I grew older and created my own world of imaginary friends and imaginary dogs, I had no Moturam-equivalent. For a long time, the only cat I knew and loved was Moturam.

Many years later, R and I were asked to cat-sit for friends. I knew nothing of cats, R didn't either, but his innate kindness somehow won over the otherwise grumpy cat. As we snuggled on the couch, the cat somehow found a way to join us. Left without its humans and clearly suffering from abandonment issues, he followed us into the bedroom at night and perched itself comfortably on my bedside table. It stared with wide eyes as we undressed and caressed each other, never taking its eyes off us as we made out. The lights were off, but I could feel its penetrating gaze. 'It's a kitten!' I wailed at R. 'It's like making out in front of a kid. We should stop.'

R stilled. We held each other, hoping the cat either went away or went to sleep or at least looked away. It didn't. Much later, when we're sure we're not going to be able to make out more that night, and I'm drifting off to sleep with our clothes still jumbled up at the foot of the bed, I feel the idiot-cat jump on me. I reach out to stroke it. Desperately seeking human companionship in the darkness is something I can identify with. But it doesn't stop. It starts sniffing all over my body before finally giving first tentative, then confident, licks to my vaginal area.

This is not the relationship I ever thought I would have with a cat.

I squeal and wriggle, but it doesn't deter the idiot. It continues with unrelenting focus, the sort that I have rarely seen even in the men who have, umm, explored my vagina.

Finally, R scoops it up, we deposit it back to the living room and try not to let its whines or our guilt ruin our sleep.

A few months later, our friends leave Mumbai, and I don't see the idiot-cat again.

A few years ago, my friend M and I were sitting in one of our favourite cafes in Kolkata, being miserable about life, as one is wont to do in Kolkata. We were talking, among other things, about how difficult it was becoming for us to come back and live with our parents for long stretches after having lived alone. We spoke about the generation gap and the occasional lack of empathy that parents show (and we show too, let's be honest). What makes living with parents so difficult, I wondered. M had a simple hypothesis, though. 'We move around too much,' he said. 'We don't have or desire to have the stability that was so essential to their generation. We don't buy houses, we shift all the time, we change jobs every two years. It's a different life.'

For years, I have craved adventure. My childhood was as regular as can be expected. I went to school, did reasonably well, then was sent off to a prestigious college in Delhi. Along the way, I made a few friends for life who led the same mundane existence I did. Nothing ever happened to me. Books made me long for more: a life of thrill, of adventure, of unconventionality. Practical considerations like money and property didn't feature in my plans.

The thing is, as I grow older, I find that the craving for stability is an evolutionary desire that has been imprinted in my brain. Try as I might, I can't avoid the thought coming up as I pay rent every month or search for the next freelance gig as to how it would be to "settle down". What would it be to not worry about making rent or my landlord finding out that we're not actually married?

It seems to be a life I could get used to.

I often feel that getting a cat would be a starting point of that stability. It would force me to make a commitment to care, a commitment to protect, a commitment that, at the end of the day, I will come back home. It has to be a cat, though. I'm not yet in that stage where I can deal with too much attachment, too much care, or too much protection. Basically no dogs or babies.

R and I often talk about getting a cat, mostly while scrolling through random cat videos on Instagram. Sometimes when we find a word or a name we like, we try using it as a cat name to see if it's something we can picture calling out to our cat. We don't discuss if we will get to carry on in the same house with a pet in tow, whether we have the capacity to take care of an extra living being, or about who will eventually clean the potty. The best thing about imaginary things is that you don't have to let practicalities restrain you.

And maybe one day we will get a cat—away from the sharp eyes of the building society uncle.

Till then, we have framed my favourite cover of the *Old Possum's Book of Cats*, and it hangs on my wall—as a reminder of the adventure and of the stability that might one day come our way.

'Do you like the name Ivan?'

'In general?'

'No. For a cat.'

'I suppose it works.'

'Ivaaaan! Ivan! Iiiiivaaaan!'

Through the Sands of Time
A Dog Person, a Cat Person, and a Mother who was Both

by Jai Arjun Singh

Anyone who has known me over the last few years—in person or through blog posts, Facebook posts, WhatsApp profile pictures, Instagram pages—will assure you that I'm a dog person. An obsessive dog person, even.

Much of my life currently centres around Lara, the second of my two major canine loves—the only two creatures I have seriously been able to describe as my "children". (Falling deeply in love with her predecessor Foxie—chronically unwell, short-lived Foxie—in the summer of 2008 was what unlocked my Dog Person-ness.) I have also been increasingly involved with street dogs around my two flats in south Delhi's Saket. These animals have helped me feel more rooted in a neighbourhood I have lived in for over three decades, more aware of it as a symbiotic village within an impossible metropolis. An artist friend and I have even discussed a collaborative project, Dogs and Humans of Saket.

As I write this, though, most creative projects are very uncertain. It is May 2020, there's a global pandemic underway, and a series of lockdowns have taken a crippling toll on unprivileged humans and animals; we have no idea what is to come in the next few months. If things get much worse, if the virus mutates and mutates and—to channel TS Eliot's cat analogy—becomes a yellow smoke rubbing its muzzle along the protective coverings of our inner organs, then this essay might not be published.

Meanwhile, there are jokes and memes to help us through. One goes: 'Your dog thinks you have left your job to spend time with him. Your cat thinks you have been fired, like the loser you always were.' The accompanying images show a smiling dog and a cranky cat. It is an old stereotype, calculated to pique those who have experienced the warm, loving side of cats (and such stereotypes and generalisations will crop up again in this piece)—but one also sees a flash of truth in it.

When the first lockdown began in March and the streets cleared of humans, when I realised how many street dogs—social animals, dependent on their two-legged friends—were going to be left adrift, hungry and disoriented, I got on animal-care groups, got in touch with feeders in my neighbourhood, started getting out myself. To do what little I could to quell the urgent howls that were keeping me up at night.

If dogs were my focus through all this, it was a function of the dog person I had become in the past decade; but it was also based on another simplification—or stereotype—about dogs and cats: street dogs need the kindness and attention of humans; cats, not so much.

But then, a few days into the lockdown, outside a Mother Dairy, a white-and-bluish-grey cat pressed against my leg, looked up at me, mewed desperately. I knew this cat—who lived near the local meat shop, now closed—to be one of the calmer, more dignified residents of the area. Now, fending for himself, he looked wild and lost. He knew there was paneer in the bag I was carrying.

There was something deeply unsettling about this gap between the cat's regal good looks and the hollow desperation in his eyes. In some ways, it made me feel worse than I had been feeling about the sociable, always-needy dogs.

More than that, I felt a tug from the distant past. If this cat had been of a particular coloration and had had an unusually bushy tail, I would have thought to myself, 'This could be Sandy's great-great-great-grandchild. Who knows... '

Sandy. Delicate-looking, hoarse-voiced, fleeting Sandy. Perhaps my first real experience in caring for an animal. Though there had been others before him.

Flashbacks, Fragments, Dates, Diary Entries: Memories of Three Cats

It is July 11, 1993: *(Since I began writing a diary in January 1990, and maintained it daily for the next 17 years, I can call on specific dates during this period quite easily.)* My mother and I have been visiting relatives and have just hailed an autorickshaw to go back to Saket when we see this little ginger-coloured thing, not more than 20-25 days old, looking at us through bright, intelligent eyes. Lots of things about him are surprising: he has a grand tail even at that age, and an incongruously gruff voice. Picking him up and taking him home is an instinctive move, and comes mainly out of concern (there are cars tearing about on the road). We don't think it through, we don't worry much about how our part-time cat, Kittu, will react.

Flashback to early 1990: The unimaginatively named Kittu enters our lives, just a couple of months after I begin writing my very first diary (most of the early entries refer to him only as Cat). As the year wears on he spends more time inside our flat, mainly during the day when he comes for his siesta after a long hard night of being the colony's dominant Tom.

I don't remember exactly how and when my mother started feeding Kittu, but I do know that at this point she had gone a few years—a few messy years that included a divorce and a custody battle—without having had an animal to care for. Thinking about this in hindsight, knowing her, I realise how hard that must have been.

But back to 1993, the advent of the new kitten. There are teething problems, so to speak. Things go okay on the Kittu front (he is indifferent; this newcomer is no threat to his sole-bachelor-in-colony status yet) but the kitten is wailing, restless. We feed him milk with a small dropper and fret that we might have unwittingly separated him from his mother—what if she was nearby and we didn't look for her?—when he was too small.

In the next few days, as he settles in, I offer him the entire length of my left arm as a chew toy; for weeks, all you'd see on that limb were several parallel red lines and tiny fang marks.

'We'll call him Sandy,' my mother says. 'He's so *compact*,' she adds. A beat of silence, and then: 'Do you remember Blackie?'

(*Did she really say this, or has my mind put together conversations that took place at different times? My diaries don't tell me everything.*)

Going back almost a decade, it is 1984 or 1985, Panchshila Park, Delhi. Close to bedtime, I am reading an Archie comic when mum comes in and tells me in a strained but matter-of-fact voice that Blackie has been run over, on the service lane just outside. Still breathing, but head crushed, no hope. She is going to a doctor to get him "put to sleep", put out of his suffering. It is probably the first time I have heard this phrase.

My memory is unreliable but I *think* I went to the car and saw part of a small black body (not the head, which is covered) draped in a white blanket or towel. I wish I had been writing my diary back then—not just for these details but also to know if "Blackie" was what we really called him. Or was it Sooty (entirely possible, since I had read one of Enid Blyton's Pink-Whistle books which had a black cat with that name)? I do remember my mother coming back, tearing up about how casual the doctor had been—how he was more worried about whether she had the cash on hand to pay him than getting the thing done with compassion and efficiency.

Childhood recollections often create the sense that something went on for months or years, when in reality it lasted only a few weeks. I have no idea exactly how long we had Blackie, and there is no one around now whom I can ask. Either way, he was the first animal to enter my consciousness—my first "pet". The memory fragments include mum removing ticks with a tweezer; shielding him from my father who was prone to violence during substance abuse, and who, once, bit the tiny thing's ear, causing shrieks; most vividly, a rain-soaked night when we realised Blackie had fallen into the drain running just outside the house, and our cook, Chhatar Singh, managed somehow in the dark to locate him by his wails and rescue him.

It was touch and go. How relieved we were. But this was probably only a few days before the speeding car got him.

More than three decades later. It is 2017 and I am in the same Panchsh-ila Park house where I had lived till age nine, until my mother and I escaped. It's a decaying ghost house now, with my grandmother and my father having both died in the span of a few months. It is exhausting to walk through the rooms of my childhood, sifting through possessions, trying to avoid look-ing at my father's diaries—troubling evidence that this delusional, possi-bly schizophrenic man had a writer's impulse too, that he needed to set his thoughts down on paper the same way I did.

In a room on the first floor, I draw a curtain across the balcony door. A jet-black cat is sitting outside on a ledge beyond the small balcony space, sunning himself, looking back at me—or what he can see of me through the tinted glass—in irritation.

In exactly the same space where my mother and I had found a stranded black kitten half a lifetime ago. I have another memory flash: mum getting

Chhatar Singh to climb up with a ladder and bring the mewling thing down so we could feed it. Blackie.

When I get home, I tell my mother about this, show her the fuzzy photo I'd managed to take. She smiles, seems to remember, but she is in a lot of pain; a second round of chemotherapy has left her worse off than before, and there isn't much time.

It is early 2020, and Devapriya Roy—editing a book about cats—is saying, 'I thought you were a dog-person!'

Back to 1993. Have you seen a kitten on a leash?

We weren't yet ready to let Sandy go out by himself the way Kittu freely did; but he did need to explore the wild occasionally, so every morning—before leaving for school—and evening, I would take him down for 20 minutes at the end of two leashes tied together. (This is how you distinguish walking a cat from walking a dog: a little more independence, the illusion of greater freedom.) I even gave him his first rudimentary lessons in tree-climbing; okay, that's an exaggeration but I would goad him up the trunk of the largest tree in our park and watch (holding on to the leash) as he tested branches. A couple of times, when he showed no interest in descending and I was in danger of missing my school bus, I may have yanked him down roughly—wherein he landed on his feet, and frowned.

It's hard to pinpoint exactly how I became so close to him. I know that he spent hours each day in my room, allowing me to cuddle him after I returned from school. There are photos, including one of the two cats curled up in a ball, hugging each other, and another of mum and me holding one in each arm—this being in the weeks of Cautious Peace, before Sandy became a threat to Kittu's genetic legacy.

Some of my earliest lessons about care were learnt during this time. When Kittu came into our lives, he was almost entirely my mother's responsibility —except for the tummy-rubbing, which I helped with—and it mostly stayed that way. Besides, he was already an adult who had spent time walking the mean streets of Saket. With Sandy, my relationship began (literally) from scratch, and I played a more defined role: in the feeding, the walking, the providing of general entertainment, the collecting and disposing of sand for the kitty litter. With my mother watching over us, I think I grew as a person during those months.

By the end of the year, I was letting him out for one or two hours at a time, keeping an eye on him from the balcony, occasionally going down to check that he wouldn't get too adventurous and would come home by the late evening. For weeks, this was part of my daily routine. And then, gradually, the time came to loosen the strings even more.

Feb 1, 1994: 'I'm writing this on the balcony, watching Sandy sitting on a tree, with the black dog circling around beneath. Today was a landmark day in his becoming independent. Before leaving for school I told mum not to let him down before 11.30 if at all. When I returned she told me he'd leapt off the balcony almost as soon as I'd left. And he's been out ever since!'

And a few days later: 'It's 6 pm, Sandy may or may not go down now—anyway, it's no longer my concern (and that makes me feel a little sad).'

Though I wouldn't have articulated it in such terms back then, I was experiencing a rite of passage that was parent-like, or a prelude to being a parent. And now I wonder how my mother felt as she watched her 16-year-old son undergo such emotions.

It is March 2003, in the *Business Standard* newspaper office, which I have recently joined, and I have made a new friend, Abhilasha. We bond over the fact that we are both "cat people". While I still vaguely think of myself in those terms, I haven't been close to a cat for over five years; Abhilasha, on the other hand, has a family of cats at home. We exchange stories, discuss the dumb, jowly cuteness of a certain variety of horny tom-cat; we mock dogs, especially the annoying little ones that go yap-yap. I tell her about my mother's Pomeranian, Chinky, who is just such a creature. (Despite living in the same house as Chinky, I only dimly register her presence: she isn't *mine*, the way Sandy or Kittu had been.)

Abhilasha will meet Chinky when she comes to my place for the first time nearly a year later, and will pretend to be very taken with her, mainly to impress my mother. Exiting the house, out of my mother's earshot, we will joke again about how silly these noisy little dogs are.

We don't know that a few years later, in 2008, we will find ourselves co-parenting a canine child—again with my mother as a super-parent of sorts—and that four years after that, we will experience the darkest, most devastating day of our lives in a vet's clinic.

Inching towards May 1994, and another dark day: the evening I saw Sandy for the last time.

Once he started going down by himself—even staying out at nights—his rivalry with Kittu became dangerous. They had to be kept apart if they were both in the house at the same time; my mother and I tiptoed about like scared grandparents in a Hindi film melodrama about a family divided, keeping one cat locked in a room and feeding the other one elsewhere.

Something had to give, and it did. A day came when we had pet-unfriendly guests over, my Nani didn't want to advertise the fact that our house had become a Kurukshetra for feline turf-wars, someone got careless and didn't shut a door properly, the two cats had a brief scuffle, we hurriedly threw the main door open for Sandy while keeping Kittu inside. And that's it. Sandy never returned.

Of course, that wasn't really "it". I spent half an hour each morning for the next few months scouting all the familiar spots where I used to take him walking, calling out to him. Looking at my mid-1994 diary entries, I see sentences that are still a sharp, painful reminder of that time.

Today's the 11th non-Sandy day in our lives, and we're miserable.
I'm feeling terrible about Sandy, seem to see him everywhere I look.
Today is the 23rd day—the maximum Kittu has ever been gone was 22 days.

Naturally, my diary also reveals that other things were going on. (Other things are always going on.) I was watching old films, recording music videos on VHS cassettes, obsessing about my favourite soap opera. But the absence of Sandy shadowed this period. There were sleepless nights when I imagined I could hear his croaking call outside my bedroom window (located near the main door) and got up repeatedly to check. Memories of shivering in bed as my mind started to process the possibility that I would never see him again. This was the first major loss in my life.

For years, I wondered if he might still be living somewhere in one of Saket's colonies, not too far from our house. One day, around 10 years after he had gone, it struck me—idly—that if he were still alive, he would now be old in Cat Years, and this was a sad and strange thought: my little sibling—about whom I had spent so many months worrying and being protective—being the equivalent of 70 or 80 human years, when I was still only in my twenties. It didn't seem right.

It must have been around this same time that my mother returned from a walk and mentioned that on the far side of our colony—a spot we rarely visited—she had seen an old, grungy-looking, ginger cat lying dead near a drain, its hind legs apparently tied together with string. 'He had a very bushy tail,' she said. 'I didn't go too close.' She didn't say anything more, and I didn't ask.

Sandy was with us for only ten months, compared with Kittu's eight-odd years, and it might seem odd that he occupies a more central role in my cat-memories. But apart from the heightened nature of my responsibilities where Sandy was concerned, the intensity of the recollection comes from the ephemeral nature of our time with him; there was no closure, it's still possible to wonder if we dreamt him up.

Kittu, on the other hand, was part of the woodwork for years (to the extent that a few days would sometimes go by without my even mentioning him in my diary). We watched him go from being a reasonably lithe cat into an undignified, burping mound of corruption and laziness; gluttonous, scruffy, torn from his fights, snoring away on my mother's stomach after a night of perdition and sin. With him, there was a sense of a life full-lived.

At the same time, I mustn't undermine his importance. Kittu was an essential part of my life with my mother, from our walks together to nearby Hauz Rani to buy beef for him (at a time when neither of us ate beef ourselves) to the many vet visits. And in his final months, I was very protective of him.

'I hate those dogs.'

Early 1998.

I'm tense about Kittu not being able to come up because of those damn dogs—for

the past hour I've been trying to keep them away with stones.

Those bloody dogs hanging around downstairs all the time. I wish mum had stopped encouraging them. Stupid woman has no sense.

January 24. Mum is back from hospital after her kidney-stone operation, sluggish and in pain, but very happy to see Kittu after being away for days. Kittu himself has been in poor shape over the past few weeks, slower than before, and this has caused me worry since there is only one stairway entrance to our first-floor flat, and a local dog—encouraged by my mother giving him biscuits in the park—has taken to sleeping there. There are times when I have to look out for Kittu from our balcony and then run down and shoo dogs away so he can make his way up the stairs. It is getting stressful.

When I recently revisited my diary entries, I found a disconnect between my recollection of my mother's illness and how it really unfolded at the time. I had thought the kidney operation was a necessary but minor thing that caused maybe a week's inconvenience, all told. In fact, I now realise, her illness was spread over a few months leading up to the surgery—and several weeks of frailty following it.

It was around this time that Kittu began his own decline.

February 13. Late afternoon. Kittu hasn't been seen for over 24 hours. Mum, bedridden and weak, keeps asking about him during her lucid moments. I have to pick up some of her test reports from a nearby lab. As I get into my car and pull out towards our colony's exit, I think I see something out of the corner of my eye. Staying calm, I pull the car over, get out, go across to check.

It is Kittu, lying stiff and dead, by the side of a car. No external wounds, at least none that I can see, so probably not killed by a dog—though there is a yellowish discoloration spread across his side. My mind numbly processes all this as I work out what I need to do. I drive quickly to the lab, pick up mum's report, use their phone to call my grandmother in Panchshila Park, breathlessly explain that I need to get our cat buried without letting mum know what has happened.

My dadi arrives in her car two hours later (during which time I have some-how taken a sheet downstairs and wrapped Kittu in it). Her driver callously mutters '*arre, issko toh kooday mein phenk do* (throw the body in the garbage)' and I growl at him. After calling a pet-burial centre that is too far away, we find a suitable patch of ground just outside the Panchshila house, and bury him there. There is something reassuring about having done this, about hav-ing kept him so close to a place that my mother and I had once called home. When mum gets well, she will be able to visit him there.

Thinking about it now: the spot where Kittu lies is just a few feet away from the spot where a black kitten had been run over a long, long time ago. There is a feeling of something having come full circle.

The next few days are tense, because I have to wait for the right moment —when mum is a little stronger—to tell her what has happened. When I do tell her, it is the hardest thing, emotionally, that I have attempted up to that point in my life. It is only while doing it that I realise the enormity of it: I am telling her about the death of a child she has loved for eight years.

Though my mother avoided saying irrational-sounding things to me, she would let it slip, months after Kittu's death and her own kidney operation, that in some strange way it felt like Kittu had taken her illness on himself, and helped her to re-cover (while himself presumably fading from view, like a benevolent Cheshire Cat). That he had bought her some time.

I didn't know it then, but this was the end of my "cat phase"—at least in terms of having an immediate relationship with a cat. And I certainly couldn't have known that I would ever become close to dogs. I had had a visceral dislike for the colony dogs right from the time of Sandy's disappearance, when I was emotionally vulnerable and having nightmares about the various ways in which he might have come to harm. In this state of mind, the last thing I needed to see was imperilled cats—cats mauled by dogs or cars—but fate had thrown a lot of that my way. In a lane near my house once, I had turned a corner just in time to see a kitten being scooped up by a dog, its cries of terror becoming fainter, even as one of its siblings watched from behind the water-meter grill it had escaped into. My attempts to chase the dog, shouting at it, gave way to a helplessness and melancholia that consumed me for weeks, adding to the festering Sandy-loss.

The day after I buried Kittu was the first day in months that I didn't throw a little stone at the dog sitting outside our building, the dog my mother had been putting out food for. And simultaneously I entered an animal-free decade. Later that year, I joined a post-graduation course that brought me the first set of friends I made as an adult. A flurry of intimacies and heartaches was followed by my first internship and job, a growing sense of independence, another job, then a blog that set me on the path to writing the things I wanted to write about. This was an adrenaline rush, and animals were peripheral during this time. My mother got her darling Chinky in 2000, but I never even allowed this creature into my room—it was the one part of the flat that was off-limits for her. She adored me, sought my attention, looked beseechingly into the room when the door was open; I never returned that affection. It feels now like a subconscious form of revenge directed against my mother, for my anger about her continuing to feed dogs near our flat, when our cat was so vulnerable.

Then life fell into a routine, I got married, settled down, began working from home, became more tuned in to the world immediately around me—all of which would lead up to a magical moment where, out of an indeterminate huddle of eight stray puppies sleeping together in the lane behind our house, needing food and care, one would eventually resolve herself into my own special child.

And today, in the very same space, my life is organised around street dogs who are probably descendants of the creatures I hated 25 years ago.

The Cool, the Dramatic, and the Maternal

The human mind specialises in building narratives—we define ourselves, write clearly articulated "About Mes". And for the movie nerd, films—discovered, obsessed over, re-encountered—are ways of understanding one's relationship with the world, shaping narratives about personality and worldview, likes and dislikes.

As a professional critic I have often encountered the question: 'Will this film appeal to a cat-person or a dog-person?' But for the truly egalitarian movie-buff who watches and engages with *everything*—popular and arty, realistic and escapist, across genres, styles and forms of expression, with no preconceptions about one mode being "better" than another—the question is reductive. Can't one be both extrovert and introvert? Dog and cat? Warm and gregarious and slurpy and needy, but also cool and taciturn and reserved and hissy? How flexible are these categories? Might the dog and cat sides of your personality take turns being in control, the same way a movie-buff might be in the mood for florid melodrama on one day and cool understatement on another?

When I think about my movement from "cat person" to "dog person", I also think about a parallel movement. As a child I had gorged on masala Hindi films, but around 1991 (around the time Kittu had entered our life, and Sandy was in the near future), I moved away from the noisy, emotionally

159

fraught world of these movies and submerged myself in the more restrained forms we then called "world cinema". I was (to return to the stereotype) becoming a catlike viewer, watching things a cat might like to watch.

It was only in the mid-2000s that I returned to Hindi cinema's fold and found myself stimulated again by these films: relishing the heightened dramas, the tonal unevenness, the messiness, developing a renewed appreciation for how popular cinema worked.

And is it a coincidence that it was around this time that I also discovered that I had a "dog person" inside me? I don't know. I am wary of playing connect-the-dots. The point is that the same person, at different times in his life, can be both "types"—and in my case, the journey from one type to another coincided with returning to a cinema that was drenched in puddles of emotion.

Here's the thing, though. The most important influence on my life—my mother—had no trouble being both types at once. Unlike me, she never had a "cat phase" followed, years later, by a "dog phase"—for her, they coexisted, and could be tapped into at a moment's notice.

My mother and nani used to tell me a story from the early 1970s, when they spent a couple of weeks in London. An acquaintance let them stay in her flat for this duration, their one responsibility being the daily feeding of a tomcat who spent most of his time in a loft above a room. Instructions were clearly given: this many tins of food per day, no more. But my mother overfed the cat so much that at fortnight's end its weight had doubled and it had a hard time getting up and down its stairway. 'Thankfully,' mum laughed, 'We checked out of the flat a few hours before the woman returned, so we never had to explain how we had damaged her cat.'

When I first heard this, it was just a funny anecdote about a parent and a grandparent, bumpkins abroad, trying to negotiate the unfamiliar world of tinned pet food. But years later, as I became more attentive to my mother's relationship with animals, how she indulged their every whim, it made complete sense that she would coddle a once-sleek and haughty feline into obesity. She could turn sophisticated cats into slobbering dogs.

By now, it is probably clear that this piece is as much about my mother as it is about cats and dogs. My interest in animals came from her, was steered by her, is inseparable from her matter-of-fact admittance that her non-human children were as important to her as her biological child was (and in some ways, in terms of the special responsibility one owes to a creature who can't understand our language or the workings of a human-created world, *more* important).

Mum died in February 2018, exactly twenty years after that traumatic day when I had had to tell her about Kittu's death. I could recount many stories here about the beloved dogs—Chinky aside—of her final few years. Lara, who was only a year old when mum was diagnosed with terminal cancer. Gentle Imli, whom mum used to feed once in a while, and who came to our house to spend the last night of her life in mum's lap. The handsome, golden-haired fellow downstairs who had stopped visiting us after we adopted Lara, but who still looked up longingly at mum from the park. Small and feisty Chameli, whom my mother was convinced was the living embodiment of an almost life-sized furry toy I had brought home for Foxie many years earlier.

But there was also, importantly, another cat. A cat who visited her in the balcony every day in the final years. My mother called her Heena. She was somewhat sandy-coloured, but by now I was too preoccupied with puppy Lara to think much about this.

In mum's last few weeks—when she was essentially bedridden, not walking about the house—Heena stopped coming altogether, even though there were others in the house to put out milk for her. Then, a few days after mum's death, I was sitting in the living room when I looked up and saw the verandah door ajar, Heena sitting there soundlessly, looking at me in an abstracted way, reacting and bolting only when I got up and moved towards her.

Something about that moment reminds me of mum mentioning that it felt like Kittu had taken her illness on himself. And it makes me feel like my mother had a cat spirit somewhere in her. If that's the case, so do I—no number of slobbering, love-demanding dogs will change that.

At the same time, one doesn't have to get mystical about this. For all the countless things that have been written and said, about the differences between cats and dogs, the difference can sometimes come down to a practical detail: a dog, even a small dog, might be too ungainly for a physically compromised, bone-ravaged cancer patient to hold on her lap and cuddle; while a cat might leap lightly into this person's arms and comfort her in its own aloof way, through its purring presence. When I think now of my mother in her twilight, in great pain, sitting on the balcony that had been her spot for decades—the balcony from where she had watched maternally over the many creatures she cared for—I see her with Heena in her arms, looking a little at peace.

MusCat Tales

by Sonali Singh

She gave us disdainful looks; we gave her a wide berth. It was a somewhat delicate relationship. Until she appeared one morning with two rather emaciated kittens in tow and decisively won—not only the battle but the war. The whole family went into a frenzy of activity, with me trying to locate suitable containers to feed her and her offspring, my son surfing the net in an effort to learn as much is as possible in two minutes flat, about cats and their habits. We knew nothing about cats, bar the usual misconceptions that traditional dog lovers harbour about them. A carton was quickly assembled from the recently stowed away stack ('I told you we would need it someday,' declared the wise husband). My daughter just stood around and said 'Awwww' in that most eloquent fashion kids her age do these days.

Not that we could please Her with all this frantic hyperactivity—she did what she had been doing all this while, ignored us and got along with her life. The kittens, however, soon lost their fear, became adventurous, and got used to having a couple of giants hovering uselessly around them at any given point of time. The days rolled on, with the mother and her kittens in semi-permanent residence till eventually, we were left with only one kitten. And because he behaved like a merciless thug, extracting every manner of concession from us, he came to be called The Goon/ Gooney, short for, Guninder, though we were clueless whether it would turn out to be Guninder Singh or Guninder Kaur.

Time however revealed Gooney to be the former and he took over our lives and changed our routine entirely. We bought cat food and patrolled the driveway while Gooney ate his food. We were on edge, nerves jangling, ears tuned to catch the tone and tenor of each meow from Gooney. Any untoward and unfamiliar sound would result in all of us rushing out, stick in hand, to chase away the neighbourhood cats, who no doubt thought life was an endless party with ready availability of cat food, all they had to do was appear at the right time every day. An arsenal of stones was lined up at strategic points and within easy reach to be launched at the more daring felines who were perceived as a threat to Gooney.

Gooney started climbing trees and would be perched precariously in the highest and flimsiest of branches, so that the danger of him falling beyond the fence and into the wadi below seemed very real. His piteous cries brought me out one afternoon—he had climbed right up a huge keekar tree out front and could not be coaxed down. The source of his distress was located hiding in the tall grass: a huge black cat, majestic in his bearing and with the most splendid white whiskers contrasting with his shiny black pelt. The name of that great Field Marshal Maneckshaw sprang to mind. I went after him flinging stones and expletives like some demented creature—more cause for the neighbours to think I'm certifiable, but then who cares.

Anyway, soon enough the inevitable came to pass, word got around, and who doesn't fancy a free lunch? Pop came into our lives—perhaps he was Gooney's father, perhaps not, but they got along like a house on fire. Pop was as affectionate and eager for company as Gooney was aloof and finicky. A stroll in the evening out in the drive way was fraught with peril—you had to look where you were going because Pop made it his business to constantly criss-cross a track in front of you. If you stopped walking, he would promptly flop down on your feet, or roll over wanting to be scratched. And we thought only dogs liked to do that!

My evening ritual of watering the flowers was an exciting event for both of them—there was the water hose to wrestle, and hapless displaced moths and lizards, forced out by splashing water, to catch. Gooney was partial to the yellow tennis ball and small flat stones which he would play with tirelessly, throwing them up and going quite crazy when they bounced down. Pop and he drank milk from the same container, but Gooney was a cat in a hurry, pulling the dish towards himself with his paw, even as Pop tried drinking from it. It was hilarious to watch the dish move from one end of the verandah to the other. I also had to deal with the How's Pop? queries the kids constantly threw at me whenever they were away from home. And a response along the lines of 'He was sleeping in the sun for three hours' led to the next question, 'Why, didn't he go to office today?' Hey obviously Pop the cat was sleeping in the sun and Pop (your father) has gone to the office.

Into this equation entered Bimla, so named because she was a whiner and reminded me of my erstwhile cleaning lady back in India, who had a distinctly Uriah Heep manner, and was always trying to convince me to advance her her monthly wages. Anyway, Bimla (the cat that is) was very unpopular with everyone except my daughter, who predictably said 'AWWW' even though, in my opinion, Bimla was the most un-Awwwwish cat I had ever encountered. So Bimla got the occasional bit of cat food, and flourished alongside Gooney and Pop. Then Gooney turned against her and, needless to say, whatever offended Gooney, offended us. The final straw was when Bimla grabbed a little myna chick and made short work of it. Then the anti-Bimla sentiments became so fierce that it was curtains for her. She disappeared one day, probably couldn't take the negative vibes anymore.

Gooney was a talker. We would have whole conversations while I was in the kitchen and he was outside the front door. He liked our company and complained at being left alone. His efforts to squeeze himself through the door were relentless and he demonstrated his pleasure at being finally let in by purring so deeply and continuously we didn't have the heart to throw him out. He knew every trick in the book and inveigled himself completely into our hearts. He complained to my husband when he got back from work, trotting alongside him from the garage to the house, all the while keeping up with his litany of woes, sounding like a petulant child. Pop, on the other hand, was always happy to have us around and demonstrated his affection by rubbing himself and wrapping himself around our legs. Winter came and both would be cozily ensconced in the carton, which was laid out at precise angles to the wall to allow them maximum protection from the cold wind, without restricting movement. There was that night we returned from a friend's house well past midnight, the car headlights swept over the front porch, and the carton was seen lying at an awkward angle. A little head popped out to make the point quite clear that we should have returned earlier or else, at the very least, should have set things in order in their sleeping quarters, before going out.

They would disappear for days at a time occasionally, but always did return —the amorous Pop with injuries. But come back they did and we all settled into a happy routine, each content in the knowledge that the other was there.

But Gooney disappeared one day and though we waited and whistled and called, he didn't turn up. It's been four months. Pop left too and did not return—perhaps he chased his lady too far and couldn't find his way back, perhaps he's found people that love him even more than we did. But our whistles still echo in the wadi and the wind carries their names even though they are too far away to respond.

Ambitions of Twilight

by Vibha Balaji

In many ways, my cousin Annan's heartbreak reminded me of the handover:

'So you'll take her?' I imagined Amma asking Atthai.

My aunt, a decade younger back then, might have looked at me—at my little fists balled into the tail of Amma's skirt.

'Silly girl,' I could almost hear her say. 'Shall we go home?'

And now, in that same voice, admonishing Annan for his foolish ways of coping with betrayal: 'when will you grow up?'

Every day, as Atthai oiled my hair and double folded it, using a white ribbon to fend away potential suitors, Annan would run off into the medhu-vadai heat in search of Ponnamma. The vacated house did not deter him. Annan would return from his rounds and place phone calls to relatives—to his maama who lived out of town, to my father's old electrician, Anbu, who relocated to the outskirts last year—all for her. He tried to pawn Atthai's gold chain at Kookaram's, and would have succeeded too if not for the owner recognising his shifty face and ringing my Atthai to confirm that she needed the money. Annan had come home to an open bullpen that evening.

Despite his best efforts to find her, Ponnamma seemed to have disappeared. Like most women in Nagercoil, she spent her life raveled in dreams of leaving. She did love Annan, or so Annan told me during his dramatic renditions of their courtship. It was just that Kanyakumari, a town known for its sunrises and sunsets, had no use for the ambitions of twilight.

Right now, Annan lies sprawled across the bamboo cot, mouth hanging open like a dead fish. He is good-looking, even caked in sweat, so these angles do not bother him the way they do me. Atthai hovers over him, fussing with the lapels of his jacket.

'Why would you wear this out,' she trills. 'It's for special occasions!'

Annan sighs. 'Going to meet Ponnamma is a special occasion.'

I am seated beside him, on the fringes of the cot. Annan is the kind of person that won't make space, but won't push you away either. His mind is a thousand miles away, locked in want of Ponnamma. How Atthai hated this girl! Eyes like door knobs, always roaming about with her hair untied. Everyone on Balamore Road knew it: Atthai's only son lost to the wiles of a temptress. It was one thing to be interested in her, but another to be so hopelessly in love. Atthai only prayed for the end of it.

As young children, Ponnamma and Annan were inseparable. During his frequent bouts of nostalgia, Annan would exclaim: 'You don't understand, we were close like pencil and eraser!' On occasion, Atthai would recount the story too—although her version varied considerably in its form and content. For Annan, Ponnamma was a reason to live. At sixteen, what else was there to live for? Their relationship, like most relationships in our neighbourhood at the time, drew heavily from the 2000-hit film, *Alaipayuthey*—a three hour long saga chronicling the ups and downs of young love. The girl would meet the boy on trains, overcoming the obstacles of public scrutiny and parental supervision. Every one of Annan's haircuts would involve sitting inside Raghu Anna's barber shop with a low-resolution print out of Madhavan in *Pachchadanamey*. If Ponnamma found the difference amusing, she didn't say a word.

After Annan finished school, he was determined to marry Ponnamma. In Atthai's rendition, this was when his idiocy peaked. All day long, arguments would rage inside our house. Atthai would scream "useless son" through the grill gate, and Annan would ignore her, sprinting in the direction of Ponnamma's house instead. Last week, during one of his reenactments, I asked him, 'Did Ponnamma want to marry you?'. To see Annan like this, forlorn and heartsick, was difficult. In school, he would rush to my defense at the slightest provocation. It was one of the reasons I had a hard time believing in Ponnamma's affections; nobody in this part of town could love Annan more than me. Annan's response arrived a few days later, when I was least expecting it. 'About your question,' he said. 'Of course she wanted to marry me. She never said otherwise.' In his hands, he held a thatched basket filled with memorabilia. The implication seemed to be this: if Ponnamma really wanted to leave, she wouldn't have left so much of herself behind.

Women in Kanyakumari have odd relationships with their homes. Atthai told me this was because Kanyakumari was built on the promise of patience. It was in the name too: the virgin goddess who would turn her anger into penance and wait for her man to return as a groom. 'Did he come back?' I asked Atthai as she braided my hair deftly. 'They say she was reunited with him after she restored peace in the land,' Atthai responded as I handed her the white ribbons. Suddenly, it became a lot clearer to me why the women of this town were in such a hurry to leave.

It is rumoured that the old bougainvillea tree shed its petals for Annan the evening Ponnamma vanished. As he raced through the narrow strip of land belonging to President Electronics, past the windows at Roshan's with handbags on display, making a left near the bank leading up to Ponnamma's house only to discover it empty, all around him nature wept. There was something rare and uplifting about young love that demanded kindness.

Even Atthai, who had spent all this time lamenting the handover of her son to another woman, understood Annan's pain for what it was: uncorrupted agony. Because Annan hadn't known she would leave; he hadn't imagined the possibility of it. Ponnamma was the sort of girl who kept her feelings to herself. It had taken Annan years to charm her. Everyday as Ponnamma left her home to pump water into a bucket, Annan would hover beside her, offering to carry it home. Eventually, she agreed, and with one foot in the door, Annan threw the floodgates open. Months after the initial shock of her disappearance wore away, Annan would tell me that Ponnamma's departure didn't hurt him as much as the lack of prior notice did.

When the seasons changed, the heat condensing into monsoon, Annan fell into routine. At first, Atthai was thrilled he'd found a reason to get dressed in the mornings. But that was before she discovered he was spending his days in fruitless search of a girl. In her books, there was nothing more embarrassing than a man chasing after a woman who couldn't name the forty-six different kinds of rasam. Meanwhile, Annan's trips became a measure of time for the rest of us. As he set out to Ponnamma's house, shopkeepers would know to open their stores; the Akka who delivered milk would begin her rounds. Like clockwork, the neighbourhood would rise from its slumber, the day punctuated by the rooster crowing of Annan's footsteps.

Annan himself seemed to delight in this regimen. 'Does your brother not have a job?' my friends would ask me. 'He's always running around here and there'. I never knew what to say to them. To respond might have been to confess that Ponnamma was Annan's job or worse, that she was Annan's world, but I couldn't bring myself to relay such a thing. It is a heavy and leaden matter to have your life rest so completely in the hands of another person.

Today marks one hundred days without Ponnamma. Annan is presently engaged in the process of antagonising Atthai. It is one of the few tasks he excels at, and he takes his duty seriously.

'Amma,' he says in Tamil. 'Why can't you support me? It's not like I'm out there putting sarakku or smoking.'

Atthai sighs. It is the long, fatigued sigh of a mother who set the bar for her son too high.

When she turns around to face me, her eyes appear hawkish in the dwindling light. 'I want you to follow him tomorrow,' she says. 'See what the fool is up to.'

I have never been one to disobey orders, so I nod. Next to me, Annan's yawns turn into protests.

True to my word, I accompany Annan to Ponnamma's house the next day. He waves jauntily at the people we run into, unfazed by the gossip that follows him. *There goes Maami's oldest. He's back here again.* I sense that this is a frequent occurrence—that people say terrible things about him, and Annan's affable response is nothing out of the ordinary. Although eight years younger, I am filled with the sudden urge to protect him.

We arrive at Ponnamma's house a few minutes late, out of breath from having jogged the final stretch. Leaping over the fence, Annan settles down by the entrance, reaching into his bag for a packet of milk biscuits. He ignores my presence, choosing to stare expectantly in the direction of the sealed-up house. I am reminded of the time Atthai dubbed him the sole inheritor of our family's craziness.

'Annan,' I say, adjusting the strap of my sandals.

'What?' he responds, not bothering to turn around.

'Who are we waiting for?'

This is a silly question. I know who we are waiting for.

'Ponnamma!' Annan exclaims, shielding his eyes from the sun and squinting at the shadow that emerges from the sidewall. I peer over the top of his head, my eyes glazed with worry. I am afraid he has moved past the grieving stage and into the hallucinating one. Padding gently through the smattering of glass shards and broken clay pots, Annan squats down to gather a bundle of fur into his arms. Rotating on his ankles, he brandishes the squirming cat in the vicinity of my feet.

'She's just shy,' he smiles, scratching her spotted ears fondly.

I don't know what to say to him. My expression, in all likelihood, is arrested in a state of horror. It isn't the shock of seeing a cat named Ponnamma, really. It is more the travel reporting I would have to do later, revealing to Atthai exactly what her son did with his free time. It shouldn't come as a surprise to me. Annan has always been the type of person to offer his heart without contract; to treat every situation with the same blundering zeal. To see him here, having befriended a cat that bears little resemblance to Ponnamma, is no more bewildering than all the other times he has come out looking like a fool.

'I know what you're thinking,' Annan says, cat in hand. He's sitting on the mound of cement outside the dilapidated gate, shifting the barest amount to make room for me.

I wedge myself into the cramped space, glowering at him, 'No, you don't. Annan doesn't know everything.'

Annan yanks my braid, mimicking the action of stopping a freight train. 'You shouldn't hate Ponnamma. She had many reasons to leave. Isn't that right, Cat Ponnamma?'

I snort, and it is Annan's turn to glare at me.

'I don't hate Ponnamma Akka,' I contend. 'I just hate who she turned you into.'

'Why? What's wrong with me?'

I sniffle, feeling my eyes well up. I look away. I don't want Annan to see me as someone he needs to shield. When the threat of tears has passed, I twist around to survey him. 'Don't you have dreams?' I ask him. 'What about work? Don't you want to work? Even Madhavan had more than a high school diploma when he went off chasing... the girl.'

'—Shalini,' Annan interjects.

'Annan!'

He grins, appearing briefly chastised.

'Sister,' He begins in Tamil. 'Don't you know poetry? What are they teaching you in school these days? How many Tirukurral can you recite?'

'Not many,' I admit.

'Loveless men, they say, are bones clad in skin. I'm doing alright by that standard. Look at this muscle!' Annan flexes his arm.

His audience remains unimpressed.

Back when I was a baby, just an oblong mass of flesh and promise, my mother let Atthai raise me. She had already given birth thrice, and my arrival coincided with a contraction of funds. I was too young to protest, having little say in the matter to begin with. But given the opportunity now, I do not think I would take my mother back. I love Atthai too much for that. I love Annan too, which is why I worry for him. I am afraid the world will knock him down someday, so much so that he will find it impossible to get back up.

Sitting beside him now, in the low bludgeoning sunlight, I am reminded of the day Ponnamma left. As if sensing my guilt, Cat Ponnamma nudges her head into my hand. Hesitantly, I reach out to pet her.

'What will you do?' I ask Annan. 'If Ponnamma Akka returns?'

Annan slopes back, his elbows a fulcrum for his body. 'I don't know. Will she return?' he says.

Under ordinary circumstances, this was a question that bore no answer. Like the old tomato seeds Atthai had palmed into rusty soil, the ground would remain barren, no sign of life to be found. That is until one morning Atthai wakes up and discovers a baby shoot sticking out of the loam. The miraculous flourishing dovetails with the arrival of our postman, Solomon. The metal bell on his bicycle vibrates thrice, an indication that he had additional news to deliver.

'O, Maami,' he crows from outside. 'Have you not heard?'

Atthai scuttles out, a bath towel twisted around her hair. 'What? What is it?'

'Your boy's troubles are over. The young woman has come home.'

Atthai's face darkens, storm clouds emerging from the depths of her. I don't stay long enough to witness the hurricane that follows. Weaving through the emerging crowd, I sprint out into the main road, uncaring of the way my own hair hangs loose behind me. Soloman's trail, notorious for good reason, means that this information has already made its way to the ears of everyone, information hopping over roofs and thatches like grasshoppers in the spring. Like any other day, Annan had set off on his usual path, oblivious to the murmurs that followed him. At present, it occurs to me that he might be the only person left in Nagercoil who hasn't caught wind of Ponnamma's return.

It should be a punishing task for a woman of Atthai's age to kick up dust in a nine-yards saree, but she manages. A short distance ahead of us is Annan, cricket cap pulled low over his head, a pack of biscuits clutched tightly in his hands. Sensing Atthai's wrath, I speed up, doubling over from the effort.

'Annan!' I scream, hoping my voice will travel and lessen the gap between us. 'She's here!'

From behind me, Atthai cries, 'Don't tell him, silly girl!'

Annan freezes mid-stride, his body held upright by some uncommon force. Twisting around, he takes in the sight of what is surely the most bizarre chain of command our family has ever seen.

There are many things I want to say to him, beginning and ending with come home—she doesn't deserve you, but we are at a crossroads that demands discretion. I am still a few feet away, and from this range, I doubt he will notice the imploration in my eyes. When Atthai finally catches up to me, breathing heavily from forced labour, she doesn't utter a word. Fastening me by the arm, she leads me away from Annan, not bothering to spare him or the situation at hand a second glance.

'Are you going to go? Don't go,' I squirm out of Atthai's vice-like grip and rush back to where Annan stands, rooted to the spot.

175

Annan remains silent. Of all the possible ways he could have reacted to Ponamma's return, this is by far the most surprising. There always came a point in arguments with my brother, where for whatever reason, his dismay would break and he'd begin passionately advocating the need for tension diffusion. Annan hated tension. It was always the checkered flag at the end of an argument: no need to take tension; stop being a tension-party; tension-tension, where's your pension? Looking at him now, I find a world of disquiet coiled between the folds of his eyebrows.

'I'll leave then,' I whisper, stepping back so he knows I am being serious.

There is nothing else left for me to do.

At home, Atthai braids my hair with a force reserved for bad marks and disobedience. She tugs at every tier, unsympathetic to the way my scalp tightens each time. When she is done, my head feels stitched to my body, the way a hair tie on the wrist does when it cuts off the blood circulation.

If Annan's anger is a whisper of a thing, fainter than the smell of sandalwood after a bath, Atthai's is an implacable fire. I recall a merciless night last winter when Annan hadn't come home. A late sleeper, Atthai had paced around the thinnai for hours waiting for him to show up. The sun had risen. Vegetable hawkers had begun their customary howling: cauliflower, banana flower, ladies finger, broad beans! Still no sign of Annan. We found out later that he'd sprained his ankle swinging from a banyan tree and taken shelter at the local warehouse. This was not before Atthai had taken matters into her own hands and stormed towards Ponnamma's house with a broomstick.

Unlike Annan, I do not possess any talent for placating Atthai. Our walk to the fish market is as cold and wet as Atthai's mood, the short distance made long by the eyes that follow us. Everything we do becomes fodder for town gossip, each sigh, rustle and cough infused with meaning. But Atthai is

Quarantine in an Apartment in Malad, Bombay, India

by Craig Boehman

Toby and Puchu live with two humans, Craig and Alokananda, in an apartment in Mumbai. During the quarantine, everyone was in everyone else's hair, but they coped.

The humans are both artists—a photographer and a composer—but Toby and Puchu are up to all the heavy lifting expected of them: inspiring and accounting and, on occasion, cleaning and tending to the plants. Sometimes they even take charge of the flowers.

Random moments from a day in Toby and Puchu's lives, as captured by Craig.

Toby and Puchu, 9 35 am

Puchu, 11 am

Puchu, 11 01 am

Toby, 3 pm

Puchu, 4 15 pm

Toby, 8 42 pm

Toby and Puchu, sometime around midnight

a proud woman, and even on a morning like this, she is determined to see to it that our shelf is stocked.

We are preparing to round the bend when Atthai balks. Across her is a willowy, familiar figure. Ponnamma's hair has grown longer during her time away, and her dark skin glimmers like salmon scales in the sunlight. If it isn't for the large, navy bucket nestled against her hip, I might even believe we invented her. It is the same bucket Annan used to carry for her on their daily trips to the bore pump. Clogged drains retain puddles of water, and in their reflection I see the pink of Ponnamma's clothes, the singular braid she gathers to one side. Above her, past the clamorous din of vendors exchanging profanities over our heads, the sky grows darker, squalls of grey and pink wrestling each other at dawn.

She looks beautiful—like the women in Atthai's serials, festooned in colourful sarees with flowers tucked into their hair. Maybe if Ponnamma had a wonky eye or a less than sizable chest, there would be fewer accounts about the travels of her body. It occurs to me that my own appearance, though unremarkable on most counts, would never garner the same attention hers did.

The moment of Ponnamma's arrival stretches out for an eternity. During this time, Atthai stops breathing, her footsteps growing increasingly erratic as Ponnamma walks slowly towards us. It appears that neither party is prepared for a confrontation.

'Maami,' Ponnamma finally greets, her voice exposing an unexpected diffidence.

Atthai nods curtly. 'How have you been?' she asks.

Ponnamma bows her head. 'There have been better days.' she says in Tamil.

This is the great secret of small-town living: you could despise somebody to the pits of hell and back, and still manage to worry about how little they are eating or how haggard they look up close.

Lurking behind Atthai, I take in the droop of Ponnamma's eyes; the tell-tale signs of fatigue marring her face. An ugly wave of satisfaction rises in me at the thought that she has suffered too. All this time, I have been watchful of Annan's feelings, caught in a crossfire between candidness and silence. The truth is that I dislike Ponnamma. It is different to hating her or wanting her. I disliked her for the simple fact that she'd broken my brother's heart.

Inside her bucket is an assortment of items: an old cricket cap that looks like it belonged to Annan, red manjadi seeds, a silver hair pin. If either of us finds this odd, we choose not to say anything. My loyalties lie with Annan, and Ponnamma's lie with whichever God is privy to her truest, most intimate feelings.

She shifts her smile towards me, and for a brief moment, the events of last May hang between us like a carcass.

The morning before Ponamma's disappearance, Annan had slipped a silver, U-shaped hair pin into my palm, and confessed: 'It's for Ponnamma. What do you think?' I hadn't said anything then, but I spent the rest of the day at school distracted. On my way home, I childishly entertained the idea of throwing rocks at Ponnamma's window. There was no one else around; it would have been easy. Just as I was about to leave, loud sobs filled the air. Unable to move, I craned my neck, trying to catch a glimpse of what was happening. *Let me talk to them. I know people who work at the bank!* And in a flash, Ponnamma was outside, and she was looking at me. Her eyes were bloodshot and unfocused, and I resented the way she could look elegant even at her worst. Love made many things bearable, including the heaviness of an-other person's burden, but with nothing to tie Ponnamma and me together,

I found it easy to race home. When I arrived, red-faced and panting, Annan asked me jokingly if I was running from my imaginary suitors. I never told him what I saw.

With no witness to corroborate the truth, Ponnamma's disappearance set into motion a series of rumours that, even to Annan, a firm optimist, became a source of concern. In the course of a single week, I turned Ponnamma into a prostitute, a peddler, a bad daughter, and a whore. She left her parents to fend for themselves. She moved them out of town to prevent the truth from getting out. She was poor. She was rich. Nobody knew anything about her family. Her mother looked sad, misguided, lost, lonely. Her father was a drunk, a gambler, a cheap salesman. She sold her body to strangers. She danced in dingy rooms outside the city. She was after the insurance money Annan's father left us. She loved him. She was using him.

Facing Ponnamma now, I wonder if I was shielding Annan from something I had created.

At the intersection, I part with Atthai under the guise of collecting change from a friend.

It's a lie but it doesn't matter because Atthai has chosen to retire to bed for the afternoon. An alarm clock as loud as fifty church bells couldn't rouse her.

On my way to Ponnamma's house, Raghu Anna stops me and reaches into his pocket for a caramel. I accept it blithely, accustomed to kindness from people who know my brother; it is one of the few benefits I reap from living as his immediate family. Past Preethis supermarket, beyond the canopy of bristling trees, I begin sprinting, the ground hammering beneath my feet. It was Annan who taught me to run, gripping my hand securely as we fell into a comfortable stride. Before him, I had been too afraid of losing my ribbons.

Leaping over the cornerstone, I expect to find him sitting by the doorstep,

179

milk biscuits in hand. Instead, I am greeted by the sight of nothing. Cat Ponnamma pokes her head out, expecting my brother's familiar and agreeable presence. We are both disappointed by each others' company.

'You don't eat caramel, do you?' I ask her, feeling a little stupid.

She blinks, padding over to sniff my fingers. I don't have much else to offer, so I let her climb into my lap and sit there as I stroke her head.

I have never been good with animals—that has always remained Annan's territory. I am yet to meet a dog, cat or lost squirrel my brother has not managed to charm. Atthai remarks that this is because he shares their desire to lounge under the sun and be handed his meals thrice a day. I disagree. I think it has more to do with his inability to subsist under lonesome conditions.

'I'm leaving now,' I say. 'The house owner will be back soon and I doubt she will appreciate my trespassing.'

Cat Ponnamma, lacking both tact and respect, does not budge from her self-appointed throne. Scooping her body into my arms, I set her down by the gate. Clouds fluctuate above us, gathering in scattered shapes that blend into one colour. If I squint hard enough, they morph into something recognisable—a picture of a swan or an imagined memory of my mother's smile.

Maybe I find it difficult to be alone too.

Cat Ponnamma follows me home despite the numerous attempts I make to divert her course. Ahead of us, on the thinnai, sprawled between dried chillies and sago is Annan. He looks like the clay dolls I'd build as a child, mixing silt with water and gathering the lumps into semi-solid figurines. My skill set at the time drastically limited the options available for expressions, and as result, the dolls would remain placid, with downturned eyes and a line in place of a mouth. They looked so breakable, perched on our windowsill, rivers of mud running down their bodies in the afternoon heat. I wonder if Annan feels the same way.

Hoisting the cat before she can bother him, I head inside. Atthai is asleep in the main room, her soft snores audible from the kitchen. She'd made meen puttu for dinner, two bowls of shredded fish placed in the cool shade of the water pot. Claiming both portions, for myself and the cat, I settle down by the grills and watch Annan's silhouette change colour in compliance with the sky.

With each hour that passes, my brother's posture slackens further. Cat Ponnamma curls at my feet, purring softly into her spotless dish.

It is nearing midnight when I stir awake. My body, pressed uncomfortably against the wall, pricks from disuse.

Outside, beyond the contours of wilting foliage, Ponnamma's figure is a silhouette from a painting. I have always suspected she possessed a brittleness of character, reinforced by the conceit of popularity, but in this setting, she seems solid—less bewitched by ruin. Annan stands with his back turned to me. For the first time in my life, I find it difficult to predict the arrangement of his features.

Craning my head towards the window, I lean in to catch snippets of their conversation. Beside me, Cat Ponnamma unfurls; a mystical creature in the dark.

For a long time neither of them speaks. The world feels like an old spinning top beneath me—rotating on metal—nothing to anchor it in place. Then Ponnamma steps forwards, arms like broken bamboo sticks, and with sweetness rests her forehead against Annan's chest.

Atthai said to me on our walk back from the market that love cannot nourish you. Her encounter with the siren of Nagercoil ended like this, on ambiguous terms—motherly nature counteracting her empathy. If she had admitted to Ponnamma then, that being bright here often meant receiving less, the storm might have changed course; but we are both fettered by sentiment, in many ways cornered by our shared love for Annan. The combination of these moorings made it hard to take the side of Ponnamma.

I remember when my parents had come to visit us, after Annan's father died, and I'd seen the flicker of childhood in Atthai's gaze; an unmended bone gasping for reprieve at the sight of her brother. She'd asked me then if I wanted to go back. Going back, in her mind, implied the presence of a place to return to. At the time, I hadn't known how to explain to her that I wanted something bigger—something more truthful than a lost home.

Squinting up at Ponnamma now, I am sure she is making a mistake. All those years ago, when I stayed by Atthai's side, I must have done so knowing fate would alter me; that I would escape this town even if Annan got on his knees and begged. Alongside Atthai, he is my only family, and if I was going to leave him behind, I needed Annan to remain someone I understood.

Cat Ponnamma nudges at my palm, driving my attention back to her.

'Do you want to come?' I whisper into her ear. 'We could find you a friend.'

In the star-encrusted shadows, she blinks—a pioneer of brevity.

'Okay,' I say, nodding with some seriousness. 'I think I understand.'

Across us, cloaked in tranquility, the folds of this town become a backdrop for Annan and Ponnamma. His arms soften, like pestled jaggery, yielding easily the space reserved for her; Ponnamma's hair, which retains the kinks of a past braid, hangs in a curtain around them. When the wind finally soars the force of it vaulting her locks into the sky, a flash of silver catches the light, its abiding glimmer illuminating us in shades of grey. Nestled here, in the hazard of darkness, I feel as if I am seeing the world anew.

Cats and Smoke

by Kulfi Mohammad Saidali

The *Atti* was what brought us all together. The poor, the rich, the misfits, the goody-goodies, the idiots, the cats, the dogs, even the sophisticated, all of us gravitated towards it for one thing: *gun-jah*. The word *atti* is unique. It's a place, an activity, a *thing*. It is the noun used to describe what stoners did, but also the act itself, and the place where the performance occurred. For us, it was Choudary's house.

There was Arul. He crafted hand-made pens. While you were stoned, he would convince you that the pen that he would make for you was the single most exquisite thing on the planet. Then he would sell it to you for at least a grand.

Karthik was from North Madras. He walked around Royapuram, Sowcarpet, and Kasimedu. Royapuram was where the harbour was. It was the place where all the contraband entered Chennai. The pot, specifically, would be brought to Anna Nagar, which was in central Chennai, and then it would be dealt to the noobies from there. In Sowcarpet, you couldn't survive without knowing Hindi. All the Gujaratis, Rajasthanis and Marwaris lived there. The locals categorised all of them under one broad heading: Seth-u. They lent money and made sweets all day. All the filmmakers who produced their own films, borrowed their money from there, and suffered the colossal interest rates that were charged. Kasimedu was a fantasy locale for *cinema paithiyams* like me. There were gangs, gangsters, profanity, violence, and guns. Murders happened on the streets. The cacophony of the brothels was all you heard, and cats-with-one-eye roamed the terraces. Or so we heard from Karthik.

There were also Ajay, Sriram, Anirudh, and Dhruv, about whom I knew everything. They were lame. They did nothing but stone.

'Let's put an *atti* here da,' Choudary said on the phone one afternoon. It was September, and nothing was happening anywhere.

'Alright. When?' I said.

'Now. Come.'

'On my way.'

I got out of the house. The neighbourhood mongrels, Shakeela, Ketan, and Karuppamma were lazing in the sun and peeked at me from beneath their voluptuous eyebrows. The white smudge beneath the Honda city was a kitten. She had large eyes and a pink nose. Her body was slender, but the fur didn't give away the fact that she was weak. You could only tell she was starving if you ran your fingers across her spine. The bearded uncle who lived three houses away called her Kanmani. Perhaps she was hiding from the dogs or perhaps she was waiting to chase a bird or a mouse, I didn't know.

I stopped and peeked beneath the car, and the dogs caught the cue. There was a bark. It sounded like the grunt of the Honda City itself. And then the dogs ran towards the car. When Kanmani scurried out towards the Peepal tree, I thought about how she looked longer than the time I had seen her last. She slapped her left paw against the swollen roots of the tree and somehow, that propelled her up the trunk onto the lowest branch. The three mongrels were jumping up and down, barking. Kanmani looked like a bunch of cotton stuck in the branches.

I took the shitty road that everyone who knew how to drive or ride swore at, and entered East Coast Road. The breeze was warm, and I had already begun to sweat. I walked to Cheta's tea-shop for cigarettes. It was called *Highway Snacks*. They sold everything but snacks. When I had stepped into the shop for the first time, as a non-smoker, with shivering hands, I had asked Cheta what the name of the shop was.

'I believe you can read. There's a board outside,' he had said.

I had walked outside to find an empty blue wall. Cheta laughed from inside, whacking the sweet boxes. We had become good friends from that day.

Cheta didn't know my real name and so he had taken the liberty of naming me afresh every week. Last week I was called *Vanambadi Poker*. And the week before that *David Achchan*. This week, I was *Kulfi Mohammad Saidali*.

'Ahh, Kulfi!' He shouted, as I entered. '*Varoo, varoo…*'

I nodded, grabbed my cigarettes from him and sat down. I lit one and ordered tea. Unlike in Delhi, in Chennai it wasn't chai, it was tea. And unlike in Delhi, it was less about the art, and more about the commerce. While it took a good fifteen minutes in Delhi for your chai to arrive, in Chennai, you'd have it in your hand before you completed saying: *Cheta oru chaaiya*.

'Otha! What the fuck are these cigarettes?' A man screamed. I turned around. He was clothed in a white shirt and a dirty lungi. His hair was almost gone. Whatever little hair he had left on his head was the colour of mehendi. Perhaps, it was the sun that did the colouring, I thought.

'What's the problem, uncle?' Cheta asked. The two of them had been calling each other uncle since I can remember. It began with one of them calling the other uncle. Nobody knew who started it.

'Uncle, the tobacco keeps falling out of this cigarette.' The man said.

Cheta laughed out loud and said, 'When you buy Goldflake products, you never blow into the cigarette, you only suck. *Sappu, sappu.*'

He said. '*Otha!* Are you asking me to suck *it?*' The man fake-screamed.

'I'm asking you to suck it,' Cheta pointed at the cigarette. 'Not suck *it.*'

She walked into the shop clapping her hands. Eunuchs were called the number nine: *ombodhu.* She walked straight to me, as though she saw the fear in my eyes. She clapped her hands. I reached for my wallet. '*Ettana kudu, engana udu.*' She said, pressing my cock like a button. The words, *Ettana kudu, engana udu,* meaning *put eight bucks on the table, put your dick wherever you're able,* rung in my ears like a siren. I was sweating. I fled the shop.

I walked back to ECR and took a right turn at the signal. And then I bought some gum for the goody-goodies at Singapore Shopee. There was air-conditioning and all the staff spoke in whispers. This was supposed to be a sophisticated silence. There were separate counters to bill, pay, collect, and exit. I had to go through all that trouble just for some gum. I walked out, pissed off.

Outside, I passed a dead-body, atop a bed festooned with *samanthi poo* and *malli poo.* There were men in banians, dancing *kuthu,* hysterically drunk. They moved their hands and legs in rapid motions to the percussion beats of the *thaarai* and *saavu melam.* I lit up a cigarette and walked down First Seaward Road. The breeze was cooler here. The fragrance of salt whipped my face. The nature of faces changed. The beards disappeared. The hairdos were fixed, or at least premeditated. Though the greenery increased, it was not natural. The trees were in rows and they stooped over the road, forming carpets of shade on the ground.

When I reached Choudary's, I rang the bell a couple of times. Arul opened the door. I said hi. He smiled and hugged me. Arul never hugged. He was high. I pushed him off and he fell on the ground. And then, Arul went to sleep. The fat cat, Caesar, stared at me. He was furry, and his fur was the same color as Alpenliebe. Choudary never told anyone where Caesar was from or what breed he was. We all thought he was a Persian, but his mouth bent and his cheeks rolled so much that his frown seemed like a smirk. Anyway, Caesar sauntered up to me and rubbed his sides against my jeans. Perhaps, his nostrils required some relief from the pungent smell of weed, and I was the only one not smelling of it. I kicked forward. Caesar's hind leg was tripped and he fell against the floor. He stayed like that. Caesar went to sleep.

I walked into Choudary's room. Everyone was there: Sriram, Ajay, Dhruv, Ani, Karthik, and Deepangshu Choudary of course. They were taking Bong rips.

'Take a rip.' Choudary said.

'Let me smoke a cigarette first.'

I lit up and walked to the balcony. This was when Caesar woke up. He came to the balcony and sat by me as I smoked. Outside, like a jigsaw puzzle, like a labyrinth of buildings, and with a spirit like sauntering smoke, Chennai came together. I kept my eyes on her. She was pretty. I didn't blink once. I saw Caesar watch the horizon shimmer. And then I took another drag.

Dog-Cat

by Payal Nagpal

My dog was a cat. She was a growling, hissing, startlingly flexible, incredibly cranky cat.

Spot, who was nicknamed Spotty almost immediately after we got her, didn't wag her tail when I came home from school. She didn't jump on me or lick or chase her tail. Sometimes, when I was lucky, she would trot up to me, press her nose against my palm and ask for attention. I often joked that she was Queen of the Household, that I was nothing more than her servant.

But I loved her. More deeply and wholly and unconditionally than anything else.

I found Spot when I was ten-years-old. My family had just moved into a new house in a gated community that was still mostly under construction. There were stray dogs and cats everywhere, most of whom were tame and affectionate, and befriended me as soon as I offered them biscuits. But Spot was different. She was a white-black-and-brown, bushy-tailed little thing who lived alone on a mound of sand. I'd see her every day when I walked home from school, call out to her to come down and play, but she'd just look away with her snout in the air.

After about a month of pathetic begging from the base of the sand-mountain, I decided I would climb up and pet her. I trekked up, stretched my hand out and patted her head gently. She paid no attention at first, but as time passed, she inched towards me and sighed in contentment. I spent almost half an hour petting her that day, braving a rather precarious surface with gravel finding its way under my skirt. It hadn't taken me long to fall in love. When my mother came looking for me, only mildly concerned about my absence (considering the penchant I had for getting distracted by dogs on the street and losing track of time), Spot followed me down the hill and to our front porch.

For the next few months, she lurked outside our gate, much to my parents' disapproval. My mother warmed up to her slowly, coming home from work and stroking her, offering her biscuits and milk. She'd let Spotty inside our gate—never our front door, though—buy her treats and harass her with hugs and kisses. Spotty would bark at the dhobi, at guests, and at any bird who had the audacity to enter our garden. And although she'd also enjoy running on the streets and chasing speeding motorcycles like all the other strays, she was—for all intents and purposes—ours. My mother wanted her inside, but father remained wary, still raw from losing the dog my parents had before I was born.

But then, after she went missing, we had to take her in. We had no choice.

I went to check up on Spot on the night of my eleventh birthday party and she wasn't there. I didn't think much of it, until she was still missing the next morning. I scoured the neighbourhood all day, and by the evening, my mother and I had organised a search party. We called our neighbours, worked on Missing Dog posters and went on continuous walks around the neighbourhood, my mind rifling through terrifying scenarios. I was convinced she had been run over or mauled by a group of big dogs. The thought of her dying played on repeat.

The next three days were a blur of tears and desperation. I struck multiple deals with the universe: I'd eat my vegetables every single day if she came back, I'd never not do my homework again.

We found Spot, unrecognisable, outside our door on Day Four, beaten and bloody and bruised. She had either been attacked by a pack of dogs or stoned by humans—or both. We rushed her to the vet and were told to keep her inside the house for the next few days. She slept at the foot of my bed that night and seemed content to be indoors until five days later, when she scratched on the front door to go out. We let her out, thinking she'd go back to being a carefree stray with no strings attached, using our front yard as her home base. But she scratched to be let in just hours later.

From then on, Spot would slink in and out of the house, coming and going as she pleased. She'd squeeze through the front door that we'd leave ajar, just in case she wanted to nap in our dining room in the afternoons. She learnt how to slide under our gate—my mother would lock it at night, only to find Spot on our stoop in the morning.

When a family friend, Diwakar—a man deathly afraid of dogs—came to town and spent the night with us a few weeks into Spot's new routine, he refused to enter the house with Spot in it. Grudgingly, my mother let her out and we settled into our evening routine. That night (having consumed a considerable amount of alcohol), Diwakar slept in our guest bedroom on the ground floor. He woke up around 4 am to the sound of footsteps padding at the other end of the room. When he turned on his phone flashlight, he saw a white figure and screamed. And after a few moments of contemplating his impending paranormal doom, he stood up and investigated, learning that it was in fact Spot who had broken and entered.

He informed my parents about this reprehensible situation in the morning, threatening to never stay with us again. My mother insisted it was just a nightmare but investigated anyway. She found paw-prints on the guest room window and realised the mesh hadn't been pulled all the way down. Spot had somehow jumped onto the windowsill, opened the mesh and entered the house.

'She's a ninja!' I declared when my mother told me what had happened.

'She's a cat,' my mother responded. And that's when she became our be-loved dog-cat.

I began to make note of all her cat-like tendencies, documenting them so I could boast about my rather unique pet. She'd paw at things to investigate them, instead of sniffing foreign objects. She'd find her way into the small-est of nooks and settle down in what were seemingly the most uncomfort-able positions. On Diwali, when the fireworks outside sounded like rocket launches, she'd enter my cupboard, curling up between my clothes, with my shirts cushioning her from the rest of the world.

In true cat fashion, Spot displayed affection in warped ways. I would read about dogs who jumped on their humans when they came home, sitting on their lap and continuously wagging their tail. I would have to chase after Spotty for love, and when I did, she'd glance at me witheringly, almost as if she was rolling her eyes. She slept on my bed, but if I dared snuggle close to her, she would get up and leave. One way I knew she loved me, though, was through her jealousy. If I came back home smelling of another dog, she'd sniff my hand contemptuously and sulk, turning her back towards me and plonking on the carpet purposefully. She didn't mind my mother hugging me, but any time the hug lasted more than a few seconds, she would find a way to sandwich herself between us.

Despite her cool detachment, there were moments Spot showed over-whelming protectiveness. She knew when I was upset and would sit by me and paw at my arm gently. She never licked or displayed overt affection, but she would lend her presence to me, and often. That was enough. When I was sixteen and started having panic attacks, she would refuse to leave my side during them. Soon, I found that she was the only one who could calm my attacks. I would place my hand on her chest and breathe to the rhythm of her heartbeat. My breath would steady eventually, and only then would she walk away. She was my grounding technique, far before I learnt anything about mindfulness or therapy.

Spot was my protector. When my mother yelled at me too loudly, she would growl at her and hiss. She almost attacked another dog once, when my mother and I took her on a walk. I stopped to play with my neighbour's dog—one of those bad-tempered, fluffy, tiny, white gentrified rats. I pet the other dog, only to have him growl at me. Spot, who had been calm, tugged at her leash and broke free. She lunged at the rat, barked at him and knocked him over with her paw.

Spot's bark (and growl and hiss) was bigger than her bite. She only bit somebody once, and that was for taking me away. When I left for college, she moved into my room full-time. She would sleep on my bed, right by my pillow. A month into my absence, my mother wanted my bed clothes dry-cleaned. When she stripped my bed, Spot thought it was an indication that I was leaving forever. She followed my mother to the door, barked at the man who came to pick up the dry cleaning, thinking he was trying to steal my scent. Before my mother could hand over the clothes, Spot lunged and bit the man's thigh. And although I know I shouldn't be as delighted about the incident as I am, it's something I look back on as evidence of the indestructible bond Spotty and I had, and the last time she showed how much she loved me.

Six months after that, she passed away. Suddenly, but painlessly—peacefully—on the 24th of April, 2017. One day after my best friend's birthday; a month after I found out my grandfather died, which was a month after my childhood friend lost her battle with cancer. My mother called my roommate and asked her to be with me when she gave me the news. I refused to believe it at first, but when it finally sunk in, the loss was crushing. In a series of terrible losses, hers was the most devastating. A vacuum grew in my stomach when Spot went away, a sort of blackhole that still hasn't been filled yet.

There are days I still expect to hear her barking when I ring the doorbell, when I almost instinctively scream, 'Spotty, I'm home!' as I enter the house. There are days I'm scared I'll forget her, that she'll morph into a two-dimensional memory—live on as nothing more than *the dog I once had*. But if I crawl deep enough into my blanket, I can still smell her: a combination of tea tree oil shampoo and fallen fur. There are still strands of white hair littering the sofa—my mother never had the heart to vacuum them. I carry her with me wherever I go, thanking the universe that of all the homes she could go to, and of all the families she could adopt, she chose mine. And that I had, and still have, the honour of knowing and loving the greatest dog-cat to have ever lived.

The Cat

by Bankimchandra Chattopadhyay
Translated by Arunava Sinha

I sat dozing on the cot in the bedroom, holding my hookah. A dim light shone faintly—shadows danced on the wall like ghosts. The repast for the night was not prepared yet, and so I wondered with my eyes shut and the hookah in my grasp whether I could have been victorious in the Battle of Waterloo had I been Napoleon. Suddenly, a small sound. 'Miaow.'

I looked around, but failed to identify its source. My first thought was that the Duke of Wellington had acquired felinehood and appeared before me to beg for opium. My instinct was to be as hard-hearted as a rock and inform the duke that he had been rewarded adequately in the past and could not expect a bonus. Unlimited greed was not desirable. 'Miaow,' said the duke.

Opening my eyes properly, I discovered it was not the duke but a tiny cat who had drained the bowl of milk Proshonno had deposited for my consumption. Busy as I was configuring my forces in the fields of Waterloo, I had not been attentive. And now this beauty among cats, in a bid to convey to the world the satisfaction reigning in her heart at having drunk unboiled milk, was saying in the sweetest of tones, 'Miaow.' I cannot say, but perhaps there was a taunt in it; possibly the feline was laughing to herself and saying in her head, 'Some die fishing, some eat the fish.' Maybe there was an attempt to fathom my own state of mind in that 'miaow'. It was possible that the cat wished to ask, 'What do you have to say now that I have drunk your milk?' What did I have to say? I could not determine this. The milk was not my ancestral property. It had come from Mongola, who had been milked by Proshonno. Therefore the cat had the same right to the milk as I, I could not possibly be angry. But there is a time-honoured tradition of bodily assaulting a cat who has drunk up the milk and evicting them from the premises. I had no wish to ignore this abiding custom and be considered a disgrace amongst humans. For all I knew the feline might go back to her tribe and mock Kamalakanta as a coward. Therefore it was best to behave as men do. Having arrived at this conclusion, I lowered my hookah with great determination, located a broken stick after diligent investigation, and proudly pursued the cat.

The feline knew Kamalakanta well, and showed no symptoms of fear on viewing the stick. She only looked at me, yawned, and shifted, saying, 'Miaow.' Interpreting the question correctly, I abandoned the stick, resumed my seat on the cot with my hookah, and, acquiring an all-hearing ear, deciphered the feline's statement.

I realized she was saying, 'Why this attempt at physical assault? Sit down calmly with your hookah and apply your judgment. Why is it that your kind will consume all the milk and cream and curd and fish and flesh in this world while we get nothing? You are humans, we are cats; what is the difference? You experience hunger and thirst, do we not? You may eat, we have no objection, but all my enquiries have not led me to any scriptures which insist that you pursue us with the intention of beating us up whenever you find us eating food meant for you. It is time your race accepted some advice from me. If you wish to enhance your knowledge, I see no alternative to being educated by learned quadrupeds. Your educational institutions make me surmise you have finally become aware of this truth.

'Hark, o supine human. What does it mean to be religious? Altruism is the true religion. Drinking this milk has benefited me greatly. This act of philanthropy on your part was accomplished by virtue of the milk that you had acquired, hence you shall bear the fruits of this religious act. Whether I have indulged in theft or not, I am the primary reason for your bank of piety. Do not persecute me, therefore, but praise me. I am the prop to your religiousness.

'It is true I am a thief, but do you think I chose to be one? Who resorts to stealing if food is available? Listen to me, those renowned holy men who tremble at even the sound of the word "theft" are in truth even more unholy than thieves. The only reason they do not steal is that they have no need to. But because they do not cast a sympathetic glance towards the thief despite being in possession of more wealth than they can make use of, the thief is compelled to steal. The sin is not the thief's, it is the parsimonious wealthy man's. The thief may be guilty, but the miserly rich is a hundred times guiltier. The thief is punished, but the root cause of his crime, the penny-pinching wealthy man, goes scot-free.

'Look at me. I skulk on walls, mewling, but no one deigns to throw out even a fishbone for me. They will toss the remnants of the fish and the uneaten rice into the drain, but will not leave it out for me. Your kind eats your fill, what do you know of my hunger? Will you be robbed of your glory if you feel compassion for the poverty-stricken? No doubt it is a matter of shame to be agonised by the pain of a poor creature like me. Even a man who has never offered alms to the blind can be a king. He spends sleepless nights when in trouble, and you are willing to be pained by his suffering. But sympathy for the lowlife? For shame, who will feel such a thing?

'If a renowned scholar or learned man were to have drunk this milk, would you have chased him with a stick? Au contraire, you would have bowed to him in reverence and enquired if he would like some more. Why the stick when it comes to me? You will say, they are respected individuals, great pundits. Does that make them more ravenous than me? That is not the case, but no one amongst you who offer additional butter to the well-oiled rich will ever know suffering and poverty. Banquets are arranged for those who are irked when offered meals, but those who eat your food uninvited are pronounced thieves and sentenced. For shame!

'Look at our condition, mewling about on walls, in yards, outside mansions, casting our eyes in every direction, and still no one throws even a morsel to us. Only if one of us can become the object of your love and live as a housecat—the sister of a young wife of an aged husband or a substitute for a foolish rich man's chess partner—can she expect nutrition. She will have a fluffy tail and luxuriant fur, and the brilliance of her beauty will turn many a feline into a poet.

'But look at us. Our bellies are sunken for lack of food, our ribs are visible, our tails are lowered, out teeth are exposed, our tongues hang out, we constantly wail, "Miaow, miaow, we have not eaten." Do not hate us for our dark skins. We too have some rights to fish and flesh in this world. If you do not give us food, we shall steal. Do you not feel any sympathy for our blackened skins, our withered faces, our faint and pathetic mewling? Thieves are punished, why does cruelty escape punishment? The poor are castigated for collecting food, why are the rich not punished for refusing them food? You, Kamalakanta, are far-sighted, for you are an opium-addict—can you not see that it is the wealthy who are responsible for turning the impoverished into thieves? Why should a single person deprive five hundred souls and hoard the food they could have eaten? And if he does, why will he not give what is left over to the poor? If he does not, the poor will certainly steal from him. For no one has been born on earth to die of starvation.'

I could tolerate this no longer. 'Stop, feline pundit. What you are saying is socialism. The root of chaos in society. If an individual can amass as much wealth as he is capable of amassing, and if he cannot enjoy this wealth with complete immunity from thievery, no one will engage themselves in amassing wealth anymore. Thus society will not see its wealth grow.'

'What do I care if it does not?' said the cat. 'The growth of society's wealth amounts to the growth of rich men's wealth. How will the poor suffer if the wealthy do not become wealthier?'

'Society cannot improve unless its collective wealth increases,' I explained to the cat. Angrily, she said, 'What do I care about the improvement of society if I do not have enough to eat?'

It proved difficult to convince the cat. No judge or logician can ever be convinced of anything. This feline was a wise judge and a fine debater as well, therefore she had the right not to be convinced. And so, instead of growing enraged with her, I said, 'The poor may not be important for improvement in society, but the wealthy certainly are, therefore thieves must be punished.'

Mistress cat said, 'Hang the thief by all means, I have no objection, but institute another law. The judge who sentences the thief must fast for three days before that. If he feels no desire to steal food in this period, he may award the death sentence without hesitation. You had brought out your stick to thrash me, you can try fasting for three days. If in that time you are not caught red-handed in the larder, you may beat me to a pulp, I shall not come in your way.'

Learned people are in the habit of dispensing advice when they are defeated in debate. Following this tradition, I told the feline, 'This is unethical talk, even thinking in this manner is sinful. Abandon these anxieties and concentrate on piety. I can send you Newman & Parker's book if you wish to peruse it. Reading *The Kamalakanta Papers* may be of benefit too—if not anything else, you will realise the value of opium. It is time to for you to return to your own residence now. Proshonno has promised some delicious milk cake tomorrow, if you are here at the right time, we shall share it. Do not steal food from anyone else today; if you are overcome by hunger, come back to me, I shall give you some opium.'

'I have no particular requirement for opium, but as for stealing food elsewhere, that will depend on the extent of my hunger.'

From *Kamalakanter Doptor*, Bankimchandra Chatterjee, published in 1875.

199

Cheeni

by Meera Ganapathi

Apparently Hitler feared cats. He was an ailurophobe, that's what they're called, these people who fear cats. Napoleon and Gengis Khan are a few other suspected ailurophobes. A pattern of cruel dictators who loathe cute, furry animals sounds too convenient. But if it were true and dictators do hate cats, how did Daadi like them so much?

Haha. Hahahaha.

You don't mock the dead. I know, I know. But how did I get stuck with her cat? Why aren't you here?

Remember how Daadi hid stuff under her pillow? Actually, I'm not sure if she hid her things or just kept them there for easy access. But with her, who could tell? I made a list of the stuff she kept under there. I'm sharing it with you for a reason, I'll tell you at the end of this mail.

Stuff she kept under her pillow:
1: Glasses
2: Pills
3: Les Misérables. (Remember the way she said 'Jeen Val Jeen'?)
4: Hairbands
5: Mobile phone
6: Sunday's newspaper supplement

7: Chocolate wrappers, always empty
8: Kibble
9: Daadaji's gold ring
10: Good Knight mosquito mats
11: Phone charger

The pillow should've been lumpy and uncomfortable, but she always slept well, didn't she? Daadi shoved all that was awkward and painful right where everyone could see it and feel it, but somehow none of it affected *her*.

So, last night was Cheeni's second night here. I was surprised at that name, I would've expected Daadi to call her cat something pompous, like Cleopatra. Besides, this one looks like anything but a Cheeni. Far from being sweet, she's a rough-edged street cat with a dull black coat, thinning in patches, and unblinking yellow eyes. She lies under the couch all day, ignoring me, which suits me just fine. She only moves when it's time to be fed. I know this because she makes a sound that's strangely similar to a little child. It's a disturbing sound. The first time I heard it, it sent a chill up my spine and I instinctively looked out of the window for a distressed child. But it was just her, right behind me, with her odd mew. I can't stand it.

She's all black, so I guess no one wanted her. Which is why, I'm stuck with her.

Anyway, last night I was fast asleep when I felt a crushing weight on me. Like a large football had been thrown at my chest, hard and fast, to knock the wind out of me.

I woke up to find a pair of yellow eyes peering at my face. I threw the cat off me in shock, and she's been hiding ever since. I'm cool with that too. She is clearly a moody, oversensitive cat.

Now who does that remind you of? (Don't say me.)

But while I was annoyed by her strange behaviour, I was also surprised at her sudden desire to be close.

Now I realise she was looking for her kibble under the pillow! This is how Daadi made Cheeni love her—a bribe, under the pillow. Are you surprised? I'm fixing the puzzle of Daadi through this Cheeni.

Hey. Listen. What do I do?

Daadi's lawyer called me again. She left me nothing. I know that much, because after she died, they called me solely to inform me that I had to take the cat. Yes, I asked about the house, even the old Morris, even her embroidered hankies. But they said, no, she's left you the cat.

Besides, there was that incident from '94. Of course, we were just children then, but it confirms that I will have no financial gain from this proposed meeting with her lawyers.

You won't remember the incident, but it's important so let me tell you.

When Pappa was around, we still went to the big house nearly every summer—miserable time for all of us, even him if you recall. You were too tiny to play then so I took to wandering around the house by myself, absorbed in all its interesting nooks and crannies. I loved the old room behind the kitchen, the one with the giant wood burner for heating water, I often sat there by myself, reading. And the store room, where I told you I once found snakeskin (that was a lie, by the way). But none of these places seemed half as interesting as her room.

She was secretive even then. She never let us into her bedroom, remember? We had to ask for her permission before entering. 'Knock twice and say excuse me,' she'd say. And if we ever happened to walk in abruptly, she'd shut her almirah really quick. Naturally, I was desperate to investigate her room, especially that *almirah*.

One afternoon, she'd taken Pappa to meet 'family'; of course, we weren't allowed. No one was home. I can't remember where you were. So, I took a chance and walked up to her room to look around. It seemed almost unbelievable but, in her hurry to leave Daadi had left her *almirah* door slightly ajar.

I ignored the rest of the room and went straight to the *almirah*. I opened it wider very, very softly, afraid, so afraid of even a single creak! We were terrified of her then, she didn't even have to be in the room but we anticipated her every reaction, didn't we? But no fear could stop me from trying to understand her. So, I stuck my head in and jostled with her silks, I still remember the scent of her perfume mingling with a dizzying scent of naphthalene as I looked for the secrets she hid, until I hit gold! She had a will.

I was around twelve then, so I knew what wills were. But now when I look back, it was an absolutely idiotic will. And she was perfectly healthy back then, so why did she even have one?

She had scrawled the will on a piece of lined notebook paper that seemed to have been torn hastily, its edges were rough and uneven. Both the torn paper and her unwieldy handwriting seemed to suggest something sinister, as if she feared for their life. If she HAD dropped dead then, it would've looked like she'd grabbed whatever she could find and wrote her desperate appeals on it. It had that hurried quality of a person asking for help.

Despite that, her language was impeccable. You know she always wrote like a proper lady. I can't remember the exact words she used, but I remember the tone of her writing being formal and severe.

Here's a gist of what I remember of the will:

To Whom It May Concern:

I, Mrs Aparna Tyagi, of sound mind and body, desire to leave my home and possessions, in case of my untimely death, in the hands of my surviving son, Mithun Tyagi, and no other family members. Upon his death, my home and possessions may be sold and the money from the sale distributed amongst the priests at our family temple in Vakil Street, Ashok Nagar, UP. I would further like to commission a bench to the temple with the words, 'Donated by Mrs Tyagi and family' to be inscribed on it.

'And no other family members.' She was pretty clear.

I should've got nothing but she stuck me with her cat. So why do these lawyers want to meet me I wonder? Is it even legal to pass on the responsibility of a pet? I doubt it.

Meanwhile, Cheeni has stopped that awful mewing. I think she missed Daadi and was pining for her.

Last evening, I was watching TV in the hall when I saw her leap onto the window sill and look out intently. She then poised herself for a jump, all set to leave the house. I was quick to shut the window but I can't be sure if she was a just house cat or she went out sometimes.

I know I shouldn't be bothered, and perhaps it would be great for me if she left. But everyone here knows Cheeni belongs to me. A black cat tends to attract attention.

My neighbour won't stop telling me she's bad luck.

You won't believe this!

The lawyers gave me a letter from Daadi. It's so much like her weird will.
We've never received any written correspondence from Daadi, have we?

Obviously, I'm delighted. Not because it's a heartwarming letter (imagine
that!). But I need a laugh. And this letter is very promising. A wonderful dis-
tillation of the finest personality traits of our beloved grandmother in a letter
addressed to—me! Not 'to whom it may concern' but me!

To Zahra,

Allow me to begin by thanking you for accepting the responsibility of my beloved
Cheeni. I have had no regrets about leaving this world, but my only worry has been
Cheeni. She deserves a loving home as she has been my only companion in the dusk
of my years.

And whose fault is that, now?

And a good companion too—a title that cannot be deferred on many.

Aha! First zing.

Cheeni came to me on a cold, winter afternoon in November five years ago. She
was hobbling in pain, outside our gate, mewing piteously and calling out to us, to
anyone. My maid, Sheelu, insisted on taking her in. I must admit that I was not for it,
back then.

Why would you be? You didn't take in your own grandchildren.

But Sheelu has these superstitions that the lower-classes often do and I indulged her. We cared for Cheeni who had injured her paw, broken a tooth, was running a fever and was heavily pregnant to boot! Love, attention and a healthy diet restored Cheeni's health and by the time she gave birth to her four kittens she was a robust cat, missing nothing but a tooth. The litter was soon dispensed with, as I could not tolerate the constant fighting and smells, but Cheeni, I allowed, I had gotten fond of her ways. She was so like me.

She takes time to warm up to people. But you know that about me, don't you Zahra? I take my time, but eventually I do relent. And then, the very special ones are let into my world. Cheeni does not take to everyone either, but whoever she loves, she does so almost illogically. I urge you not be sharp with her, as she is a sensitive cat.

Sheelu may have told you about her food preferences, the timings, the portions and such. But she may not be privy to the secrets Cheeni and I shared as friends. What is not a secret is that Cheeni is a flirt and a group of pining toms would routinely hang around my house in shifts. She gets pregnant far too often and I find myself unable to restrict her brood from becoming an army.

There are five here now, as you may know. But I care for none of them except Cheeni, she reminds me of myself.

Of course…

Now for the secrets.

Cheeni does not like most men. She snarls and hisses at any man that enters my home. I can empathise, historically, men, be they husbands or sons, have always let me down.

Ugh…

Cheeni likes to sleep by my bedside, she might sleep by yours too, one day.

If I bribe her, sure.

Cheeni does not drink milk. It's not very good for cats anyway, so I would request you to not bother with milk.

Cheeni is bound to disappear for weeks at a time if she finds new love. Allow her. I did not allow my children many things, but by Cheeni I did right.

For some reason, this, finally this… infuriates me. And I had only wanted to laugh. I can't add the whole letter here, because it goes on for four long pages about Cheeni's minutest details and I can't help but feel cheated. Even now.

You would've been so much better at this Resham.

I suppose it's a gift but I can't be sure.

There's a dead cockroach outside my door.

The dead cockroach was not a gift. It was just a dead roach. When the pest control people came by to take stock of the situation today, I realised Daadi's man-hating theory was correct. Cheeni took one look at the poor man who entered my door, hissed at him with all her strength, and fled!

It was almost comical. Like a weak, half-hearted defense raised by a losing army. The last display of courage before running away with one's tail between one's legs.

I wonder what will happen when I bring a guy home? If I bring a guy home....

Cheeni *is* strangely like Daadi, Resham.

She does not acknowledge my presence. And yet, she expects my subservience.

I forgot to feed her one night and the next morning I woke up to a terrible scent in the air, like sulphur and rotten eggs. I traced the scent to the living room only to find a dark, damp circle in the middle of my *divan*. She had peed to punish me.

When Daadi was diagnosed with cancer, I was surprised she called me. Later, I realised that she had no one else to tell. But if a person has never bothered to share their joys, why must they burden you with their sorrows?

I want to find the strength to give away this cat, where she won't remind me of the uncertainty of our childhood, of Ammi's sickness, of Pappa being broken... and of you not being around to take Cheeni away from me.

I suppose the cat is my only family now, an inheritance I did not want but the only one I have. Which is why, I struggle to sever ties.

My therapist told me I should stop writing to you, it's unhealthy apparently. I disagreed.

I said, 'Look! It's almost like therapy. I write down my thoughts like I'm speaking to her and it gives me clarity about my own behaviour. It helped me understand just why I can't seem to get rid of the damn cat!'

My therapist said, 'Zahra. These are all signs of you refusing to let go.'

She's right. But I miss you, and it hasn't been that long since you've been gone.

Let me tell you about something funny instead.

I was feeling generous one evening and decided to buy Cheeni a cat tree. It's one of those contraptions with varying levels where a cat can jump from one platform to the other, much like an actual tree. I reasoned that a cat used to a big house, would probably be unhappy within a 2 bhk like mine.

The delivery arrived last night and I fixed all its bits and presented it to her, by leaving it beside her spot near the couch. She didn't even sniff the thing. Instead, she crept into the empty delivery box and made her home there. She and the cardboard box have been inseparable ever since.

I have thrown out the tree.

Yesterday was your birthday and I missed you so much that I went out and had a few drinks with him. I just...I wanted to take my mind off things. Besides, he used to know you too.

When the pub closed, he wanted to come over and continue drinking. I agreed, I wanted him to come over too.

A mistake which was immediately brought to my notice by Cheeni who spat at him! She hissed and spat. I was sure she'd run and hide like she had earlier, but she would not relent. He bent down to pacify her and she nearly

leapt at his face. He refused to come in after that.

I can't tell you how glad I am this morning.

Cheeni has a boyfriend.

I haven't written to you in so long, I know. Maybe this is a good thing? I'm sorry, I feel guilty for telling you that.

Work has begun in earnest, so I've been quite busy. And, the other day, I kind of met someone nice.

But I will never know until I bring him home to Cheeni, will I?

Speaking of Cheeni, I'm considering getting her neutered. The neighbourhood has begun to complain about the sounds of horny tomcats that gather around outside my apartment whenever she's in heat. The din, the sexual tension in the air…it's all very overwhelming. And because I'm on the ground floor, it's even harder to ignore.

I feel sad to have to deprive her of what nature has clearly blessed her with —an abundance of charm. But it must be done or I will go insane. Or worse, I will be asked to leave the apartment.

Last night I couldn't help but think how ridiculous it is that Daadi compared herself to Cheeni!

If Cheeni is like anyone, she's like you, Resham. She's easy to like and quick to forgive. If I'm not careful, I might also write a lengthy letter about her one day; four pages long, and brimming with madness, addressed to my embittered granddaughter.

Got her neutered. Got him home.

There's a connection between the two sentences. She did not spit at him.

Does this make him a good man?

Or has she lost some of her spark?

I'm sorry Resham, but my jaded heart tells me it can only be the latter. Still, I have decided to give most things in my life more of a chance.

He is kind to me. And he's nothing like *him*. He and I haven't spoken since that incident with Cheeni.

Cheeni allows this one to pet her. Something that he taught me to do as well.

'Scratch her behind her ears, cats like it,' he said.

'Your grandma sounds like a prejudiced old bat,' he said.

I can't help but like him. He also has the kind of nose we both admire, proud and sharp. I also like his Adam's apple, it bobs when he talks.

No kibble under my pillow, and yet Cheeni sleeps next to me.

I don't like to overdo the affection, I don't want to invest too much in anyone, anything. But her presence in my bed is comforting. I allow myself a little warmth, how else will I go on?

It is your anniversary today, the bad anniversary, the one that should be mourned, not celebrated, not yet. He's not been in town for a few days, maybe I don't even want him here. I don't know Resham, this day, I have only felt it twice before, and I don't know how deal with it. Not yet.

It's been two years since you left, six months since Daadi died.

It's easy to use the word 'death' with people you don't care about. But with the ones you cherish, it's less painful when you make their departure sound casual. They haven't died; they've simply 'passed', 'left', 'gone'.

The other day, I heard my neighbour's house-help describe the death of her mother in the unforgiving language of Bombay, 'meri mummy off ho gayi'—my mother went off—like a light. Also, a sort of casualness, I suppose.

Cheeni was there when Daadi died. I was around when you passed. We've both seen death up close, but I'm not sure how cats interpret it. Still, I heard Cheeni mourn Daadi in her childlike lament, that awful sound of a lost child. I find it funny sometimes that Daadi of all people found it in her to love a black cat. Don't superstitious Hindus fear black cats? Not any more than they hate Muslims I suppose. Maybe Pappa should've learnt from Sheelu about how to persuade an old bigot into accepting her Muslim daughter-in-law and grandchildren. But I don't want to dwell on that anymore. My preoccupation now is only with letting go.

But I still hold onto you in this pathetic string of emails you will never read. Cheeni however, has moved on. In fact, on the fourth day she stopped looking for kibble under my pillow. In two months, she began to greet me at the door. These days, she sleeps next to me, and just like that Daadi is forgotten, by both of us.

I no longer think of her when I see Cheeni. I only see a cat I have grown to like.

The Secret Life of Cats

by Ipsa Samaddar

Before there were people on Ramlal Bazar Road, there were cats. Or at least, that's what my mother tells me. When her father bought some land in this locality in the 1970s, the street could hardly be called a street because of the abundance of wilderness all around. Gradually, more and more people started to move in and build houses until that ratio was reversed. But the cats have always been here. So have the dogs, but they don't claim ownership of the street with nearly as much nonchalance as the cats do. The dogs might sit by your feet at the market and then follow you home, hoping for a kind treat. If you befriend them, they'll visit you every day at the tiny chai shops or your backyard for a meal and some head pats. But the cats have expanded their territories far beyond this.

It seems to me that when humans decided to colonise the street with their concrete and their dour faces, the cats simply decided to treat the houses as their own territory. So you will find several cats sunning themselves on mossy awnings and verandas if you take a walk down the street. Some of them spend their day chasing one another through neatly planned gardens, leaving a trail of mud behind. If you peek into a house at mealtimes, you will find a cat or two sitting around several pairs of feet, gazing at everyone with round, pleading eyes. Some cats have even found their way onto sofas and beds, or sought out strange spots like the narrow gap between two closets.

In short, the street belongs to the cats as much as it does to anyone else. They maintain a fine balance between being pets and frequenting each nook of the neighbourhood. We wake up and fall asleep to the sounds of their activities. A pair of cats quarreling in high-pitched howls often serves as an effective alarm clock. Throughout the day, you can hear them leaping from awnings to asbestos roofs and rolling around in grass so that homes turn into mini-Parkour courses. In the mating season, as you prepare to go to bed, cats traipse around the street yowling mournfully for their lovers, who might be peacefully curling up to sleep right next to you. If you happen to stay up, you will hear this all night and begin to feel like you've unintentionally walked onto the set of a *Romeo and Juliet* production. Just as the cats have grown accustomed to the myriad lives humans follow, we too have had glimpses of what their lives might be like. We manage to keep track of which cat is dating whom. My mother can even tell if a cat has descended from one of the majestic creatures of her childhood.

Her knowledge comes from having grown up with a cat in her twenties. Named Kichi, the cat holds pride of place among other deceased family members in a yellowing framed photograph. And a family member she certainly was. My grandfather would buy fish exclusively for her from the market, and bandage her wounds after she'd fought with some other neighbourhood cat. Kichi would express gratitude by running around the house in delight when someone returned home from work. However, it was my mother who glimpsed sides to her that others in the family hadn't. Once, Kichi sat by my mother all day when she was sick and confined to bed. It was my mother that Kichi had frantically called when she gave birth to a stillborn kitten. Somewhere along the way, my mother had begun to intuitively understand Kichi's inner life.

Since then, our house has seen a never-ending series of new members who came for one meal and decided to stay. But sadly, never for too long. Some would just leave one day and never return. For the others, we would regularly wake to terrible news. So, my mother told me, 'Beshi maya e jorash na.' Don't get too attached to them, because you'll inevitably outlive them. That's what she'd trained herself to do since Kichi had passed. I tried on

215

this stoic armour as I went about feeding the cats who visited us. And every little kitten I'd watched growing up before my eyes and gamboling about our garden eventually left us. I thought of them as passersby who wanted some love and care before they went on their way. Until, of course, a particular cat came along.

I was walking to our backyard one afternoon to give some chicken bones to a black cat—the current resident of our inn—when I found two furry kittens cowering behind her. Their mother was probably trying to wean them off, but they were all tensed up, fear etched across their green-blue eyes. I gently left the bones on the ground so as to not scare them, and watched from a distance. They had beautiful fur—white with brown and black patches on their backs, heads and tails. Very slowly, they sniffed at the food and began nibbling at it.

Over time, as the kittens began to grow up, they came back every now and then. Soon, one of them chose another house as its permanent residence. The sister then started visiting us every day, sniffing curiously around the house and our ankles, and rubbing her head against them when she wanted food. Very soon, she began waiting for my mother and I to return home from school or work. It was rather delightful to come home after a long day and find a little ball of fur sitting patiently on the doormat with her paws tucked in. My mother remarked that she'd begun to behave like Kichi.

And she lived up to that reputation. When I was studying for my board exams, she'd climb upstairs to sleep in my room every morning. Maybe she was just curious, but her presence in the room would gradually pull me away from my freefall to anxiety. As we got used to her seeking out new places to sleep in the house, we decided to name her. I chose the name Magan-lal Meowrani (Meow for short), based on one of her sitting postures; she'd look exactly like Maganlal Meghraj from *Joy Baba Felunath* reclining upon his pillows. Meowrani was my mother's addition. She decided that Meow's pickiness about food, and her habit of frequently grooming herself, was royal behaviour. (Yes alright, it's a fancy name, but so is Choupette and Shanti Om bb, okay!)

Much like a queen, Meow was adept at balancing her private life with us and the long queue of cats outside who kept trying to court her. Soon enough, she was being followed by small kittens of her own, as she acquainted them with the world, her chest puffed out in pride. There was a level of familiarity we'd established by naming her, and it deepened when we saw her nursing her children, looking utterly at peace with the world. But then she started losing her kittens.

We could tell when a cat was expressing affection or asking for food. But how does a cat express grief? How do cats deal with death? For some reason, not one of her kittens made it past a few months. Sometimes it was a car, sometimes it was dogs. Meow would mostly seem confused by their absence for the next few days, purring around the house and waiting for a reply. My mother would pet and scratch her for a long time to comfort her, as she'd done with Kichi, but we'd never know if it was helpful enough. When I realised that a horrid pattern was repeating itself, I tried to distance myself emotionally again; more so, because I'd be leaving for college soon.

But no matter where you go, when you return to Ramlal Bazar Road, you always return to its cats too. As the world shut down in March 2020 to counter the coronavirus, I returned home from college and desperately tried to navigate Zoom University and a spate of assignments. In the face of all the changes around the world, it was the cats who restored some normalcy to the street, going blissfully about their lives as if nothing had happened. Meow, too, resumed her usual post in my room, quite delighted by my return. But the uncertainty of this time has bled into everyone's lives, and it wouldn't be long until it bled into ours too.

When I came downstairs for breakfast one morning after an online class, Meow immediately began circling around my ankles and beckoning me towards the back door. Thinking that she must be hungry, I followed her with some biscuits in my hand. But instead of leading me to her meal bowl, she took me around the house to the garden. She came to a stop before a patch of turmeric plants and stood staring at me. I stared back at her and looked around the garden, completely clueless. Then I noticed that Meow's stomach looked a bit sunken, and realisation dawned on me. Fearing the worst, I peeked around the aloe vera plants, and there it was, hidden beneath a turmeric leaf. The kitten was so thin and black that I could hardly tell her apart from the mud. Meow walked over to it, purring softly, and began licking it. But it was no use. I tried to call Meow to follow me back into the house, but she refused to leave the kitten's side, licking its tiny body over and over again. I gently patted her head and then I couldn't watch any longer.

Meow didn't turn up for lunch. I returned to my classes and nearly forgot about the morning's events. When I finally turned away from my laptop after 4.30 in the afternoon, I suddenly heard mewling. Meow had forced her head around the veranda door and was asking to be let in. As soon as I opened the door and crouched to greet her, she hurried in and rubbed her head against my knee. Then she remained standing that way, eyes closed and mouth open in a soundless whimper. It was the first time she'd come and asked for comfort. I petted her slowly and carefully and tried to get her to sleep, but she only lay on the floor with her eyes half open. My mother came and held her close after she found out the news, but Meow wouldn't move. I tried to read her face; it wasn't unlike those of people in several press photos on my news feed.

After we coaxed her to have some dinner, Meow followed us upstairs, rather than going out to roam with other cats. She curled up quietly on the chair by our bed, watching us prepare to sleep. While my mother and I were ready to tuck ourselves in, Meow simply stared at us. I tossed and turned for long before I fell asleep. Suddenly, I thought I heard someone calling me in my sleep and sat up with a startled, 'Yes??' It was Meow standing next to the bed and yowling loudly. As soon as I got out, she started circling my feet frantically, a wild expression in her eyes. Rather bewildered, I thought she needed to visit the bathroom or eat, and walked downstairs, intending to let her out. But she simply turned away from the open door and started following me.

Finally, it hit me. I crouched and petted her and she began to calm down, so I held her close until I began to feel sleepy. But no sooner than I'd stood up did she start following me again, winding herself round and round my legs so I could barely walk. Over an hour, I stopped to pet her again and again because she got agitated the second I moved away. When I finally tried to climb into bed, she grabbed my leg with both paws and looked up at me with watery green eyes, whimpering in protest. I could feel her despair and restlessness seeping into my body, but I couldn't understand what to do with it. A sick feeling crept into my chest and I woke up my mother for help. She managed to distract Meow as I finally got into bed. I was feeling nauseous like I'd never felt before. My hands and feet tingled and I felt like I'd begin to moult like Gregor Samsa. When I finally drifted off, I dreamt of all the cats who'd died in the house sitting on a branch of our bel tree, their fur translucent, and their eyes burning into mine. When I woke up with a start, I discovered that Meow had been sleeping right next to my head.

I could barely focus on work the day after, still unnerved from the previous night. Meow came upstairs that night too, still in bad shape. I stayed up to finish some ridiculously dense reading while my mother went to sleep. At 3 am, I gave up trying to understand Lacan and shut my laptop. Meow immediately jumped off her chair. I knew what was coming, but in no way was I equipped to deal with it. She seemed doubly frantic this time, staring at my face questioningly like I held all the answers to something. But all I could do was pet her until I grew too tired to keep my eyes open. I tried to climb into bed, but in vain. Meow began to whimper desperately, clinging to my legs. Suddenly, I felt everything inside me hit some kind of wall, and I sat on the edge of the bed and broke down. Maybe some stress from the workload and the newsfeed had fuelled the tears, but I was feeling utterly helpless. 'Is this grief?' I wondered. This must be what Meow was expressing, and what I always turned away from. It was so incomprehensible and frightening that it felt violent. I'd never felt so close, and yet so far, from Meow.

She came up to me, still whimpering, and I cradled her head. She calmed down immediately and sat staring into my tear-streaked face. She still seemed exhausted and despairing, but she was gazing at me with utter relief (although I'm sure I was looking rather red-nosed and disconcerting). And that was all she was asking of me. To calm her down, to stay beside her and give her love and warmth because she was badly shaken. It was something all my friends had been asking of each other over WhatsApp, it was what had been floating desolately around Twitter, what was echoing from almost every video of patients and healthworkers. I had been trying to think of some complex solution, when the answer was all around me. I began to realise that shielding myself from grief was never going to make it easy to face. So I let her climb onto the bed and sleep next to my head. It took her several restless nights before she could resume her stately demeanour. But she often came back to sleep by my head afterwards.

It is winter now; several months have passed since Meow's loss, and the onset of the virus too. Nothing seems to have changed on my street. Of course,

I've been lucky enough to not have to leave it. The cacophony of animals still moves our clocks from day to night. But that only seems to be the surface of things. What the world has seen this year can be termed nothing short of extraordinary, and perhaps there is much of that extraordinariness in the cacophony I'd assumed as normal. I still feel sick when I remember the force of the emotions I'd encountered that night. But now, when a cat, or any animal, stops by our house for food, I try to make sure I feed them and send them on their way with a head-pat. Meow, of course, is still around. She often climbs upstairs to the veranda to bask in the wispy sunrays of winter mornings. Sometimes, when I start feeling overwhelmed by everything around me, I go and sit beside her, and we quietly enjoy the winter sun warming our faces. And amidst the chaos of our times, it feels more than enough.

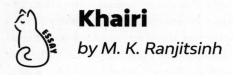

Khairi
by M. K. Ranjitsinh

The Tiger Project had been initiated in 1972, and the Task Force of which I was a Member Secretary had selected Simlipal as one of the first nine Tiger Reserves of the country. My friend and colleague, Saroj Raj Choudhury, a most dedicated conservationist and the head of the newly started wildlife training faculty in the Forest Research Institute of Dehra Dun, volunteered to become its first Field Director. Thereafter, Saroj chose to make the village of Joshipur, which was within the Tiger Reserve, his headquarters, unlike other Field Directors who chose their headquarters in faraway towns and cities.

One day, tribals seeking forest-produce close to the Khairi stream in Simlipal, found an abandoned female tiger-cub and brought it to Saroj. He named her Khairi. Khairi is the name of a rivulet in the Meghasini massif in the Simlipal Tiger Reserve, in northern Odisha. Quickly she became a part of his family in the Joshipur Forest Rest House.

A few weeks later, local tribals brought to Joshipur a male fawn chousingha or four-horned antelope, the only animal in the world with four hard horns, one which has evolved in India and is endemic to it. Khairi and the chousingha soon became inseparable, fast friends. They would eat, play and sleep together, their bodies touching one another. The fawn would initiate play, jumping up suddenly and racing away, whereupon Khairi would pursue it, bowl it over, hold it gently in her jaws or paws and the two would roll over and play.

In three years, the antelope grew to about 15 kg in weight; Khairi, in comparison, to about 150 kg. One day, as they laid side by side, the antelope took off in play all of a sudden, as usual. Khairi grabbed it as she must have done scores of times before. But this time she broke the neck of her friend. Carnivores often do not realise their own strength as they grow in power, as don't pugilists!

Saroj was furious. He whipped Khairi with a cane. She took the beating quietly, with her face averted, and when he buried the antelope, Khairi sat beside the grave for three days, ignoring her food and not even drinking water for a day.

During this time, I had moved to the Regional Office of the United Nations Environment Programme (UNEP) at Bangkok, as a Senior Regional Advisor in Nature Conservation for the Asia and the Pacific Region. In 1976, the International Union for the Conservation of Nature (IUCN) and the World Wildlife Fund (WWF) International, which had donated a million dollars to Project Tiger in India, wanted an appraisal of the Project. A three-member appraisal committee was constituted, with me as the third and only Indian member. I was assigned five of the fifteen Tiger Reserves, Simlipal being one of them. I went to Joshipur and stayed with Saroj Raj Choudhury.

It was love at first sight. Khairi strode up and stood a few paces away, rock still, ears afore, mouth shut, her piercing amber eyes fixed on mine, sizing me up. Then the ice broke. A couple of quick steps forward, and raising herself slightly on her hind legs, she gently clasped my mid-riff with both her forearms and paws and closed her jaws on my forearm, firmly, but without exerting pressure, all the while careful not to put weight on me, which would have toppled me over.

She would not leave me, following me to my room and elsewhere, but ever so dignified, without being over-effusive or intrusive, as dogs are so often wont to do. Saroj said Khairi had not taken such a fancy to any of his previous guests. Perhaps Khairi, with her extrasensory perception, realised that I was in greater love of her than she of me!

During my entire four-day stay in Joshipur, Khairi was constantly looking for play, hugging and embracing me, and clasping my hands in her jaws ever so gently. She would never unsheathe her claws, but tigers—indeed, no cats I believe—have adequate control over their dew claws, the fifth one a little higher up the foreleg. Whenever Khairi hugged me or gently slapped me with her paws, her dew claws would tear my clothes and scratch my skin and sometimes cause bleeding.

Simlipal was then riddled with the problem of poaching, including what was called 'Akhand Shikar', where tribals would systematically set fire to all the forests in rotation, snaring the terrified, escaping animals, or killing them with bows and arrows. Hardly any large animal was visible by day, so Saroj would drive me around in the park till the wee hours of the morning, to show me and prove that wild animals did exist in his beloved Reserve.

At daybreak, when I'd barely had a short nap, Khairi would enter my room. Not wanting to offend her and cause her to bang against the door, I would not latch it. She would circle around my bed, slowly purring, wanting me to wake up. I would feign sleep. Soon she would blithely jump upon the foot of my bed and, careful not to tread upon any part of my body, she would straddle my prostrate figure and thrust her face a few inches above mine, continuing to purr gently. Opening my bleary eyes, I would meet the stare of those lovely amber eyes. But however much one loves a tiger, it is difficult to countenance the stench of their mouths, so close to one's nostrils. Then there was another factor to consider. A sudden movement in a befuddled state of mind could trigger an involuntary, instinctive, friendly grab, as happened with the luckless chousingha! If, after all these proddings, one still did not get up, Khairi would lower herself ever so gently on my body, and I would feel the pressure of her substantial weight.

Saroj, I think, fed Khairi with some indulgence and she was overweight. He tried to re-wild her and to train her to catch natural prey, especially langurs which were plentiful and mostly terrestrial around Joshipur, and the easiest wild prey to catch. It did not work. One day, she caught and ate a feral dog that had entered the premises of the Joshipur Rest House. It turned out to be a rabid dog. Khairi contracted rabies and died a miserable death.

I saw Saroj a few months after this incident. He was half the man he had been, and told me he had lost interest in life. He died shortly after.

Reference
Ranjitsinh, M.K. *A Life With Wildlife: From Princely India to the Present*, Harper Collins, 2017.

These Particular Cats

by Sonal Shah

The cat appeared soon after Delhi's yearly smog, in early November: a stocky, marmalade feline with intelligent green eyes, chatty and insistent, following us with frequent mewls into our balcony. We soon discovered that she had given birth to two kittens, who were ensconced in an upturned, unused sofa-set at the top of our building. I took to calling her Doris, after the writer Doris Lessing, whose life I was involved in researching at the time. At times, Doris-the-cat seemed more interested in conversing with us than in her kittens. Her namesake, over the course of her life, was constantly needled by interviewers about her 'decision' to leave the two young children from her first marriage in Southern Rhodesia when she finally left the colony for London, to become a writer (taking her third child, from her second—also defunct—marriage).

Additionally, Lessing was a cat person, and wrote prolifically about them in both published essays and in her diaries. She loved cats deeply, sometimes grieving more straightforwardly for them than she did for people. But she could be as incisively unsentimental about her relationships with cats as she was in describing relationships between people in most of her work.

One of the most brutal bits of writing about animals I've come across is the opening chapter of her book *Particularly Cats*, later collected with other essays in *On Cats*. During the course of sketching out life on the farm in the veld where she grew up, Lessing describes, in just a few pages, kittens being carried off by hawks, killed by snakes, running away—seduced by local wild cats, or being drowned at birth. The wild cats are routinely shot. Occasionally, domestic animals get caught in the crossfire. As a girl, Lessing mistakes Minnie, the runaway half-Persian, for a feral creature, and shoots it dead herself. She also causes her mother to shoot the side out of another beloved cat, by mistaking its tail for a cobra in a woodpile.

Lessing's mother, a former World War I nurse, desperately trying to hold on to English social status in colonial Africa, is responsible for all the 'hard work' of the cats. 'Farm work for the man; housework for the woman...' Lessing notes drily. But beyond this demarcation, her mother 'was of that part of humankind *which understands how things work*; and works with them. A grim enough role.' Unlike her father, a soldier and amputee, who passed reluctant comment on the violent necessities of nature, Lessing's mother was 'nature in her element', with no time to waste 'on sentimental philosophy'. She was 'humorous if it killed her; but resentful of course, for it was not my father who drowned the kittens, shot the snake, killed the diseased fowl, or burned sulphur in the white ant nest...'

Finally, presumably fed up, one year Lessing's mother goes 'soft-hearted and can't bear to drown a kitten'. The farm becomes infested with an exponentially multiplying clowder of increasingly inbred cats, conjuring up illustrations from that classic children's book, *Millions of Cats*. Lessing's mother pats her favourite, an old matriarch, goodbye, and leaves the family to deal with the mess.

Resigned, they attempt a 'humane' killing method involving a chloroform-soaked tampon and a biscuit tin, but eventually Lessing's father decides to round the cats up into a room, like the Romanov royal family, and shoot them with his old service revolver. After describing the massacre, Lessing remarks that while she was angered by the preventability of this 'holocaust', she had been inoculated against grief by the death of a beloved Persian cat (it fell into a tub of scalding water), a few years earlier.

As Lessing goes on to describe the cats of her adult life, it emerges that she, like her mother, understood the grim reality of *how things work*, though this knowledge did not blunt the sharp sensitivity that made her such a powerful writer. She might at times feel sad, or write movingly, about dispatching a cat to the RSPCA, but rarely did she belabour the decision. When it came to leaving her children, Lessing had less choice in the matter than perhaps people realised. Yet it was still a momentous decision to depart for England to become a writer, a feat Lessing felt she may not have been unable to accomplish while still enmeshed in the British colony's rigid arrangements of race, class, and gender.

I admire decisive people, but I am not often, in my domestic life, one of them. In December, my landlady ordered her live-in maid to cast out the upstairs kittens—not quite the '*bulala yena*' (Kill it!) that Lessing heard frequently coming from the Black workers in her childhood kitchen—but it was a cold enough winter. I tried and failed to emulate my partner, who could coo over them or feed them, even name them, while remaining emotionally unencumbered, seemingly still capable of leaving nature to its devices. I directed my helpless anger at the small claims they were making on my heart, with their tiny paws and button noses, at my partner instead, attempting to explain to him why blind disregard was the only way forward. Love, I tried to argue, was not a thing to be dispensed so frivolously; it meant duty, responsibility, and other things I hoped to keep well clear from my life for as long as possible.

A line from *The Gift of Death*, Jacques Derrida's reflection on Christian sacrifice, floated up from the murky memories of a college classroom to the surface of my mind. 'How would you ever justify the fact,' Derrida asked, 'that you sacrifice all the cats in the world to the cat that you feed at home every morning for years, whereas other cats die of hunger at every instant?

Not to mention other people?'

The French philosopher's emphasis was on how responsibility binds one to the singular other, entailing a sacrifice of universal ethics, or availability to the 'other others'. But I was thinking about the sacrifice of my untethered life, my dreams—like Lessing's—of wider skies and future freedoms. I sensed, as perhaps she did while raising an elemental resistance against everything her mother stood for, that selfishness might be an important component of freedom. Once you were locked in a relationship you had to take decisions, often messy ones. You might hold life in your hands, or possibly wield death. I thought about my own mother, who used to inject the plump, elderly cat of my childhood with two insulin shots a day. And about the ageing dog my parents had now, who required a great deal of her attention.

But do we, can we, ever really choose who we love? Subject to 'the gaze, look, request, love, command, or call of the other' as Derrida might describe it, I found myself endlessly distracted by the perpetual exploration of these two inquisitive balls of fur: a whiny tortie who stuck close to her mother's side, and an elegant ginger with a white belly who tended to venture further. There they were, chasing each other happily across the park, or crawling like commandos across a high, iron fence. There they were, sleeping in a flower pot. With no say in the decision nature had made for me, I began to take other decisions. A box in our balcony seemed better than the dubious driveway where they were taking shelter. When each of the three disappeared, one by one, returning haggard and ill after a few days, we took them to the vet for rounds of antibiotics and vaccines. When the ginger kitten got pregnant at four months—much to Doris's hissing indignation—we got all three of them spayed. Through the winter, they began taking shelter in our living room, our cupboards, even, delightfully, our bed. We graduated from setting out eggs or milk to buying cheap, feathery 'pet meat' from the local butcher, then chicken, then boneless chicken, and soon enough, pricey cat food. Once you start caring, you are doomed to continue. And the appalling thing is how little say you have in the matter: how great a part circumstance plays in the bindings of love that constrict, pull and shape one's life in one direction or another.

Things changed. Soon, my partner moved in, and we decided to get married. We began to consider what we'd do with our cats when we went out of town. We drew closer to fellow cat parents, slipping often into that particular realm where we would dissect in hilarious detail picky feline eating habits, the best litter to buy, and their fascinating peculiarities. Our phones filled up with pointless but undeletable photographs.

The day came when we had to move, and the question of how to continue caring for the cats became central. We found a flat nearby, but the building was not as well-suited to allowing our wards the liberty to come and go that they previously enjoyed. After one terrible night in the new place with the three of them, we decided Doris ought to live free in her old familiar block, fed generously by us. Her children, quite randomly named Kaddu and Keema, became housecats with access to netted balconies.

I found it difficult to feed Doris, however, because she would invariably follow me after eating, calling and running at my heels, until she reached another cat gang's territory. Trading house chores, I convinced my husband to take on the psychologically burdensome task, which he did with less worry and likely less punctiliousness than I would have imposed on myself. 'She's fine,' he insisted whenever I worried, and I swallowed down my guilt and pretended to believe him. About a year or so later, he largely stopped feeding Doris, insisting that she was quite able to fend for herself. This cat, who had once curled up to me purring as I slept, who was far more grateful and affectionate than her progeny, had slipped out of my responsibility, back into the care of nature. The prospect of seeking her out, only to curtail whatever feral freedom she still enjoyed, was too daunting.

Three years after Doris first appeared, another cat brought her litter of two kittens to the enclosed area below our new house. With great interest, Kaddu and Keema watched them suckling and playing, from above. If I looked at them at all, it was askance. They might get a packet of food one day, or a bowl of water. Perhaps we'll get them neutered. They are not to be named. They are not to be loved. I see how easily two cats become four, then six, then hundreds of cats, thousands of cats, millions and billions and trillions of cats.

In a later chapter of *Particularly Cats*, Lessing describes the heroic, muddy rescue of a semi-feral cat and her new kittens, from an abandoned shaft near the family farm. While countless others were routinely drowned, these kittens 'grew up and found homes; and she stayed a house cat'. There is possibly nothing more arbitrary. Love, as I've learned from my cats, is an unavoidable claim, but its particularities are just as unaccountable.

House of Saints
by Anukriti Prasad

'I'll lock him in your room.'

'One day, your body will disappear under mysterious circumstances,' Rhea says. 'One day.'

Surya—he doesn't go by Suri now—picks up the feline and croons something inane into its humongous ears.

Rhea kicks at his ankles as she passes by. 'Keep that thing out of my room.'

'Don't tell Maa,' she hears, even though Preeti Aunty had promised she would have a lovely time rooming with Surya. *He's still a sweetheart*, Rhea was told. *A little unaccommodating sometimes but you just call me the moment he gets stubborn, beta, I'll sort him out.*

'We decided no animals before I moved in.'

Surya's face turns to her, finally, irritating in its absolute symmetry. 'Mommy's so mean,' he whines, tone pitched high, cat shaking animatedly in his arms. Rhea longs to grab his hair and tell him no cat would sound like that, if they ever spoke. His radiant features pull into an exaggerated grimace. 'Why doesn't Mommy love me?'

Rhea takes a step forward, and Surya hurries backwards. 'You look beautiful today.' She advances without pause. 'Have a good day at work, I love you.'

His bedroom door shuts in her face but Rhea doesn't mind. Evening will coax out a hungry man. Her patience apes that of vigilant lions. Slow, she murder-hums. Steady.

'I remember when I was twenty.'

'How?' Rhea questions, burying another page in the printer till it spits out a copy. 'You were twenty many decades ago.'

Jonathan has no sense of humour. He makes her fetch coffee for the whole department during the four pm break. 'Decades ago, when I was a twenty-year-old intern,' he continues, punishment delivered. Rhea doesn't offer any quips. 'I was only allowed to bring coffee and rub my nose at my boss' feet.'

Everybody watches Rhea over the lid of their caffeine tankards. 'I'm so grateful I have a generous boss,' she recites. Tension dislodges itself from the air. Then, 'Truly overjoyed my boss only overworks me instead of putting me on coffee runs.'

Silence is rare in their big multistoried office. She's a star, setting trends. 'It's costing me an arm and a leg to pay you, brat.'

'His arm and leg aren't worth a lot,' Rhea tattles to Manya over the phone, after-hours. 'I'll find you a better fiancé.'

Her cousin, the preschool teacher, sighs like Rhea has offered something more unreasonable than an excuse for eating crayons. 'I'm not marrying Nat for how much his limbs cost.'

'He offered me an internship here in exchange for your hand, didn't he?

That's why you're marrying him?'

Manya tells her if he cancels the wedding, Rhea will have to work sixty-hour weeks to cover the down payment on their new apartment.

'She's spent a total of four hours with him on this whole trip.'

'Pay attention. They only need four hours to realise they're in love.' Surya's tone edges between forlorn and reverential. On screen, Naina walks away from Bunny without confessing her four-hour love. The furball rubs needily against her feet and Rhea, benevolent to the core, shoves it away only lightly.

'If this film doesn't get better, you'll only need three minutes to realise I'm trained in taekwondo.'

Movie nights are a weekly plague and every fresh wave brings a headache only the film choices of an insufferable housemate could inspire. The warmth of Surya's extended arm behind her head does no favours.

'You don't like Bunny?' His eyes flit over her features, lightning-fast and aggravating. There's a brief reprieve as he smiles wide. 'I thought you'd love his character.'

Mortification licks at her face. His words are rarely tossed forth without careful consideration of how hard they'll hit. Bastard. 'You think I go around falling for every flighty asshole with three seconds of charm?'

Surya's face leans closer in its curiosity. 'No? I used to be an exception?'

Rhea holds the popcorn bowl tight and plots a murder.

'Incredible work.'

Rhea singsongs the words every time Jonathan tries to admonish her. 'Uh-huh. Your boss thinks I'm doing "incredible work" here.' Without her, the branch would retrogress to doom. She's a productivity marvel.

His teeth grit so hard she worries Manya's wedding pictures will come out with an uglier-than-usual Jonathan disgracing them. This, too, will have to be a topic of conversation shelved for when they mount his traffic-worn Hyundai, and Jonathan suffers her concern till Surya's quarters are in sight.

Presently, Rhea contents herself with humming sacrilegiously at her work-station.

'Extend your contract for a few more months,' Fiza wheedles from the cubicle over. 'The boss already likes your work and the work-ex really won't hurt. Even Jonathan thinks you should.'

Jonathan's mutiny-detecting ears prickle. 'You. Swap absurdities when work hours are over.' Portly files crash-land on Fiza's busy desk. '*Off* company property.'

'It would take someone offering me three times Jonathan's salary to get me to stay,' Rhea surrenders later, when the smoke break stretches into its last few minutes. 'I don't like Bombay.'

'Is it the traffic?' Lata-from-Marketing wonders.

'It's Jonathan's incessant nagging,' Fiza posits.

'No cute guys.' Vijay-from-HR stills. 'Present company excluded, of course.'

Rhea lets free a flying kiss in their direction and prances back inside. A chorus of complaints follow. Fine. 'It's my flatmate,' she concedes when they move like a pack, prey cornered. 'I'm allergic.'

'Choco-chips.'

'I'll add them later.'

Self-preservation instincts misplaced, Surya waggles his outstretched fingers impatiently. Rhea packages her ire into deep breaths and passes him the container. Sundays necessitate synergy, when they prepare breakfast together, and between the early hour and the theatre of busying himself in a cute apron, Surya is imperceptibly less trying.

Under the veneer of derisive supervision, Rhea spectates with naked interest. Shravi always sums it up precisely. *No bad angles with a face like that.*

Over and over, his hands work the ladle, flipping out neat circles till both plates are stacked full. Axel meows gratefully when his bowl is lowered.

'You get a plate,' says the waiter.

'And you get a plate,' Rhea rolls her eyes.

'Everybody gets a plate,' Surya crows, settling opposite her.

'If you've added too many choco-chips—'

'You'll thank me anyway?'

Rhea tears into the pancake, demonstrating. 'You'll book a hospital room.'

Inspection renders her threat obsolete. Apart from a straggling few on the surface, the small chocolate pile occupies a nervous corner of the plate. Whipped cream dollops rest on the pancake and the picture it makes might as well be a perfect facsimile of their breakfasts years ago.

'Last time's was prettier, wasn't it?'

The breezy interjection fools no one. Rhea allows him to squirm silent, then eats without comment.

'Will your speech for the wedding be equally rude?'

'Depends,' Rhea simpers. 'Will you still be the groom?'

'Rhea,' Manya snaps.

This is a fun game. Jonathan's fingers wrap white around his stress-ball steering wheel. 'Walk back the rest of the way.'

It's drizzling. Ugly Bombay weather only the natives are conditioned to be grateful for. 'Maybe I can keep things civil for my boss. Spare you some dignity.'

'Isn't it too soon for you to be bringing up dignity?' Everybody in the car waits, caught between the red-light and the punchline. 'The fiasco with that boy didn't happen all too long ago, I'm told.'

'Beloved brother-in-law,' she sings. 'I've never dated.' This, of course, is an easily mended lie but Jonathan has a face that inspires insincerity.

It lifts into a curve now. 'Is that right?'

Humiliatingly, Manya picks up the thread before she does. Jonathan doesn't react to the smack he's gifted, not moving even to grab her retreating hand and press a kiss to it. In the back, Rhea sits up, hound-nose sniffing a rare fight.

'Nat, don't.'

'I just think it's bold of her to talk,' he gossips, without any pretence of concern the building aunties back home affect. 'If my crush had dumped me without a word to run off to another city, I wouldn't even step foot in the place, breathing the same air.'

This isn't information Jonathan's entry-level keycard should have access to. Rhea's toes struggle back into her heels. 'Stop by that tree.'

Manya, her wretched breach, turns in the passenger seat. 'Rhea, sweetie, I'm sor—'

'Right here is fine.'

An obedient chauffeur, Jonathan pulls over to the melody of Manya's excuses. 'Will you get back okay?' he worries, exaggerated, through the window.

Rhea kicks his tail light before she leaves.

'Let him go.'

The kid hesitates, Axel tucked in her arms like the obligatory animal side-kick to every asinine kid-protagonist. 'Want to play with kitty,' she snivels and Rhea's mile-wide mean streak distends. Rotten luck to have someone gatecrash your poorly-planned heist but even worse that it's Rhea, exiting the elevator, drenched and homicidal.

The hallway floor is a community locker room when she squats down wetly. 'In that case,' Rhea beams, 'go get your own fucking kitty. Yeah?'

When she's done, the girl cries; Axel is returned to their flat. Win-win.

'Thought you'd be more pleasant after hanging out with Manya.'

Rhea punts a cushion at him. Surya gathers it to his chest romantically.

'Did something happen?'

'Fuck off, Suri.'

'Were you crying?'

'Are you blind?'

'What did she say?' Surya frowns. 'You look like a wet cat.'

Rhea helps out his negative IQ. Gestures towards the balcony door where rain is now beating down like an incensed woman pouring fury on her churlish brother-in-law.

He swivels to push in on the edges of her patience. 'Hey. Why didn't you let Krishi take the cat?'

Tracking ill-humoured droplets into the house, Rhea seethes at the name. Krishi. Little wonder the kid was a nightmare.

'Take a shower, at least,' he says, face puckered, looking rather dry. Rhea contemplates changing that.

Psychic, he smiles and takes several steps back. 'I'll get the geyser.'

'Rhea? No, she isn't home yet, why?'

Surya's innocence leaks through thin bathroom walls and Rhea has to relinquish a grin to the safety of the mirror.

On the counter, her phone starts to vibrate with Manya's sixth call.

'That soup is a bribe.'

'Should've made tomato, then. I stopped liking mushroom.'

Surya's fingers grope the hand-towel over his shoulder, eyes pasted to the sight of his concoction depleting rapidly. If it weren't for Jonathan's motormouth words strangling her, Rhea would've said they look like a modern age domestic dream.

'You've gotten good at being stubborn,' Surya suggests.

'Your soup sucks.'

He's gotten better at being insulted. 'What did Jonathan do?'

This is a fantastic time for the universe to wrap up the joke. Explaining the several branches of this evening's humiliation to the man who planted the seed seems cruel punishment. Hardly deserved for making Krishi burst into those ugly sobs.

'Meow,' says Axel, and Surya's attention goes skittering over.

'Just tell me what happened,' he invites after the ceremonial petting. 'Then I can fix it.' This is new. It knots in her throat like one of Shravi's culinary experiments. 'We'll be even for the cat.'

Fucking cat.

His torso looks foolish leaning over the kitchen island, anyway. 'You don't fix problems, Surya, you spawn them.' A confutation deflates under her unforgiving steamroller. 'Even Jonathan knew how to get a good dig in about what you did.'

At last, silence blankets their dark hall. It takes another minute before their ears are accustomed only to the paper-light tapping outside and when a low clap of thunder shakes their frames, Surya remains still.

'Go on,' Rhea smiles, feeling her dimples crack as she ruptures another safe centimetre. 'I got out of his car to walk back in the rain, Surya. Fix it.'

Handsome men make cowardice look becoming.

'So much for getting even,' she parrots into his strained face, shoulder brushing his goodbye.

'Pretty boy alert. Lobby.'

'Will he finish this for me?' Rhea asks, two clicks from completing a spreadsheet that will hopefully leave Jonathan a committed headache.

'Mm. Looks too pretty to understand Excel.'

'You can have him.'

Their slavedriver glares at Fiza's wolf-whistle. Rhea concludes Jonathan would do well with taking the nearest fire extinguisher to his skull.

'I hope he's a Libra. Libras together are very compatible.'

'Other compatible pairings include you and a termination letter, Fiza,' Jonathan reminds helpfully.

'He's a Leo,' Rhea disappoints when she joins the ogling camp, but it's through bubble wrap filling her mouth. The model parked outside their glass walls has his gaze fixed on her like the stupid yellow flower that follows the sun's familiar amble.

'Surya, Fiza,' she introduces, minutes after his wave and smile have sent realisation dampening Fiza's daydreams. Jonathan clears his throat, ignored.

'What are you doing here?' Rhea chirps.

Surya's eyes crescent. Against the mild beige of their office, he looks abnormally tall in the black trousers. Rhea feels a little slow, forgiving. 'Fixing a problem.' Trying another soup, he means. 'Let's go.'

Jonathan refuses. 'She's my responsibility. I'd be worried.'

Rhea wants to study him. 'You kiss my sister with that lying mouth?'

When he struggles it back to his face, Jonathan's smile is beatific. 'If you leave her in a ditch somewhere, Surya, I won't tell.'

Fiza trades her an eyeroll. Jonathan waits, joke outstretched, reception pending.

'You must be interesting at family dinners,' Surya compliments finally, bite so deep in his tone, it slices even through her. Pleasantly shifting so their warmth bursts into a shared bubble, he arranges his features just right. 'Later.'

'A *kidnapping*.'

'A detour,' Surya corrects, patient even though her allegation has boomeranged other customers' attention to them. 'Ten minutes, tops.' Rhea glowers away the lone hero who sidles closer to investigate and Surya's corners flatten prettily in the dwindling sunlight.

Three minutes into the shopping trip, the proprietor cosies up to him like the girls back in school, senses honed to divine a generous hand. Rhea's philanthropy crouches till it's invisible. 'That's ugly.'

'—shopping for yourself?'

'—putting that on your pet is animal cruelty, I think.'

'Take a hike,' Surya advises when she's only halfway through her list. His sycophant's hiatus, begun somewhere after Rhea's fifth jibe, remains unbroken, but she can taste the lingering resentment coating her neck like sweat.

'No collar?' Axel's a smart cat, hardly needs any of the accessories Surya's just spent top coin on. Watching him burn a hole in his deep wallet is funner than obediently waiting, though. If he wants her compliance, he'll have to wrench it from her like nails from soft skin.

When the bags have been folded into the backseat, Surya pulls up by an ice cream vendor. 'Cornetto, I'm guessing?' he says in a tone that doesn't much sound like he's guessing. Rhea's cold wrath fragments.

This is sorrier than the soup.

'Today is not a bribe,' comes the retort and if Rhea squints till his face is a dark blur in her vision, she can even spot a shade of sincerity in it. That jawline is wasted on scowling. 'I'll pick you up, we'll hang out. No Jonathan. Problem solved.'

Rhea waits till her old friend reappears on the traffic signal. In the pause that follows, she gathers her Cornetto and purse singlehandedly like those independent women on Netflix shows, and pulls the car open.

'*Bribe,*' she educates her flatmate sweetly through the window.

'Be honest. You're a little desperate.'

'The party can happen without you, you know.'

'But without my hot flatmate?'

Lata's silence splinters under Axel's insistent meowing as he coerces pats from Rhea. Fiza's noticeboard mouth had spared none of their absent co-workers the minutiae of Surya's public pickup. The consequence—evidenced by this early morning call—is elevation on the social pyramid.

Rhea's fingers practice against the back of the phone case. 'I'll ask,' she yields. 'He doesn't seem the party type.' This is firsthand falsity. Without him, you have no party. But that's not for Lata and the others to delight in.

'Why me?'

'They've decided you must have a sterling personality to go along with the face,' Rhea tells a deadline-bound Surya later, hunched over his obnoxious iMac. 'Personally, I believe in breaking people's daydreams at the earliest. You should come.'

An invitation like those return-to-sender packages. Surya's preoccupation with his work outranks every conceivable temptation the devil could sing about. No one knows this better.

'I'd love to be your date,' he decides.

Rhea bolts his door from the outside.

'Are you still shit at holding your alcohol?'

'Lots of murders happen in dim-lit alleys,' Rhea intones as they pass a serendipitously dark backstreet. When their limbs disengage post a quick round of shoving, she fights down the lightness humming in her chest and their steps fall back in lock.

Further down, Lata's farmhouse glitters like a monstrosity from a Bhimji Zaveri ad.

'God, I hate Bombay.' She's broadcasted as much from the moment Manya picked her up at the airport a month ago but looking into the colossal mirror sparkling beside Lata's main door reinforces the sentiment. Surely something so ornate outside is meant as satire.

'Looks loose,' Surya notes. 'Could fit perfectly above our living room sofa. No?'

Yes. 'We are not stealing from Lata,' she asserts, sweeping over their matching figures in the glass before digging at the bell. Surya protests before all social etiquette abruptly evaporates and he's stooping down in the dark entryway, cooing at a dark blob.

'Don't bother,' Lata smiles when the door has opened to the Renaissance painting of Rhea struggling to tug Surya upright. 'Luna only wakes up at mealtimes.'

His disappointment slips congruently under a winning smile and a brighter greeting. Rhea follows them in with a last look at the black cat napping outside. Boring, she settles. Axel's much friendlier.

'Like a monkey-ladder, even.'

'I got it when you called him a tree, Vij,' she snaps. How many climbable fixtures can one man be compared to?

'Look at that,' the HR angel whispers, eyeing the spread opposite them. Rhea lets him indulge. Surya's figure towers and parts and still, people make to push coyly closer. An entertaining spectacle, if slightly repetitive. 'Where did you even find him?'

Last layer of hell, one could say if they'd spent too long gazing at Surya's exposed collarbones tonight. 'Kolkata,' she answers instead, which isn't too far off. The inconsistency goes unquestioned. Surya's figure cuts a distracting image, walking up from the bar.

'Still talking about work?' he teases, leaning easily along the table behind Rhea's back. Her goosebumps know to behave themselves.

'Oh no,' Vijay says breezily. 'Just thinking about trees.'

'Left cheek.'

'I'm busy.'

'I'll get it.'

Despite his words, Surya doesn't move. Rhea, focused singularly on the Babel tower of party cups she's erecting, feels the slow turn of impatience.

This is not the time to play impossible waiting games.

Shifting just means they're both staring now. It sits discordant against the thumping bass. 'A written invitation, perhaps?'

That one is foolish, no bite. Words you'd find in her sixth-grade mouth.

Surya feigns oblivion, moving carefully to concentrate on the apple of her cheek. 'There,' he says when the eyelash is released, and it's softer than anything you could pull from her innards.

Thanks, she means to say, but the dimples are faster. She wraps them back instantly, turning, focusing, chiding, but in the very corner of her peripheral vision, Surya is grinning back.

Shravi would have a field day.

🛕🙏🛕

'He's a writer.'

Fiza sounds tortured. 'I asked for *flaws*.'

'His spine will be a horizontal parabola before we hit thirty.'

Across the room, the conspiracy custom-made for Rhea's derangement bends low over the table, taking aim. The ball plopping neatly in a cup for its fifth consecutive trip can't distract from the way Surya's waist intersects the precise line of his back.

'Oh yeah,' Fiza deadpans. 'It definitely looks like he's headed down that road.'

Surya is winking at his poor adversary when their little spectator sofa creaks under a new weight. 'Rhea,' Lata says around a smile that looks nothing like smiles should. 'Could you…handle your flatmate? I actually like my date tonight.'

'What's his name?' Fiza quizzes. Lata's muttered this about her last three boyfriends.

Only a moment's struggle, this time. Poetic against the backdrop of her plus one's own losing match. 'Ahan.'

'You—'

'I'm not exactly calling him by name during our fucking honeymoon phase.' Even frustrated, Lata's face refuses to wrinkle into anything unsightly. 'But I do like him. Sober.'

Rhea's shoes gain sentience. Surya's next ball jumps into her waiting hand, cheeks bunching up when he looks askance. 'Stop hogging sweet Ahan. Lata sulks easy.'

Predictably, Lata's waiting arms resemble a cage when Surya's opponent lumbers back to make amends.

'Jesus. It's just beer pong.'

Lata's latest is sulking. 'You could stand to not be perfect at one thing, Suri.'

On a list of indiscretions she doesn't usually care to keep track of, this careless remark has just climbed to the top. He blinks.

'If you're down an opponent, Surya, Rhea's rather competitive, too.' Always the ones you trust.

Surya laughs with Fiza. 'Drinking game against a lightweight. Which level of hell does that make for?'

'My fists, if you don't shut up.'

His cheeky grin wilts to poorly-hidden consternation when five minutes creep by and Rhea's shots have grazed no cups.

'Have you been cut off at parties?' Surya questions casually post-win, when Fiza's eyebrows rise at the confiscation of Rhea's impending beer cup pile. 'Worse punishment than having to drink. Trust me.'

'I do,' Fiza promises, flustered, but he goes to replace Rhea's drinks with mini Bisleris, and her colleague's gaze pricks into her, brazenly implying all manner of the unthinkable.

Rhea mutters complaints about her climbing buzz. 'Washroom.'

'You checked?'

Surya's amusement brightens in the face of her uncharacteristic fidgeting. 'Wait.'

Two beats, then—

The mute air in the narrow hallway cracks with a solitary pleasured note. Rhea's flush crawls free, feet already moving to find another washroom.

'Bombay parties suck.'

'The worst.' Slippery slope, endorsing her in this state, but nothing devolves without Surya's permission.

'You know what would make us feel better?'

Rhea's laugh spills from her chest like the first ray of sunlight scaling the horizon. 'Put it back, Suri.'

Even his disappointed sulk looks pretty in the aureate hand mirror he's lifted off a side table. 'Tell me if you change your mind,' he conspires. Rhea feels only a slight resistance when their tangled fingers tug her forward.

'What was it, twenty-six minutes?'

'Jonathan made me stop timing Rhea's rants after the Stapler Incident.'

'Pity. I gave her at least an hour's worth of material with the laundry fuck-up,' Surya sighs.

Sweet Ahan looks slightly ruffled when Lata giggles with Surya. 'We were worried she'd strangle you that night.' Ergo, the impromptu dinner they forced her to attend. Ah.

Fiza, essaying the role of Surya's lackey for the evening, hands him consolations. 'Maybe if you manage to befriend her, your neck will be safer.'

'Oh no. If friendship was the key to surviving Rhea's wrath, I should've scored my immunity years ago.'

A lone moth spots the lightbulb of Rhea's gentle buzz. Approaching, it calls to its eclipse.

When a delayed round of titters goes up in the cluster of couches they're lounging around, the confusion juts out, fractured bone peeking from torn flesh.

'Rhea didn't mention? We grew up in the same building together, back in Kolkata.'

Tell them your blood type while you're at it, she thinks, asphyxiating under the moths. Maybe throw in the time you and Shravi scared me on the stairs and I had to wear a cast for two months.

Betrayal slopes down the curve of Fiza's profile. 'Wait. You—'

'Oh, you have to listen to the details.'

Jonathan's inauspicious arrival sets little ripples aquiver in the still water of their cluster, unexpected. Rhea wonders if Manya is tiring of keeping him home. 'They used to be inseparable,' her boss unveils when the bait goes untouched by Surya's careful pause. 'Same school, joint vacations, hand holding during roller skate lessons, you name it.'

Sweet Ahan is won over. 'We should try roller-skating too.' Lata giggles, thighs slung possessively over the plagiarist's lap. Vijay stifles a retch.

Fiza's lack of nauseating dates clears her for cross-examination. '"Used to be inseparable"?'

Rhea's insides unhinge, crawling unchecked through her frame.

'Maybe they still are. But there was that whole college fiasco.' Jonathan's tone activates a dormant homicidal cell. 'Pretty hard getting past things like that.'

'What college fiasco?' Sweet Ahan begs, eager as though his stupid paws will catch another date idea if he pries harder. Rhea hopes Lata breaks up with him in the morning.

Jonathan's wide mouth distorts, preparing to enlighten, but he's missed the gunshot. 'It was more a fuck up than a fiasco. No points for guessing whose.'

Rhea can sense every taut vein along their brushing arms but Surya's voice is light when he abandons subtlety to cock a thumb at himself. It's a lame little line and yet the blessed curse of popular boys means landing a sitcom laugh track every time they open their mouths.

'I'm not surprised Rhea didn't mention me after the stunt I pulled.'

Fiza's curiosity sediments on the downturn of her lips. 'You didn't attend the same college.' It's not suspicion, Rhea notes amidst the throes of her humiliated battery, but the diligent lackey is retiring.

'We were going to. I bailed the morning of our flight.'

Rhea's tongue is a cheap glue stick left out in the sun for too long.

Why would he do that?

'Well, Lata,' Surya answers sweetly, warmth hollowing. 'There's only so long you can keep a crush on your best friend under wraps. And it's definitely easier under the invigilation of building aunties compared to the wild freedom of university. See?'

Even their mention brings her spine up straight, heart kicking, humming-bird, itching to crawl through an arbitrary cage.

'You liked her.' An incorrect hypothesis. Jonathan's slow systems have been reassessing while this conversation landslides, eyes pinching down to their shared loveseat and after all that, he's set aside the truth only to string Rhea higher for the fall.

Surya's laugh feels like a waste of air. '*Liked?*'

Her stomach feels strapped. Fists curled to brace.

'Jonathan, why would I ever stop?'

And release. Rhea's body locks in some immobilising terror but the mercy of her muscles is apparent when she's allowed to glance at him.

To drag her wound out in the open, only a pithy lie slapped on as band-aid, is bad enough. But Surya's setting up the rope barrier now, snapping sharp warnings for visitors not to inch any closer. 'Do not touch' he's saying, except her shame isn't his art and neither he nor Jonathan have the right.

Rhea tugs him close, burning hand on his strong wrist and—

'—what the fuck are you doing?'

Surya's nose is almost kissing hers. Rhea ignores it, searches his face, hissing the words till he shifts and his lips stop shy of her earlobe.

'Trying to make the right soup?'

'We're leaving.'

Six pairs of eyes watch her carefully. Surya's inertia prompts a repeat. 'Thanks for tonight, Lata. Lovely place. I'll see you Monday.'

Monday next year. Maybe.

A few tactfully aimed pokes later, her flatmate rises. 'It's our cat,' he explains, sounding much sorrier than he looks. 'Axel gets anxious if you leave him alone for too long. You know how it is.'

Everybody nods, pliant under the command of his smile but Rhea spots the edge in their docility. The aftermath of his little confession is clear: a hole in an impenetrable exterior.

The hyenas back in their building had found themselves with some similar version of this realisation. Then followed the glee; Rhea lying open to the bite they had kept in loose check thus far.

It's upsetting that Surya gets to pick his time, choose the manner of his reveal and so squarely manage to shift narratives till he takes the fall without mutilating his attractiveness.

It's not entirely his fault. But Rhea's borne this weight in front of strangers, building aunties and friends alike for years. He can swallow a little unfairness.

Ahan—tipsy, no longer Sweet, and seriously beginning to test Rhea's patience—pouts. It'll haunt her for the rest of her days. 'It must've been hard for Rhea too when you left her alone.'

The party of eyes swings to him, disbelieving.

'I'm surprised Rhea even said yes to rooming together. Unless she forgave you. Did you forgive him?'

Like the inside of a black hole, everybody's breath tightens, squashing together. And then, a warmth on her back.

Luna's tiny mews greet them when they walk through the doorway a minute later, but Surya's steps guide her right past.

'Meow.'

'No.' Rhea's heels wrest independence from stiff, sturdy pumps before she storms into the kitchen. 'It was a travesty. I'm never going to a party again.'

'Meow,' Axel consoles, pit-patting daintily across the marble to rub once against her feet, conscious of bone-china patience.

Surya hovers outside the kitchen like an aloof guardian angel. 'Schemes?' he echoes. His brain is still looping their elevator conversation. Maybe if the universe feels kindly, Rhea will be allowed a chance to whack his skull back into function.

'Tactics. Strategies. Whatever you want to call them. They're not going to work.'

'I'm not trying any strategies.'

Rhea's scoff fogs up the glass of water. He thinks her dumber than the time she got halfway through his toothpaste mousse before the other kids told her she was burning her compliments on a prank.

The memory welts her shame. Moistens her chords for a fight. 'Picking me up from work,' Rhea lists. 'Lying at the party, sweet-talking me in the Uber. I'm not fucking stupid.'

'You couldn't be if you tried. Always the smartest—prettiest—in any room.'

Flattery now. She wants his spine for a slingshot.

'What do you think this is going to bring you?'

Chink in the armour, she expects to hear. Maybe something non-verbal. A slow lean forward till he's staring up at her, perhaps, so he can really stick the landing for that hopeful, heartbroken look she's seen regularly dispatched.

But.

'I didn't lie,' Surya murmurs instead, sliding close. Rhea's lungs pluck off-key like ukulele strings. He means the compliments.

'At the party. Just now.' A Surya list. 'Before the flight. I never lied to you.'

It fits so well in his mouth. Rhea wonders how he can group them so easily. One was childhood instinct, another was unmasked sincerity, and one was an apology undelivered to her face.

The last two press into her bruise like unkind curiosity. Singling out the first battle is self-care. 'Some friendship this is.'

Here's the bit Jonathan, with his secondhand steal, will never know: growing up inseparable charges more than roller-skating lessons and sitting next to each other on the school bus.

Beyond the pranks and the fights, their little knot of friends withstood the ravages of teen tragedy and tantrum because friendship survives on the ritual of sticking a hand into the dirt to grab the other and lift.

Instinct would not allow Surya to see a comrade disgraced publicly at another's hands.

'Rhea.'

She thinks of the duality a kindness-shaped sword can embody. 'I go to bed thinking we're going to board a plane together in the morning but I wake up to Preeti Aunty at the door and a burning in my throat that won't lighten for the next six months.'

A nightmare etched into memory. She forgot her boarding pass at the security check, her phone was carted off in an abandoned trolley and the seat beside hers mocked every last tear emptily.

But still it shrinks, her pocket of anger.

Surya expedites the process, lips and brows and muscles wet with guilt. She wants to tell him there's no use keeping all that distance if he'll look at her like that anyway.

'I didn't want to go to college, Rhea.'

Hysterical. The whole world knows now.

'I didn't leave without an explanation.'

Liar. He never once said—

'Independence Day lunch. Club balcony.'

Rhea's face burns. Oh.

She remembers well enough. He'd worn a red kurta and Rhea had taken unmerited pride in how it stood out against the other boys' saffron and white outfits. Something about its combination with the promise of impending collegiate freedom had rendered her extra playful, while Surya stayed un-usually impervious.

'You wouldn't listen.' *You kept laughing about it every time I said I'd rather go on project-based work-ex trips than waste four years in college and I got so—I was so angry, Rhea.*

A weapon of pure ice. Rhea only experienced it once. A week of the silent shoulder and she had crumbled like Parle-G in hot tea.

Low pulses of panic massage her temples. The shimmer of long-term cog-nitive dissonance is slipping.

'It was a really good offer,' Surya confesses quietly. The years shed away, they're back on the terrace and no one else witnesses his admissions. The details she'd extracted from Shravi—writing programme, individual mento-ring, paid opportunities—but this moment has been sealed, reserved solely for her. 'I didn't expect you'd block me so quickly.'

A common misbelief among the spoiled. She wore her anger for skin to college. Moulded a reputation of being so sharp-tongued boys would stam-mer in conversation and girls would pout, being handed no-nonsense life advice.

259

Rhea enjoys herself like this. Confronting the source, however—

She fills another glass. Slides it across.

It's not a bribe. Barely an apology. 'What happened isn't fixable.'

Surya's throat bobs smoothly when he downs the water. 'Then I'll do the next best thing.'

'Pick me up from work? Make me soup? Don't waste your time.' Friendship: do not force.

'Are you really so thick?' His frustration is punctuated with an indignant meow from their companion. Rhea has been ganged up against. 'Genius, it can't be a waste of time if it's for you.'

Disarmed of her usual counters, Rhea pauses. Inches dwindle before her eyes.

'Even Jonathan figured it out,' Surya mutters, index finger acquainting itself with her cheek before pushing back a strand of hair. Rhea needs to hold her breath. Up close, he doesn't look so unattainable. 'I've never lied about you.'

Sneakers tapped while she tied her shoelaces, absurd quips filled horror movie night, and the treasure trove of birthday paintings still litter her old room; Surya could be the best friend in an alternate dimension.
But Rhea's theory tilts a different way.

The mini-sun above them warms his words as Axel curls around her toes, finds a chink. Rhea pushes closer. Swallows the little voice. Surya's ears seem to twitch.

'Hold still,' she instructs, studying her options with lightheaded sleep deprivation.

'Or?' Surya tests, teeth peeking from under talkative lips. 'Another round of taekwondo threats? Eviction? Mid-sleep asphyxiation?'

Pretty and insufferable. It demands punishment. Rhea plants two hands on angled cheeks and kisses him.

Cat Food

by Priya Sebastian

Talent

by Gautam Chintamani

The arrival of an actor on a set is often accompanied by whispers, hushed enough not to raise the alarm but loud enough to let everyone know that 'talent' has arrived. Everything before this moment is but preparation—hammering out the perfect dialogues, designing and redesigning elaborate sets, intricate camera movements perfected to the last detail, background artists, sometimes in thousands, dressed to the nines and choreographed—all for the actor to deliver a line or a look. Everything fades into the background, and everyone else becomes secondary. Unlike most humans—and other creatures I suppose—cats don't like to play second fiddle, and that is perhaps the reason why furry felines aren't the first thing to pop into one's head, when one thinks of animals in cinema. Although there have been many iconic cats in movies worldwide, Bollywood, the world's biggest film industry, invariably relegates cats to a secondary spot, a few notches lower in the pecking order.

It's not as though filmmakers don't like cats, but this apparent lack of fondness possibly results from certain technical factors. For starters, cats are, well… famously moody, and when it comes to cinema, the 'M' word is dreaded like the plague. Why? The inability to get into action mode on cue is a factor that can make or break careers, and cats, to put it mildly, are not known for their ability to compromise on the matter of mood.

Unlike dogs, who have saved the day in many films such as *Hum Aapke Hain Koun..!* (1994) or avenged their mistresses and masters in *Noorie* (1979) and *Teri Meherbaniyan* (1985), or horses that get you out of a sticky situation, say a la Dhanno in *Sholay* (1975), or become an inseparable part of your identity such as

Raju-the-horse in *Azaad* (1978), who was immortalised by the R.D. Burman-Anand Bakshi song 'Raju, chal Raju, apni masti mein tu... '' cats, more often than not, are embellishments. Glorified props that are needed to convey something about the character, without doing any heavy lifting of their own. It is assumed that cats aren't team players, and therefore it would be impossible for a screenwriter to come up with a cat version of, say, the scene in Manmohan Desai's *Mard* (1985), where Raju Mard Tangewala's sweet Labrador, Moti, and trusted stead, Badal, team up to save him from drowning to his death in quicksand.

Then there is the question of framing—a cat and a character can share the frame in limited ways. Nearly most cat appearances in mainstream Hindi films, or for that matter Hollywood too, can be traced back to the super-villain Ernst Stavro Blofeld, James Bond's nemesis, who was frequently portrayed stroking a white Persian. First seen in *From Russia With Love* (1963), the Blofeld character singlehandedly crafted the onscreen image of the cat that pretty much remained unchanged for decades. The image was further cemented in what is considered the greatest cat-appearance in cinema, *The Godfather* (1972), where screen-legend, Marlon Brando, found a stray cat on the shooting floor and included it in the scene, to give himself something to do. Interestingly enough, the cat purred enough to ensure that director Francis Ford Coppola did not edit it out. By the mid-1970s, this particular image of the cat in a villain's hands had become a regular motif in popular Hindi films, as seen in *Rafoo Chakkar* (1975), *Jay Vejay* (1977), *Paapi* (1977) and *Maha Badmaash* (1977), where the mysterious villain was called 'Mogambo'.

The onset of the 1980s, a decade often unjustly derided as the worst for Hindi films, saw the *filmy billi* share the screen with one of the greatest screen villains, Amjad Khan. For Khan, having enjoyed the high of *Sholay's* Gabbar Singh, nearly everything else that followed ran the risk of falling short, especially when playing the baddie. While he had well-etched characters in *Inkaar* (1977) and *Muqaddar Ka Sikandar* (1978), there was little that he could explore as a villain, at least, on the face it. In *Bombay 405 Miles* (1980), Amjad Khan fiddled around with Baoding or Chinese mediation balls as a prop and took it a notch up to play the classic cat-stroking villain in *Katilon Ke Kaatil* (1981). Khan played the 'Black Cobra' and could be seen talking to 'Ginny Darling', a black Turkish van. The 1980s were a significant period for animals in Hindi cinema, with Ballu, the Eagle, playing Allah Rakha opposite Amitabh Bachchan in *Coolie* (1984), Tarzan and Ruby having a ball in *Adventures of Tarzan* (1985), Moti, the dog, being a good boy in *Teri Meherbaniyan*, snakes ruling the box office along with Sridevi in *Nagina* (1986), and Handsome, the pigeon, saving the lovers in *Maine Pyar Kiya* (1989). But it was essentially the same old tale for cats. With a bit of horror interlude in Ramsay Brothers' *Veerana* (1988), they continued to be props for the villain. Although cat-stock rose a bit, with them being the super-pack for criminal kingpin Roshi Mahanta in *Khal Nayak* (1993), and even doing a bit of the dirty work for Gulshan Grover's Billa in *Gambler* (1995), the 1990s, too, were no different for cats. Just to provide some context, this was an era where some creatures, such as a snake, even got to play the hero Jackie Shroff's brother in *Doodh Ka Karz* (1990)!

Today though, the cat is no longer an afterthought or a villain prop in Hollywood, something more than apparent from the space given to the tabby both on the poster and in the narrative in Joel and Ethan Coen's *Inside Llewyn Davis*. How long then before Hindi films re-imagine the cat? For an industry where most writers proudly wear the cat-parent badge on social media profiles, it's strange that no one's really come up with a great role for a cat. They might not have spent as much time in front of the camera, but one thing's for sure, cats are the only other bunch that deserve the moniker 'talent' on a film set.

Do My Parents Have 4 Cats and 1 Child or Just 5 Cats? A (Millennial) Reflection

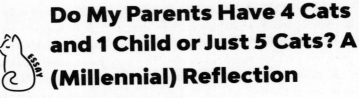

by Teesta Rawal

I haven't always been feline. Or at least I think I haven't. My friends, however, would beg to disagree. Consider for yourself, I suppose, who is right. Let's weigh the evidence.

1. Cats: Sleep all day, awake at night.
Me: Everyone I've lived with will agree. I woke up at 2 in the afternoon today.

2. Cats: Extremely fussy about food, often refuse to try out new things.
Me: Fussy is my middle name. Teesta F Rawal.

3. Cats: Aloof, mysterious creatures. Crave attention at specific times, in specific ways only. Always on their own terms.
Me: People often ask me why I prefer being alone instead of with a group of friends. Well, I enjoy my own company. And being more social would kill the "oh-so-mysterious" vibe, wouldn't it? Which isn't to say I despise attention. I will shamefully admit that sometimes I even demand it aggressively. But only sometimes.

4. Cats: Ensure people are at their beck and call at any point in time.
Me: Look at my Whatsapp messages. If your reply takes longer than 15 seconds, I will claim that you have ghosted me, that you deserve to be mercilessly cut out from my life.

5. Cats: Don't like being touched. Will scratch or bite in case of accidental

(or deliberate) contact.

Me: Absolutely the same.

6. Cats: Sleep in weird positions, often curled up. Their spines can support it.

Me: Also sleeps in weird positions, often curled up, inviting spinal issues in the future.

7. Cats: Don't appear to love baths.

Me: Showering is torture. Orange soap makes it only slightly more bearable.

8. Cats: Practically wedded to cardboard boxes.

Me: My college roommate will tell you that I had a box to sit in for a good three months, before she put her foot down and threw it out.

9. Cats: Love hiding in nooks and crannies, observing surroundings silently.

Me: Blends in effortlessly, knows things about people and places that others do not. (Should any persons or organizations require such skills, you know where to find me.)

10. Cats: Warped sense of what counts as fun (read: doing things you are absolutely not permitted to, and then getting away with it, such as tracking dirty pawprints across the kitchen counter, sleeping on the dining table, getting inside cupboards stacked precariously with crockery, clawing holes in bed linen, or sleeping atop neatly folded laundry and shedding fur all over it. This is a highly abbreviated version of the original memo on the subject.)

Me: Definitely have a long list of things under this category. (Cannot list here as my cat-loving parents are likely to read this book. Or in case the aforementioned individuals and organizations actually consider hiring me. Or wait, maybe they'll actually like that?)

11. Cats: Always seem unapproachable, unfriendly. May be said to have cold eyes.

Me: Glares at strangers on the street, prefer never to be spoken to as far as possible. (This article was commissioned by text and delivered on email.)

12. Cats: Actually very affectionate and unwaveringly loyal to those they trust.

Me: Will protect those I love with my life, cannot stand disloyalty. For example, either you buy this book or you're in deep trouble.

Having put down eleven—no wait, twelve—points now, I can see why people would think as they do. However, I must acknowledge two dissimilarities between me and the feline species. One, I detest fish. I *cannot* stand it—neither the smell, nor the taste, nor the texture. Would rather eat bones than fish. And two, I am upsettingly klutzy. Not even a tenth as nimble and agile as a cat is. Really restricts my climbing onto walls and high platforms—for the greater good, I think.

I personally am vain enough to ignores these minor blights on my otherwise stellar near-cat impersonation (if im-*person*-ation is even the right word for this). Now if you'll excuse me, I must leave to preen in the mirror for a bit. Lord knows it does not end well for anybody who tries to ruffle my hair.

16 Things About Cats (and Boys)

by Gurmehar Kaur

1. Sometimes you spend a lifetime daydreaming about a life with one.

2. Sometimes they show up unexpectedly.

3. A few are abandoned, in need of care and affection and a home (with no promises of staying of course), instantly transforming you to your domestic goddess best.

4. Others walk in, proud and entitled. Often wailing for attention (with no promises of staying of course).

5. Some you find on the internet. In a friend's Instagram story. In a friend-of-friend's Facebook post. On their own profile, with the bio screaming out their unadopted-needing-to-be-adopted status.

6. They both like scritches. But only when asked for.

7. They do ask for it often enough. Once a day.

8. As you begin to get slightly comfortable, leaning into the scritches-cuddles session, mildly hinting you might expect some action back, they slide out of your arms immediately and leap over into the next room.

9. They love the cosy indoors, but invariably keep an eye on the door to make sure it's open for when they need to be back out in the rugged wilds. (Even when

by rugged wilds I mean the back alleys of Purani Delhi.)

10. Not all of them are alike. #NotAllCats.

11. Umm, am I beginning to sound like a cat-hater? Another thing to note: whenever you begin airing your tiny complaints about either category, even to yourself, you sit back and wonder if they are really so bad or if you are just a hater. 'No, I don't hate men.' 'I AM NOT A CAT-HATER.'

12. In fact, I love them. Maybe too much for my own good. (Not all of them love me back as I would prefer. Nevermind.)

13. My family labels all my cat friends and boy friends as unsuitable, even unlucky. They would prefer it if I picked someone stable, family friendly, attentive, ridiculously demanding of my time, refusing to give me personal space, a completely different species from my usual type.

14. My cat friends' and boy friends' brooding, scatterbrained, often neglectful behaviour forces me, from time to time, to imagine what the future would look like if I just bought into my family's endorsement for a dog-partner—stable, family friendly, attentive, ridiculously demanding of my time, refusing to give me personal space.

15. God no.

16. Return to Step 1. and go through list again.

(This piece is dedicated to all the cats I've loved before and the one I love now.)

Scenes from a Marriage (with Cats)

by Varun Grover

In the last decade, the internet has genuinely helped the growth and wild popularity of only three things—fascism, cryptocurrency, and cats. And only one of these three things is life-affirming. But as it happens with all things popular, we tend to box them into easy stereotypes, fed to us by machine learning software. Things get endlessly meme-fied and painted in shades of black or white. Hence in popular internet imagination, cats are either cold, evil, calculative assholes or cute, funny, fascinating creatures with a master's degree in self-love.

But in reality, living with cats is as layered an experience as being in an intense relationship with an extra-terrestrial being. In Ted Chaing's sci-fi short story *Story of Your Life* (later turned into a much-loved movie *Arrival* by Denis Villeneuve), linguist Dr Louise Banks spends years trying to decipher what the aliens, who have suddenly appeared in 112 places all over our planet, are trying to communicate. She even manages to crack some of the language code, but then one day the aliens pack up and leave. She never manages to find out why they had come, why they left, and what (if anything) they were really trying to communicate. Her successes in understanding the aliens are huge but equally huge are her failures.

That's what I feel about cats too. Unlike dogs, they have managed to evade being 'defined' by humans in easy terms and that has given them an aura of complexity tinged with eccentricity. Living with cats is undoubtedly fun but away from instagram cameras, it's many other things too. And sometimes it is as ordinary, frustrating and odd as peeling garlic while wearing woollen gloves.

ONE

It was a Sunday morning and I stumbled groggy-eyed to the mega-sized litter tray we have set-up in the corner of our hall for our three cats. I don't know why the English language uses the same word for a bunch of newborn kittens and the improvised cat-toilet full of fast-clumping sand and odor-reducing chemicals, but *litter* it is.

The spaceship-like tray was shipped from Hyderabad and is one of the fanciest-looking things in our home. On occasions, guests have mistaken the covered-tray for a laser-printer. My job is to clean it first thing in the morning but on this Sunday a more urgent requirement is to check the shape and size of the pee-lumps, giving me an idea about the volume of cat-urine that went into the litter.

Over the last five years we have witnessed as many shapes of pee-lumps as there are geometric designs on this planet. Our first cat Jaaneman's pee generally makes circular disc-like lumps, of roughly four-inch diameter. Dilbar, our second cat and the alpha of the house, pees deep and ends up making iceberg-type lumps. Chhenapoda, the third cat, is a bit of an artist though. His pee-sculptures have the mark of an auteur. Circular, conical, rectangular, cube-like—he lets his mood guide the shape. On a few occasions in the last four years, we have discovered perfectly heart-shaped pee-lumps made by Chhenapoda. Maybe he loves us.

On this particular morning, I wanted to check if Chhenapoda had stopped peeing multiple-times in small volumes (a sure sign of urinary tract infection) and had gone back to his healthy, artistic peeing in big volumes. He had been on medication for a week now and no perceptible improvement was visible till the previous night. The threat of an ultrasound scan loomed large if pee-lumps were still small and many. I picked up the scoop and started gently dredging the sand, much like a trained archaeologist looking for dinosaur bones. To my relief, the tide had turned and Chhenapoda was back to his boss-level peeing. I was so happy that I broke my own rule of never disturbing a sleeping person on Sundays and woke Raj Kumari up to share the pee-lump update. She walked with me to see the lump with her own eyes and then we hugged.

TWO

Jaaneman wouldn't have sex with Dilbar.

Both were of marriageable age (that is 6-months or above for cats) and of opposite genders. Both wanted to mate, as confirmed by the various mating sounds and signs they were emitting. A male cat pees in random places to leave the trace of his attractive smell for prospective hook-ups, while a female cat rubs her forehead in various corners to spread the news of her availability. They had been together for eight or nine months now and not been spayed/neutered yet. They were a perfect match but something was stopping the union. Maybe they didn't vibe. Maybe they were like Akshay and Madhuri of *Dil Toh Paagal Hai*, '*Maine tumhein kabhi uss nazar se nahin dekha.*'

Ideally, this problem shouldn't have even existed. They should have been neutered as soon as they came of age because cats live happier, healthier lives if rid of the sexual organs/hormones. Also, there are enough cats dying on the streets for lack of resources, and every cat neutered gives a chance at survival to five more cats.

They were not neutered because of a strange and stupidly human moral dilemma we were facing. We wanted them to 'experience' sex at least once before the surgery. We understood cat-sex in human terms only—an elaborate act done for pleasure, a performance that defines our desirability and even personality. We kept waiting for them to experience it and promised that we would take them to the clinic the very next day.

Once we took Dilbar on a playdate to a friend's place with two cats and he immediately fell in love/lust with a female cat there. They didn't fuck, probably they wanted to take it slow, but enough promises were made and smells exchanged for a future date. At the same time, Jaaneman started sending me strange signals and a cat behaviourist confirmed that she probably wanted to mate with me. Yes, let me explain.

Cats think of all creatures as cats. In their idea of the universe there doesn't exist any 'other' species. A pigeon is a flying-stupid cat, a dog is a ferocious-naive cat, a lizard is a crawling-furless-bonsai cat, and a human is a tall-moody cat that is obsessed with failed concepts like money, deadlines, and water.

Feline experts believe it is this utopia, hardwired in every cat's psychology, that gives them the power to command equality and respect. (In a twisted way, it also forms the basis of their typical neurotic behaviour worthy of a million viral memes.) Cats can demand attention and me-time from their human companions with equal ease simply because they don't view the relationship through a master-pet or master-slave or slave-master lens. They think of it as comradeship, where a no is as welcome as a yes from both sides. It won't be wrong to say that cats are Sufi-Marxists, with an ever-fluid idea of boundaries and proprietorship.

In 2016, we had rescued an 8-week-old kitten from a ventilation shaft in our building where her mother had probably left her to figure out life on her own. She was a malnourished and easily scared baby. Both me and Raj Kumari had never had cats or any pets in our homes ever, and this was new territory for us. We called our friend Pallavi, who was living with cats for a while, for help. She taught us the first lesson of living with cats—'respect their space'.

I still remember Jaaneman sitting in a bucket, wrapped in a towel but still shivering, when Pallavi told me to caress her forehead. The thought of touching another creature—a tiny one with alien skin and features—gave me a strange kind of fear in the stomach. I still went ahead and Jaaneman hissed. That was the beginning of a relationship that culminated in her allegedly wanting to mate with me.

Of course, I told her am happily married and, in addition, it would be too insulting for Dilbar. We tried to set them up for a mate-date—locking them down in a room with sexy music and mood lighting. Nothing materialised till we found our third cat, Chhenapoda. I found him in a horrible state on the street and brought him home. Raj Kumari decided to nurture him back to health and keep him with us, if Dilbar and Jaaneman didn't show much resistance to the idea.

Jaaneman and Dilbar were more than a year old, when the 10-week-old Chhenapoda joined us. Adding a third cat to the mix did magic to Jaaneman and Dilbar's feelings for each other. I don't want to psychoanalyze what happened but the fact is, within a week of Chhenapoda entering our house, Dilbar and Jaaneman mated like two wild cats—quick, moderately violent, and boring. (All these adjectives from a human perspective.)

We watched parts of this rite of passage with fascination and slight awkwardness. But above all, with relief. Our babies had grown and we could get them neutered now. We hugged.

THREE

Jaaneman's favourite trick and personal joy is finding new places to hide. She can spend hours alone in some new, yet undiscovered corner of the house and won't step out even when lured with her favourite treats. We have spent at least 100 working hours in the last 5 years trying to figure out 'Jaaneman kidhar gayi.' It's probably a survival tactic for her as she's the most unsocial of our three cats. She keeps sharpening her hiding-skills, in preparation for every time a new person walks into our house. For her, every new visitor is a potential serial killer.

In 2018, we had just shifted from a higher-floor flat to a lower one in the same building. We wanted a change of space despite knowing that cats hate such stupid ideas. Humans make things their own using symbols. Flags, rings, books, walls, abstract lines drawn on paper—these have all been used as territory-markers at different times in history. Cats are slightly more evolved. They spray urine or rub pheromones on objects to mark them as their own. When Jaaneman head-bumps me and rubs her face on mine, she's basically saying 'you are mine' but less in a lover's way and more in a colonizer's way.

The fact is that cats find their confidence by the familiar smell of the surroundings. House cats especially are absolutely obsessed with rubbing their smell on every object—walls, edges of tables, fruit baskets, rubber slippers (their favourite things!), cloth racks, the bare floor. Moving house is the equivalent of being transported to a different planet for a cat. We knew our babies would face this issue so we tried our best to acclimatize them to the new house as much as possible before moving in. We would take them to the empty house for days, helping them prepare mentally for the shift.

We had cat-proofed the new house to our best capabilities, pigeon-netting every window and opening diligently. And still, only a couple of days into the new house, Jaaneman went missing. We looked for her in every possible corner, knowing fully well that she loves hiding, but after a two-hour extensive search, we were forced to reluctantly admit the possibility of her escaping through the door or a loosely-netted window.

We started our search from the top floor of the 24-storey building. It was a hot day, like all bad days are. I was sweating and thirsty and angry and in despair, all together. Another couple of hours of search through the entire run of the staircase and ventilation shafts and I just wanted to sit and cry. She had never been out of the house, had no awareness of the exterior world, and was an anxious cat in general—and my mind kept imagining horrible scenarios.

At some point, I was on my knees, bending down to check below every car parked in the lot to see if she could be spotted. At another point, I asked the building security, throat choking up, if they had seen a cat falling from a higher floor to the courtyard. Nobody had seen anything unusual, except a grown-up man on the verge of a collapse while asking questions about a cat named *Jaaneman*.

One bargain with reality we make, when we bring an animal home, is to accept the fact that we would (in the normal course) outlive them. That a day would come when we would take them to the vet's clinic and the doctor would tell us the lack of options, we would plead, hurt, vent, hug our baby, say our goodbyes, bury them, and then be bitter for the rest of our lives. This possibility, this voice, sits on my left shoulder like a mini-Satan, and keeps whispering in my ear every day—'You don't have enough time, sir. You won't ever have enough time.'

I returned to our apartment after a long and unsuccessful search while Raj Kumari had done another couple of rounds through the staircases. She looked as lifeless as me and we didn't have the courage to even look each other in the eye. I opened my phone and, like a loser, typed 'where do cats hide' on Google. One comment on some reddit-type story about a missing cat said that cats can sometimes hide in the springs under the bed or sofa.

This new house we had moved to had an old king-size bed in one of the rooms, exactly the kind of bed mentioned in the reddit comment. I tried to look under the bed but there was no visibility at that angle. In fury, I tried to lift the (very heavy) bed at an angle but failed. Just then, I sensed a small movement in the wardrobe behind me. We had scanned every inch of that wardrobe at least ten times before that, and still my hopes had not given up, so I headed there. I absent-mindedly pushed a bunch of hanging shirts on one side and there she was—Jaaneman!

Was she hiding in plain sight all this while? Was she somewhere else for a long time, at one of her secret spots, and had recently moved here? Were we just unlucky to not spot her for four hours or we severely lacked in cat-finding skills? Many questions popped into my head like a committee of crows, but above everything else, there was relief. I screamed for Raj Kumari and she came running. Jaaneman sat there, right on the center-shelf of the wardrobe, looking at us all nonchalant, while I finally let myself go. I cried and cried—the thousand horrible possibilities I had imagined vanishing and a deep feeling of love and gratitude washing over me. We hugged. Me, Raj Kumari, and a very reluctant Jaaneman.

Love story
by Vidya Rao

One: Sufi

She comes to greet me, limping a little.

As she grows older, her bad leg, injured in her childhood, gives her trouble. Yet when she was young you wouldn't have thought she had a bad leg, she was so limber!

She stands on tiptoe and she tells me how much she's missed me. I hug her and tell her I've missed her dreadfully, too. I tell her how happy I am to be back, home again, home to her.

We've shared this house for so many years now. We were both young when she came to live with me. We had met, quite by chance one rainy afternoon. She was dodging the traffic at a busy intersection. She had no umbrella—she never carries one—and she was soaking wet. I'd stopped at the traffic lights. And I saw her. I had offered her a ride in my car. She had jumped in, settled herself comfortably—and before I knew it, I was inviting her home. She accepted that invitation, she was looking for a place to live. And I was happy to have someone like her to share my home. How trusting she is, I'd thought then. But perhaps we were both trusting. I'm glad we were. Or where would I be now, without her?

That was many years ago. She was young then, and as I said, limber. I was younger too. Now we are both getting on. I have an assortment of aches and pains, and I tire easily; she has trouble with her liver, and has to be on a diet which she hates. Now we are two old people. We stumble along, glad to have each other.

A few days ago, travelling in the mountains, I had awoken to a bright cold morning. Spring in the mountains, I had thought, as I watched the sun's rays glimmering on the still snow-clad Dhauladhars. In the clean air I could hear birds; further down the mountain, children calling to each other, the bleating of goats, temple bells chiming. I'd thanked my life for this gift of work that takes me all over the world, has shown me mountains and oceans, snow and burning sand, and given me friends from a hundred countries. And I thanked my life also for the gift of my home, for her presence in my life.

I'd reached for my shawl—sunshine notwithstanding, the air was cold. Then, I saw it on my shawl, a single hair, variegated, two-toned, as mine is too. But this wasn't my hair. Mine is soft, wavy, long. This straight, short, slightly wiry hair could only be hers. I plucked the hair off my shawl and held it up to the light.

In that instant, she is very close. This one small hair brings her into this room that's so far away from the home we've made together.

I miss her, her body's warmth, her cool affection.

And now I am back. She is here with me. Contentment seeps into my bones.

I wash my face and hands, getting some of the train's grime off myself. I brush my teeth. Then I switch on the geyser. Soon the water will be hot and I can take a shower.

She watches me intently as I unpack, tossing soiled clothes into a bucket full of soapsuds. Lots of clothes to wash, I tell her, grimacing a little. It is always so after a trip. She doesn't help me. She never does; I don't expect her to either. It is enough that she sits by me as I work, that she looks at me, that she lets me know how happy she is.

She follows me to the kitchen where I fill the kettle with water, switch it on, and make myself a cup of herb tea. I don't make any for her. She doesn't share my passion for tea. Or in fact for fruit, salads, or soups… none of this soppy herb-tea-heath-food stuff for her!

I ask her if she'd like some warm milk. It's good for you I tell her. She agrees to have a little. Just to keep me company.

I take my cup and sit by the window that looks out over our tiny garden-in-pots, and she comes to sit by me, quiet as always. I offer her a biscuit and she takes it straight from my hand. Her mouth nuzzles my fingers.

A squirrel scampers up and down the garden wall, chittering cheekily at us. She looks at the squirrel, so focused, she might be meditating on the form of her ishta devata. I remember when she was young and could move so swiftly, so lightly, despite her limp. She'd run races with the squirrels. I used to think she'd leave her shadow behind. She was so swift.

I hold her close. Are you thinking of how it was when you were young? I ask her. There is a small pause. Then she turns to look at me with her large beautiful eyes. Is that reproach? Have I upset her by reminding her of those days?

She turns back to look at the squirrel. A parrot joins the squirrel. It perches on the railing of the balcony, green and gaudy against the grey of the cement railing. Two pigeons waddle up to the water-bowl. Beyond the garden, in the forest, I hear a koel. The first koel of this year. I tell her I want to celebrate that. She smiles benignly and accepts another biscuit.

I finish my tea, but this time that we spend together is so precious that I don't want to get up and start the usual rush-rush-rush. Time enough for that, I think. Now is a pool, quiet, still, deep as her eyes. We sit in silence for a while, a golden, full silence that is as nourishing as a bowl of hot soup.

It is so good to be back, I tell her.

She jumps off the table by the window. She jumps into my lap. She reaches out and touches my face with a little velvet paw. She licks my cheek with her pink sandpaper tongue. Then she curls up in my lap, moulding her body to mine, and she begins to purr.

Two: Butterfly Soul

Wednesday, 13 October 2021

Two years ago, around 2.45 in the afternoon, my beloved Sufi-cat left her mortal body. She was 20 years and 4 months old. Two years, and I still miss her; my house still feels empty; I feel empty. Something in me feels unravelled, unmade.

Yesterday afternoon, remembering her, our many years together, I'd wept, almost wailed with grief. This morning, calmer, I thought of her again, as I do almost every day, and I sent out a message to her. Just to tell her how much I love her, how grateful I am that she chose me to be her friend in this lifetime, how much I miss her.

Earlier this year, in early February, a year to the day I'd immersed her ashes, her 'flower-body', in the blue waves off the coast of Goa, Sufi came to me. I am sure it was she. An enormous kite—an eagle-like bird—came gliding out of nowhere, right up to my window, so close I felt I could touch it if I stretched out my hand. The kite stopped there for a long moment, looked right into my eyes, waiting…

Sufi?

Another moment. And then the huge bird flapped its wings once and soared away.

Sufi.

Today, on this second anniversary of her passing, I look out of my window and see now an enormous butterfly, many-splendoured, like her own calico fur. And again, it comes right up to me, stops in mid-air, inches from my face.

I've seen butterflies before outside my window, in my verandah. But never one so huge and so multi-coloured.

I remember that the butterfly is a symbol of the soul, of the psyche.

Just a very big, brilliantly-coloured butterfly? Or my dearest friend?

Sufi.

My beloved Sufi, I whisper. My eyes are too small to hold the flood of emotion. Loss, pain, emptiness, loneliness, and with all of this, also gratitude, acceptance, wonder, joy.

Sufi, oh Sufi!

The butterfly hovers in the air for a long moment. Then it flutters its huge wings and flies away.

Part One was published before in Namaste *magazine.*

Author Bios

Saba Imtiaz

Saba Imtiaz is a freelance journalist and author who currently lives in Karachi, does not have a cat, but has somehow been conned into feeding a group of neighbourhood cats. Her first book *Karachi, You're Killing Me!* was published by Random House India in 2014.

Janice Pariat

Janice Pariat is chief doorman to Vincent in a house in Delhi, India, where he lives rent free. She is a good doorman. Mostly. Though not when Vincent wishes to be let out at 3am. In between feeding Vincent, playing with Vincent, and letting Vincent in and out of the house, Janice writes. Sometimes Vincent also helps by lying on her keyboard. In this way, he helped her complete *The Nine Chambered Heart*, best selling in India, though was not around when *Seahorse: A Novel* and *Boats on Land: A collection of short stories*, were published. Janice teaches at Ashoka University, and also makes soap, knits, and concocts her own creams and cosmetics—none of which interest Vincent. He likes to sleep.

Anushka Ravishankar

Anushka Ravishankar mostly writes books for children. She wrote a book called *I Like Cats* long before she realised that she did, indeed, like cats. Now that she is aware of her predilection, she finds it difficult to write about anything else.

Sakshi Agarwal

Sakshi Agarwal graduated from Ashoka University with a Bachelor's in English Literature and an inability to write about anything that isn't linked to the act of resistance. Under the mentorship of her professor (and general-snark-mentor), Arunava Sinha, she translated Abhishek Majumdar's award-winning play, *Muktidham*, for production in the United States. In 2020, she published a translated collection of short stories by Subhadra Kumari Chauhan with Bee Books. Later, she worked with the NGO, The 1947 Partition Archive, and completed translating her second full-length novel from Hindustani. Currently at University College London, she is pursuing a master's in comparative literature and an associate degree in dreaming of chhole-bhature.

Anukrti Upadhyay

Anukrti Upadhyay has post-graduate degrees in Management and Literature, and a graduate degree in Law. She writes fiction and poetry in both English and Hindi. Her English works, twin novellas *Daura* and *Bhaunri* and novel *Kintsugi* have been published by the 4th Estate imprint of HarperCollins in India. Her Hindi works, a short story collection, *Japani Sarai*, and novel, *Neena Aunty*, have been published by Rajpal and Sons. Her writings have been in Scroll.in, Kitaab.sg, The Bombay Review, The Bangalore Review, The Bilingual Window and several Hindi publications. When not counting trees and birds, she can be found ingratiating herself with every cat and dog in the vicinity.

Gayathri Sankar

Gayathri Sankar graduated from Ashoka University this year with a major in English Literature, a minor in Creative Writing, and an unfortunate tendency to (mis)use the word "dichotomy" in daily conversation. She writes the occasional book review for *Scroll* and scripts for Accelerate, a program striving towards better sexual health for the gay and transgender community in India. Her writing career began with two prizes in the Scholastic Writing Awards when she was in school, one of which was a love letter to Captain Underpants that she refuses to comment on.

The story published in this anthology will be the pinnacle of her writing career so far.

Natasha Badhwar

In the months following the writing of this essay, Natasha Badhwar's family has adopted 11 cats and kittens from their neighbourhood. Their home is better described as a cat campus, and there is always extra cat food and nutritious soup for visiting felines. This is the enduring legacy of Rahat, their first cat who had to leave too soon.

When she is not stirring a bubbling pot of chicken stock and oats soup, Natasha is an independent film-maker, columnist and author. She leads the media team at Karwan e Mohabbat (Caravan of Love)—a people's campaign in celebration of the values enshrined in the Indian Constitution and in solidarity for victims of hate crimes.

Her books include the popular memoirs, *My Daughters' Mum* and *Immortal For A Moment*.

Meenakshi Madhavan Reddy

Meenakshi Reddy Madhavan is the author of several novels and one short story collection. She has variously cohabited with cats all around India and is currently living with three—Bruno, Olga da Polga and Squishy—in Berlin. They try very hard to keep her from writing, but she perseveres anyway.

Vangmayi Parakala

Vangmayi Parakala is a culture writer with *Mint Lounge* in Delhi. She has previously worked at *The Hindu*; she holds an MA from the English Department at Delhi University, and an MS from the Medill School of Journalism, Northwestern University. Her forthcoming work includes a biography of Homai Vyarawalla for children (Niyogi Books). Most of these things essentially keep her distracted from the primal sadness of being unable to adopt a dog currently.

Aneela Babar

Prior to attaining work-life balance in clearing cat litter, writing on popular culture, baron ki izzat, hum umro se apnaapan, and chhoton se pyaar, Aneela Z Babar was pursuing a career in research within the development sector in South and South-East Asia and Australia. Recent published works have been *We are all Revolutionaries Here: Militarism, Political Islam and Gender in Pakistan* (Sage/Yoda Press) and *Texts of War: The Religio-Military Nexus in Pakistan and India* (Sage/Asian Institute of Technology). If you ask her what the high point of her life has been, she will be torn between 1989—the year of *Chandni* and Benazir Bhutto—and the time in Delhi when she lived in the house where *Chashme Buddoor*, her all time favourite film, was shot.

Arhaan Babar Ray

Arhaan Babar Ray is a middle schooler at Vasant Valley. He divides his time meeting homework deadlines, playing the piano, deliberating about the Marvel Universe and thinking up tech codes that can teach cats to clean up his room.

Aditi Sriram

Aditi Sriram teaches Writing at Ashoka University, near Delhi, and earned her MFA from The New School in New York City. Her first book, *Beyond the Boulevards: A Short Biography of Pondicherry*, was released in 2019. She freelances for several publications including *The Indian Express* and *The New York Times*. This story is dedicated to Steven Millhauser, and exists thanks to D.R., V.B. and A.P. For more details about Aditi's work, visit www.aditis-riram.com.

Maneesha Taneja

Maneesha Taneja teaches Spanish in Delhi University. She is a sucker for reading murder mysteries and watching crime shows, much to her husband's chagrin. (It has been noted of late that he is now a convert to the genre). Maneesha lives in a pet-friendly house in Noida, with her dog babies and cat child, and with her parents and siblings in the near vicinity. After having translated Gabriel García Márquez, Pablo Neruda, Nadine Gordimer and Amitav Ghosh into Hindi (among many others), she hopes to now write her own novel!

Nilanjana Roy

Nilanjana S Roy is the author of *The Wildings* and *The Hundred Names of Darkness*, and is a novelist and editor who lives in New Delhi. She is often the cat's whiskers and occasionally the cat's pajamas, except for occasions when she has overshot a deadline and must retire to the doghouse.

Sandip Roy

Sandip Roy is a writer and radio host living in Kolkata. His work has appeared in numerous outlets including the *New York Times, San Francisco*

Chronicle, *The Hindu*, *Firstpost*, *The Times of India*, *BBC*, *NPR* and *Scroll*. He is a columnist for *Mint Lounge* and *The Hindu* and hosts the Sandip Roy Show for *Indian Express*. His audio dispatch from Kolkata airs weekly on public radio in San Francisco. His first novel is *Don't Let Him Know*. He once had a cat named Beato and a dog named Panic, where the cat was bigger than the dog. These days he and his partner co-parent a plushie, Chewie @this_is_little_chewie, who has more Instagram followers than either of them.

Shreemayee Das

Shreemayee Das likes to believe she is a writer, a stand-up comedian, and also a sensible adult. She has a degree in English Literature and bookshelves to prove it as well. She mostly writes on cinema and culture for publications like *The Telegraph* and *Firstpost*, and also works as an editor and a teacher. She has a lot to say about books, but can't seem to write any.

Jai Arjun Singh

Jai Arjun Singh's books include *The World of Hrishikesh Mukherjee*, *Jaane bhi do Yaaro: Seriously Funny Since 1983*, and the anthology *The Popcorn Essayists*. Most of his columns, essays and reviews are collected on his culture blog Jabberwock (http://jaiarjun.blogspot.com). Like a true cat, he is usually suspicious of people and hisses a great deal at two-legged creatures, but is also capable of being sweet and purr-ful if things are going his way or when a bowl of curd is placed in front of him.

Sonali Singh

Sonali Singh is a senior bureaucrat in the Government of India. She is an alumnus of St Stephens College (BA Hons) and Delhi University (MA), where she studied History. She also holds a degree of Bachelors in Mass Communication from Panjab University, Chandigarh, and a Master's degree in Public Administration from the University of Malaya, Kuala Lumpur. Sonali was first adopted by the cats Gooney and Pop when she was living in Muscat, Oman, in 2009. She has since been adopted numerous times, in other parts of the world—most recently by the tiny (but fierce) Piddoo in Delhi.

Vibha Balaji

Vibha Balaji is a writer (and professional overthinker) based out of Chennai. When she is not working on her stories, she can be found in her apartment, swatting flies and watching bad reality TV. She is currently pursuing an MFA at The New School in NYC.

Vikram Mervyn

Vikram Mervyn is Kulfi Mohammad Saidali when he walks, or when he writes, or when he enjoys life. Kulfi Mohammad Saidali, who doesn't usually roam around searching for narcotics, is in love with Chennai. He enjoys any sort of cinema, walking about, and chai. He attempts to write in the "non-chalant-tense" about the minute tragedies he sees as he walks.

Payal Nagpal

Payal Nagpal is a Type A anthropomorphic cat, writing and residing in Florida. Once of Ashoka University, she is currently pursuing an MFA at the University of Florida.

Arunava Sinha

Arunava Sinha translates classic, modern and contemporary Bengali fiction and non-fiction from Bangladesh and India into English. He also translates fiction from English into Bengali. Over sixty of his translations have been published so far in India, the UK and the USA. He has twice won the Crossword Award for translated books. He teaches at (and memes out of) Ashoka University, and is the Books Editor at *Scroll.in*. His dog, Tingmo, might be unhappy with his participation in this anthology. His students, however, are likely to be happy about it.

Meera Ganapathi

Meera Ganapathi is a writer and founder of the independent digital publication, *The Soup*. Based between Mumbai and Goa, she writes books for children and essays and short stories for grown-ups. An accidental cat lover, Meera has not had a fur-free black tee-shirt since 2015.

Ipsa Samaddar

Ipsa is a third year Literature major and History minor at Ashoka University who's sold her circadian rhythm to Satan in an effort to complete her assignments. The formalities of academic writing have nearly put her off creative work, but she continues to pursue fiction (and cats) in the one city and one college campus she's spent nineteen years of her life in. Right now, she's probably procrastinating by binge-watching crime shows or crying over fictional queer characters.

M.K. Ranjitsinh

Dr M.K. Ranjitsinh has had an unparalleled role in India's wildlife conservation history. He was the prime architect of the Wildlife (Protection) Act of 1972, and of the Central government schemes to assist national parks and sanctuaries. Formerly of the royal family of Wankaner, he joined the Indian Administrative Service in 1961, and his passion for saving endangered species continues even after his retirement, whether in planning the relocation of the Asiatic lion from Gir forest, the reintroduction of the cheetah into the grasslands of central India, or in saving from extinction the Kashmir stag, the Manipur brow-antlered deer and the Great Indian bustard. He has always had a soft corner for felines, big and small.

Sonal Shah

Sonal Shah is an editor and writer who lives in New Delhi, though she grew up near Washington, DC. She has led and been part of editorial teams at *Time Out Delhi*, *The Caravan*, and VICE. Passionate about adding beauty and complexity to the world, Sonal cooks, dabbles in music and drawing, and takes way too many pictures of her cats.

Her website is www.sonalshah.in.

Anukriti Prasad

Anukriti wrote her first story at six and decided not to make that mistake again, till many years later a creative writing course at Ashoka University changed her life. She has published two short stories with Juggernaut and is currently writing an ongoing web novel for Mintworks Publishing. Anukriti usually splits her time between writing too little, thinking too much, and on some bright days badgering friends into illegally streaming bad Bollywood flicks together.

Priya Sebastian

For about seventeen years, Priya Sebastian lived in a home within a lush jungle-garden inhabited by fierce thug-cats. The biggest of these cats was Gundappa. When she wasn't feeding the mob of demanding cats at her door, she managed to illustrate editorials for magazines like *The Indian Quarterly* and *The Caravan*, as well as make cover illustrations for various Indian publishers, with her distinct black and white charcoal drawings. Her first picture book titled *Is It the Same for You?* was published in 2019.

Priya's work can be found at
https://priyasebastianillustrations.tumblr.com/
Prints of her work are available at her shop
https://shopforplums.blogspot.com/

Gautam Chintamani

Gautam Chintamani is a cinephile-historian and the author of five books. He loves dogs, Labradors in particular, and hates cats. He believes that terrestrial beings take themselves all too seriously and extraterrestrials will save 'em all. As it's all downhill anyway, he intends to enjoy the ride. When he is not writing, reading or analyzing movies, he is being reminded by his wife to get their Enfield Desert Storm serviced.

Teesta Rawal

Teesta is a semi-professional cat-sibling, currently living her best life in London. She spends most of her time taking random buses and loafing around the streets, until she remembers she's doing a Master's degree in Gender Studies as well. In her spare time, she enjoys staring at stocked shelves in Sainsbury's, and mooning about Bombay, where her Mum Nina continues to care not only for her own four cat-siblings but also a dozen strays.

Gurmehar Kaur

Gurmehar Kaur doesn't understand cats. Or boys. However she is obsessed with both. In the time that is not spent decoding cat signals or boy signals, she writes about young people, politics, and the brilliant women in her life. She is a social activist and advocate for Digital Peace Now, a non-profit organization advocating for Cyber Peace. In 2017, Kaur was listed by *TIME* magazine as a 'Next Generation Leader', a global listing of ten young men and women making a difference in the world. She graduated from Lady Shri Ram College in 2019 and holds a Masters from the University of Oxford. Her first book was *Small Acts of Freedom*, a deeply personal family history published by Penguin Random House India in 2018, and her second book *The Young and the Restless: Youth and Politics in India* was shortlisted for the Sahitya Akademi Yuva Puraskar 2021.

Varun Grover

Varun Grover is a screenwriter, lyricist, and stand up comedian based in Mumbai. He thinks of himself as Neo of Cat Matrix, constantly in awe of multiple revelations that he's been blessed with by the divine felines. His upcoming projects include the lyrics for *Badhai Do, Monica O My Darling*, and *RRR*.

Vidya Rao

Vidya Rao is a performer of thumri-dadra and ghazal. For many years the disciple of the legendary singer, the late Vidushi Naina Devi, she continued her study of this form under the late Vidushi Shanti Hiranand and the late Vidushi Girija Devi. Her initial training in khayal was under the late Prof. B.N. Datta and thereafter under Pandit Mani Prasad. She is also an editor, teacher, researcher and writer, and most importantly, a cat-sakhi. She lives in New Delhi.

Craig Boehman

Craig Boehman is a Mumbai-based photographer who specialises in fine art and street photography. He got his start when one of his images was selected for a magazine cover in 2015. Since then, it's been everything photography while entertaining daydreams of encountering and photographing a tsunami, which has been on his bucket list for more than three decades. His other bucket list item has been to thwart his clone. You can catch his work on his website www.CraigBoehman.com

Priya Kuriyan

Priya Kuriyan is a book illustrator, comic book artist and animator. A graduate of the National Institute of Design, Ahmedabad, she has directed educational films for the *Sesame Street Show* (India) and the Children's Film Society of India (CFSI), and illustrated numerous books for various Indian publishers. In 2018, she published *Indira*, a graphic biography of Mrs Gandhi, co-created with Devapriya Roy. She once had a cat with the memorable daak naam, Phunty, and bhalo naam, Phantom. Phunty continues to inspire her cat art.